T0168645

Stories of Chicago

Stories of Chicago

GEORGE ADE

Edited and with an Introduction by
Franklin J. Meine

Illustrated by John T. McCutcheon and Others

University of Illinois Press
Urbana and Chicago

First Illinois edition, 2003

♾ This book is printed on acid-free paper.

Previously published as *Stories of the Streets and of the Town: From* The Chicago
Record, *1893–1900* (Chicago: The Caxton Club, 1941). Reprinted from
that edition, with a new title, by permission of The Caxton Club.

Foreword

To write an adequate historical and literary introduction to George Ade's stories and John T. McCutcheon's drawings is a task of almost book-length proportions. In this limited space it has been possible to make only the very briefest comment, with the hope that the train of thought, once started, would gather momentum.

The selection of only a few stories and pictures out of thousands has been exceedingly difficult. There are literally hundreds more equally good — plenty for a more extended production, but again it has been necessary to select severely in order to keep this anthology in proportion. Emphasis has been put upon those sketches which are important for their value in revealing the social life of Chicago rather than for their literary significance, although the latter phase has not been overlooked.

All notes and footnotes are gathered briefly at the back of the book, and are referred to by number in the text.

On behalf of the members of the Caxton Club, the writer wishes to express sincere appreciation for the enthusiasm and co-operation of Charles H. Dennis, John T. McCutcheon, and George Ade in giving generously of their time and in contributing their reminiscences especially to this edition.

F. J. M.

OLD LA SALLE STREET

Contents

Introduction

CHICAGO—Port of Humorists—supreme and unchallenged—the home port of George Ade, John T. McCutcheon, "Mr. Dooley" (Finley Peter Dunne), Eugene Field, Bert Leston Taylor, Ring Lardner, Franklin P. Adams, to mention only a favored few. Two of these humorists were born in the city proper; others were born within the reaches of the afterglow of the Chicago Fire; most of them enjoyed their happiest creative years in Chicago.[1]

George Ade's earliest memory of his youth at Kentland was "that one night in October, just as far back as I can reach into the past, we sat on the fence and looked at a blur of illumination in the northern sky and learned that the city [Chicago] which we had not seen was burning up in a highly successful manner."[2]

"Other cities have produced other humorists," observed Tom Masson, who for twenty-five years was editor of *Life*, the old humorous weekly, "but Chicago appears to be the right atmosphere for a humorist to grow up in. After he has grown up, has suffered enough from his environment, so to speak, he may go elsewhere with personal safety, but it is doubtful if he will ever do anything better than what Chicago has given him to do."[3]

Great humorists, yes. Great artists, yes. Great literary men too, for humor was only *one* of their many creative qualities. Theirs was a literature of everyday life, a native literature, that found unique expression in the Middle West. In Chicago that life found focus, and these humorists, in jest and in sober thought, captured its spirit and sketched it quickly and colorfully on a broad canvas, delightfully, spontaneously, with a friendly heart *warmpth* that was the pulse of Chicago.

* * *

Life in Chicago in the Gay Nineties was brilliantly and vivaciously mirrored in "Stories of the Streets and of the Town," a feature newspaper column or department, written by George Ade and illustrated by John T. McCutcheon. For seven years, from November 20, 1893 to November 7, 1900, this department appeared anonymously on the editorial page of *The Chicago Record*. There this feature held spot space: it occupied about one and one-half columns of type and pictures in the center of the page, with a two-column head across the top. "The daily grind, allowing for the breaks on account of cuts, had to be anywhere from fifteen hundred to eighteen hundred words in order that the stuff would get well below the fold on the second column."[4]

The "Stories" drew upon all phases of city life, as a glance at the table of contents will quickly reveal. They ranged from candid-camera shots to phantasy and fiction based upon everyday life: one day a story about "The Junk Shops of Canal Street"; the next day "Hobo Wilson and the Good Fairy"; still another day, "Effie Whittlesy."

Curiously enough, although the column was exceedingly popular, the author remained anonymous to his newspaper public. Said Ade: "I kept my two-column department going for seven years. Before I retired to the clover pasture and began to steal money by syndicating, I had published four books, all of the material having first appeared in the paper. I was somewhat known at the bookshops, but to the readers of *The Record* I was still an unknown speaking from the darkness. Never, by hint or suggestion, was it made known to our subscribers that behind the story department there might be hiding a human being with thoughts and emotions worth recording. I peered through the camera for seven years and never stood in front of it once. The compositors working on my hand-written gems never had to reach for an upper-case 'I.' "[5]

Selected stories, after their newspaper appearance, were issued in series in book form in paper wrappers.[6] In all there were eight such series issued by *The Chicago Record*, and sold to their readers at twenty-five cents each. *The Record* boastfully advertised that these stories and sketches were "commonly conceded to be the best things of their kind printed."

This newspaper feature and the resultant series of eight "paper-backs" constitute one of the choicest contributions to Chicago's literary reputation and to Chicago's social history. Indeed, the First Series, dated April 1, 1894, is the first appearance in book form of George Ade and/or John T. McCutcheon, and antedates by years their better-known, hardbound books subsequently published by Herbert S. Stone & Co.

These stories of the streets are important Chicagoana: they are candid-camera shots of Chicago by artists, literary and graphic, who knew how to select their episodes and characters, and how to highlight them. Yet, unique in Chicago's literary history, these browned "paper-backs" are now almost unknown; few of them have survived the rigors of well-thumbed reading or of the housecleaning activities of the gentler sex.

Ade's stories and McCutcheon's sketches appropriately appeared in *The Chicago Record*. It was a distinctly cultural paper, with an accent on an elite Society tone. Here the Hoosier humorists found their port, and a suitable setting for their artistry; they enjoyed at least a favorable audience.

* * *

The Record was the morning counterpart of *The Chicago Daily News*, both of which were owned and operated by Victor Lawson, whose managing editor was Charles H. Dennis. To Charles Dennis Chicagoans owe much, for, among many notable achievements, it was he who recognized the genius of his young reporters, Ade and McCutcheon, and provided adequate opportunity for their expression. This same fine stalwart gentleman, Editor Emeritus of *The Chicago Daily News*, tells his story in a letter to the writer:

THE CHICAGO DAILY NEWS
DAILY NEWS PLAZA, CHICAGO

July 2, 1940

Dear Mr. Meine:

In response to your request that I set down on paper my recollections of the circumstances under which "Stories of the Streets and of the Town," George Ade's famous series of sketches published in *The Chicago Record*, of which I was then managing editor, came into existence, I give you these particulars out of a clear memory of the affair.

Ade joined the reporting staff of *The Record* in, I believe, 1890. His close boyhood friend, John T. McCutcheon, already was a member of the newspaper's staff of artists and their friendship doubtless led Ade to apply there for a reporter's job. From the outset Ade was a brilliant success as a news gatherer. This fact, together with his skill as a writer and his fine sense of humor, brought him rapidly to the front. Consequently, when I made up a staff of reporters to work on the grounds of the Chicago World's Columbian Exposition some months before it was opened to the public in the spring of 1893, Ade was the star writer of that small galaxy. I established then on the editorial page of *The Chicago Record* a feature occupying the last two columns, which appeared daily for considerably more than a year under the heading, "All Roads Lead to the World's Fair." Ade wrote many of the sketches which appeared there and McCutcheon made many of the illustrations. The feature was markedly successful.

When the Exposition closed in the fall of 1893, the "All Roads" feature came to an end. Ade returned to the newspaper's regular reporting staff, where he went on writing articles and sketches in his own delightful fashion. His copy went to the copy desk in the city room, where, in the massacre of copy necessary to bring everything down to volume that would fit the restricted space allotted to local news, Ade's articles suffered grievous mutilation. Knowing that whatever he wrote was amply good enough to appear in print exactly as it came from his hand, I shared his exasperation over the terrible hash made of his articles. So I told Ade soon that he and McCutcheon might have the two columns on the editorial page lately vacated by the World's Fair feature and that they might use it every day, subject to my supervision, in any way they liked. I chose for the new feature the title which it bore from first to last.

Ade and McCutcheon went to work with pencil and drawing pen. It is my recollection that Ade consistently shied away from the typewriter and that his copy always came to my desk in his own bold and very legible handwriting. The immense success achieved by him through the inimitable sketches contributed daily is now generally accepted as a bright spot in newspaper history. McCutcheon's drawings were as excellent in their way as was Ade's light and friendly touch in depicting with convincing fidelity phases of a city's everyday life. It is further to the credit of those two fine young Hoosiers, upon whom for many years the American public has looked with peculiar affection, that—and this fact is not generally known—while they carried on their editorial-page feature, Ade and McCutcheon were collaborating every day in the production of a cartoon for *The Record's* first page. Ade would come to my office fairly early in the forenoon and he and I would talk over ideas for a cartoon. Having hit upon one satisfactory to both of us, Ade would carry it to McCutcheon, who would sketch it out. In that early part of his career, McCutcheon drew many cartoons that ranked well up with his later and more finished work.

Sincerely yours,

Charles H. Dennis

* * *

In the "Stories of the Streets and of the Town" Ade and McCutcheon achieved a joint artistry in which their separate arts, the literary and the graphic, were perfectly blended. The turn of the phrase and the simple pencil line were expertly woven into a rich tapestry which revealed the mood and the manner of Chicago in the Gay Nineties. For their most enjoyable effects these "Stories" depend upon this harmony of prose and picture.

Mark Twain—he of the piercing eye—immediately sensed this artful blending when, in a letter to William Dean Howells, he said of the "Pink Marsh" stories:[7]

July 22/08

Dear Howells—

Thank you once more for introducing me to the incomparable Pink Marsh. I have been reading him again, after this long interval, & my admiration of the book has overflowed all limits, all frontiers. I have personally known each of the characters in the book & can testify that they are all true to the facts, & as exact as if they had been drawn to scale. And how effortless is the limning! It is as if the work did itself, without help of the master's hand.

And for once—just this once—the illustrator is the peer of the writer. The writer flashes a character onto his page in a dozen words, you turn the leaf & there he stands, alive & breathing, with his clothes on and the African ordor [sic] oozing out of him! What a picture-gallery it is of instantly recognizable, realizable, unassailable Authentics!

Pink—oh, the shiftless, worthless, lovable black darling! Howells, he deserves to live forever. *Mark*

This weaving together of their arts derived largely from the unusual similarity of backgrounds, talents, desires of author and artist. Both native Hoosiers, they had been "buddies" in college: at Purdue, George, class of '87, in search of fraternity pledges, found John T., class of '89, "stalking around in a long cut-away coat," and induced him to join Sigma Chi. After McCutcheon had obtained a toe hold on the old Chicago *Morning News* in 1889, he wrote "glamorous letters about life in the big city" to Ade in Lafayette, who was then writing testimonials advertising a tobacco-habit cure. Previously Ade had been struggling on Lafayette newspapers, which paid mostly in meal-tickets on a cheap restaurant which was a heavy advertiser.

"The following June (1890) George came up, and was presented to the editorial powers at the *Morning News* office where he was given a tryout, doing weather, at $12.00 a week." Immediately, Ade put Weather on the Front Page. The *Morning News* later evolved into the *News Record*, and then into *The Chicago Record*.

"George came up to Chicago before the Blackstone was built, so we were obliged to take a room about a block farther south near the corner of Peck Court. A tablet now marks the spot. It says 'Peck Court.' This was the beginning of our hall-bedroom days, days when both of us worked on the old *Morning News*, he writing and I drawing—days when we weren't quite poor enough to have beautiful ladies bring Christmas baskets to us and not quite rich enough to buy the Christmas baskets ourselves.

"This hallroom that we inhabited was not a mere figure of speech. There was no vulgar display of wealth in its modest appointments—nothing to distract our minds from the calm contemplation of our literary and artistic aspirations. It was called a comfortably furnished room for refined gentlemen, but this was fulsome flattery and most misleading. It was not comfortably furnished. Fortunately, at that time, we didn't know the difference between a hall bedroom and one in the Blackstone.

"The room, third floor back, extended in sweeping perspective twelve feet in one direction and ten in the other.

You had to take accurate aim to walk between the bed and the sofa. One window opened to the west, admitting a flood of sunlight in the afternoon when we were at the office. To one standing at the window, a varied view was disclosed—in the foreground a morgue for empty bottles, barrels, and old packing-cases; in the middle distance a row of chimneys, and in the distant prospect the stately uplift of the Polk Street Station tower outlined against the western sky. It must have been beautiful at sunset."[8]

Thus began their long brilliant journeys, enriched by more than half a century of maturing friendship. So intimate, so delightful, a friendship must needs find expression in their arts, as indeed it did during their five years' collaboration on *The Chicago Record*.

Of that early copartnership Ade reminisced to the writer in an interview at Hazelden Farm, September, 1940:

"McCutcheon had no desire to be a cartoonist. He wanted to be an illustrator; he was a realist and simply wanted to picture people as he saw them. In fact, he resented and resisted as long as possible the burlesque and exaggeration necessarily implied in cartooning. In the early days when McCutcheon and I were on *The Record*, 'Mac' did not always originate cartoons; the idea of cartooning simply didn't appeal to him. I would go into Charley Dennis' office (Dennis was then managing editor) to discuss with him suggestions for a cartoon, and after writing out the text for the cartoon—the title above as well as the legend below—we would take it to McCutcheon with the story, and he then drew the cartoon. At first, especially in the column 'Stories of the Streets and of the Town,' McCutcheon's work was entirely that of illustration. Later he found that people liked some of his quaint cartoons, and he began developing them slowly, by adding such features as the little dog in one corner, the little boy in another. He developed these various 'props' through the series called the *Bird Center Cartoons;* the name 'Bird Center,' typically Hoosier, was my suggestion. McCutcheon later became a world-famous cartoonist, but the point is that in the beginning 'Mac' didn't want to be a cartoonist. He wanted to be an illustrator, a realist; and much of his best work appeared in the 'Stories of the Streets and of the Town.' "

* * *

Greater praise than that of Mark Twain and George Ade could hardly be accorded an artist and illustrator. McCutcheon's pen-and-ink sketches were the talk of the town; and McCutcheon, William Schmedtgen and Frank Holme were celebrated at exhibitions in the Art Institute. There developed a Chicago "school" of artists and illustrators; McCutcheon led the parade. Beloved of them all was "Billy" Schmedtgen, the head of the art department of the old *Record*. At first Schmedtgen and McCutcheon started the tradition in the "Stories of the Streets and of the Town"; later other artists shared the honors, notably Charles D. Williams, Carl Werntz, Charles Sarka, Clyde Newman, Frink, and Dom. J. Lavin.[9]

McCutcheon illustrated the books *Artie, Pink Marsh*, and *Doc Horne;* Clyde Newman, *Fables in Slang* and *More Fables in Slang*. In most instances the illustrations in the books are quite different from the sketches in the original newspaper columns.

Mr. McCutcheon has contributed for this Caxton Club edition some of his reflections upon his sketches, and the circumstances under which they were drawn for "Stories of the Streets and of the Town."

CHICAGO TRIBUNE
TRIBUNE TOWER
November 11, 1940

Dear Mr. Meine:

By way of refreshing my memory, I have just looked back through my old copies of *Stories of the Streets and of the Town*, of which I seem to have seven of the eight volumes. It was a pleasant reunion. From page after page, old friends looked out at me. It was as though I were opening gateway after gateway upon well-remembered gardens in which strolled old friends of the Nineties.

My association with George Ade as his illustrator began with the first of his "Stories." This feature made its appearance on the editorial page of *The Chicago Record*, November 20, 1893, after we had completed our work out at the old Columbian Exposition.

Tagging along after George, he chronicled and I illustrated almost every phase of Chicago's life and activities. As a historical record of those times, these old paper-backed reprints of the Ade stories will be of great value to the future historian.

At that time, we didn't suspect we were passing through what, in future decades, was to be called "The Gay Nineties."

As I remember it, there was joy and zest and adventure in our work. And there was an awful lot of work, but as seen in fond retrospection, it didn't seem like work. Besides we didn't have anything else to do. I don't remember any square envelopes with R.S.V.P. on them.

In looking through these old volumes, I quickly discover that I used my associates in the old *Record* office as models. For example, here in the very first volume is an article called "Since the Frenchman Came." It was all about the basement tables d'hôte that bravely flourished their brief moment and went their way. Here are our two friends, Albert C. Wilkie and Fred Richardson, toasting one another just as though they were in gay Paree. I have drawn them as devil-may-care young boulevardiers—Chicago style.

Other unmistakable faces leap out of the pages at me. Here is a gentleman whom I recognize as Frank Hoyne. And here is John M. Glenn, later prominent in the Illinois Manufacturers' Association; and also Jack Priest, now a distinguished railway official in the West. I remember going down to Henderson, Kentucky, to see his sister marry Will Iglehart. The bridal party drank bourbon out of tin cups and a lovely time was had by all.

In this first volume is a story, "The Intellectual Awakening in Burton's Row," showing that George was beginning to branch away from the sordid realities of the Harrison Street Police station on Monday morning to something beautiful and uplifting.

I don't seem to have a copy of Volume II. Perhaps it is in the rubble of my treasures and misplaced possessions, lurking somewhere as a "potential headache" for my executors.

But here in Volume III is a picture of the new and shiny Masonic Temple, and nearby, the Lake Street L, evidently then regarded as worthy of attention. George's questing pen, like a wand, touched with light The Newberry Library.

Evidently I wandered off the scene during part of Volume III, for Mr. Schmedtgen, the kindly head of *The Record* art department, to whom so many of us cubs owed so very much, aided by Charley Williams—now Mr. Charles D. Williams, successful painter in New York—pinch-hitted for me.

As soon as I got in circulation again, I drew both their pictures—

Smetty on page 87 and Charley on page 98—but whether in grati-
tude or reprisal I don't remember. [All page numbers refer to the
original series.—Ed.]

Opie Read appears in the story "A Plantation Dinner at Aunt
Mary's," and a little farther along, I illustrated George's classic
story about the young man and the gallumphing lunatic, "Mr.
Benson's Experience with a Maniac." I have made a huge success
telling this story to my children, animated by startling activities
and facials.

There were 400 drawings in Volume III!

In 1895, after saving up for a year, George and I "announced"
to the editor that we were going abroad for four months. Mr.
Dennis, whose wise counsel and coaching nursed many a budding
genius to fame, wished us well as we departed. The paper paid our
weekly salaries of $35.00 (each) during our absence, conditional
upon our sending two illustrated feature stories a week. This
collection of stories bloomed later into a paper-back called, *What a
Man Sees Who Goes Away from Home.*

My fedora hat was the first seen in London. I was stared at by
crowds of Londoners.

On page 27 of Volume IV of the *Stories of the Streets and of the
Town,* I see Mr. Ade posing for me. Then Mr. Schmedtgen took
over for thirty pages but I came back strong with some Aubrey
Beardsley drawings for George's "Chicago High Art Up-to-Date,"
showing that modern art was just as modern in the Nineties as it
is today.

After this there seems to be some sort of a hiatus on my part.
Mr. Schmedtgen presided at the drawing board from page 102 to
134. Maybe I took another vacation, which by that time was
becoming an incurable habit. Or maybe it was due to a new chore
added to my daily duties. This was in late 1895. The editor thought
it would be nice if I would do a front page daily five-column
cartoon in my odd moments.

Mr. Ade was to provide the ideas during his spare moments from
the "Stories of the Streets," the Music and the Drama Depart-
ments, and his other literary activities.

Those were days when we weren't being spoiled by coddling. As
a matter of fact, we loved it. Seeing the paper every morning with
our stuff featured was a major adventure. Whether or not we knew
it, opportunity was knocking at our door every morning.

The first story in Volume V is a "Doc Horne" story—later to
reach a cordial host of readers in book form. And on page 10 is the
first of the "Ollie and Freddie" stories, the saga of two of Chicago's
gilded youth.

George was now going stronger for fiction. *Artie* (1896), *Pink Marsh* (1897), and *Doc Horne* (1899) came out in book form, published by Herbert S. Stone & Company; and many thousands of admiring readers were learning for the first time the name of the writer who had written them. I don't seem to locate these three classics but I remember illustrating them.

The fifth volume presented that delightful story "The Barclay Lawn Party." In later years George was to receive $2500 for such a story.

The man who succeeded Eugene Field as conductor of "Sharps and Flats" is portrayed at a piano which is being played by a lovely young lady [p. 59]. I remember the portrait perfectly and his name is Carl Smith, but as for the young lady, I regret that I have wholly forgotten her.

On page 70 is my younger brother Ben and on page 108 is Sewell Collins—afterwards a distinguished artist in London. Hugh Fullerton, famous sports writer, is on page 110, and on 116 Charley Alling, loyal Sigma Chi and life of countless Sig gatherings, once more rallies the lagging spirits of his less dynamic colleagues.

In the fifth volume, I seem to have done all of the 251 drawings all by myself despite the diverting effect of a daily five-column cartoon.

When the sixth volume left the press on July 1, 1898, my days of co-operation in the series had reached an ending. In August of 1897, I accepted an invitation from Assistant Secretary of the Treasury, Frank Vanderlip, to go around the world on a new U. S. revenue cutter, booked to leave the Cramp Shipbuilding Yards in Philadelphia the following December. A trip planned for six months stretched out to nearly three years, during which I attended three wars and collected a notable assortment of Asiatic microbes of a most disagreeable character.

With my drawings in the fore part of Vol. VI, my connection with the "Stories of the Streets" ended. I was away on the bounding deep or dodging unfriendly bullets.

Incidentally I picked up some material about the Sultan of Sulu which George Ade used in his first musical play—a huge success.

Carl Werntz, Charles Sarka and Clyde Newman alternated in illustrating the Ade columns; and it is the drawings done by these three young comers that appear in volumes six, seven and eight. They have all marched onward to fame and distinction in wide fields. It was Newman's brilliant illustrations that adorned the first of the famous Ade *Fables in Slang*.

Although I missed the final volumes of the *Stories of the Streets and of the Town* I note that I began to appear again in *The Chicago Record War Stories* (1898), *Notes from Foreign Lands*, (1899) and *Stories of Filipino Warfare* of which I was author and illustrator (1900); so I was not entirely left out.

John T. McCutcheon

* * *

The "Stories of the Streets and of the Town" played a tremendously significant role in George Ade's literary development. It was the matrix of all his work. Everything that is crucial in the development of Ade as an interpreter of the great American scene is present: the rich, colorful everyday life, the vernacular, the character studies, the fables, the dramatic forms, the jingles—as well as the moods, the sly humor, the turn of the phrase, the quaint artistry of indirection which was so peculiarly his. It is all there; you cannot know George Ade without knowing these seven years of daily literary production.

Heretofore Ade has been pigeonholed as a fabulist, a humorist, a playwright, a character delineator, a short-story writer. Now for the first time it is possible to see Ade in his true literary lights. Sketch upon sketch from the "Stories of the Streets and of the Town" reveal the true George Ade, the many-sided genius sparkling through many facets.

Chicago was his workshop and his laboratory, as well as the backdrop against which his characters lived and talked realistically. He rambled about town, and made notes enough to fill an unabridged dictionary; but never once did he put himself into a story. When Ade was out of town or on vacation, able members of *The Record* staff were selected by Mr. Dennis to take over the column. Ade recalls that Mr. Dennis was a choosy picker when he selected "Billy" Iglehart, Trumbull White, Malcolm McDowell, Kennett Harris, Ray Stannard Baker, who later became famous as "David Grayson" and as the biographer of Woodrow Wilson.

As Dennis and McCutcheon have pointed out, Ade's was a roving assignment—he got his materials from all corners of the city. "It is doubtful," observed McCutcheon, "whether any other newspaper man has had equal opportunities for studying every class of people in a big city. . . . He had the faculty of making an interesting story of anything, whether it was a ride in a streetcar or a dissertation on the probabilities of rain. . . . In each story there was a freshness and charm that compelled the expectant interest of thousands of readers."[10]

"So I started on a seven-year Marathon," relates Ade. "In a little while we discovered that readers became more interested in our 'Stories of the Streets and of the Town' if they could find familiar characters recurring in the yarns. The first to bob up about once a week was a brash young office employee named 'Artie' Blanchard, a very usual specimen of the period. Then 'Pink' Marsh, a city Negro of the sophisticated kind, became a regular visitor. He was followed by 'Doc' Horne, an amiable old falsifier, not unlike 'Lightnin',' so delightfully played by Frank Bacon."[4]

Although "Artie," "Pink" Marsh, and "Doc" Horne are probably the best known because of their subsequent book publication, there were other popular series, of both episodes and character sketches. The most notable of these were "Min Sargent" (the office girl, the counterpart of "Artie"), "The Frisbee Club," "The Hickey Boy," "Ollie and Freddie," and "Stories of the 'Benevolent Assimilation.'" The burlesque boys' stories (*Handsome Cyril, Clarence Allen,* and *Rollo Johnson*) later issued in colorful pamphlets by the Bandar Log Press, appeared first in the column, and are included with the original illustrations in this volume.

The "Artie" stories appeared at intervals from Dec. 9, 1895, to May 30, 1896; "Pink Marsh" from Dec. 15, 1896, to May 22, 1897; "Doc Horne" from June 3, 1896, to Dec. 8, 1897. But even before these characters *propre* had emerged in full stature, preliminary figures had preceded. Artie slowly came to full focus out of character delineations of young men typically occupied in downtown offices. Pink Marsh began to take shape through a synthesis of real persons involved in real episodes. Two sketches will show some of the aspects of this process: "How 'Pink' Was Reformed" (p. 98), and "How 'Pick' Caught the 'Battle-Row'" (p. 153). Thus two important facts become quite clear: first, these characters have undergone an important literary development; and second, they are realistic products fashioned out of everyday life.

Consider Ade's form of the Fable in Slang. The first fable in slang appeared Sept. 17, 1897, without caption; and the same fable was published in *Fables in Slang*, 1900, under the title, "The Fable of Sister Mae Who Did as Well as Could Be Expected." This fable in its original form has been included in this selection (p. 220) for purposes of comparison with the final book version. More significant, though, than the first appearance of the actual fable *form* itself, was Ade's tendency to write in the fable *style*. Ade apparently had a flair for the fable. From the very outset he seemed naturally to drop into a concentrated literary form as telling in its dramatic economy, as McCutcheon's art of the simple pencil line was strikingly effective in shaping the mass. Indeed, the very first sketch Ade wrote for his column, "A Young Man in Upper Life," the very first story written for the column, suggests the beginning of a fable technique which is the keynote to his literary style.

Even Ade's plays, successes which he achieved later, find their roots in the "Stories of the Streets." Of his earliest sketches, "Mr. Pensely Has a Quiet Day Off" (p. 23) and "Il Janitoro" (p. 177) are clearly and consciously cast in actual dramatic form, as were many other subsequent sketches. For materials too, Ade was indebted to his newspaper column, as for example the *Sultan of Sulu* (1902), which made considerable use of a series of "Stories of 'Benevolent Assimilation.'" His short-story writing, of which "Effie Whittlesy"[17] is an American masterpiece, evolved out of his daily stories of fiction. Some of Ade's best short stories and local-color sketches were later collected and published under the title *In Babel*, 1903. The story "Effie Whittlesy" appeared originally in *The Chicago Record*, March 13, 1896.

Selections from each of these major lines of growth have been included in this volume to show how implicitly Ade's finished literary productions evolved out of his daily newspaper department.   *   *   *

To his job of capturing and sketching the American scene,

Ade brought a number of significant talents, which have best been pointed out by his collaborator, John T. McCutcheon:

"In 1890 Ade went to Chicago armed with the following equipment: A wonderful memory, an X-ray insight into motives and men, a highly developed power of keen observation and the benefit of four years of literary work in college and three years in professional fields. He had lived in the country and had retained, as on a photographic plate, the most comprehensive impressions of country life. He knew the types, the vernacular, and the point of view of the country people from the inside. He had lived in a small town and had acquired a thorough knowledge of the types and the customs of this phase of life. He had learned college life during four years of observation and had learned the life of the medium-sized town. With a memory that retained his observations of these four distinct elements of life, and an intelligence great enough to use this knowledge, he was ready to learn what a great city could teach."[12]

What that city did teach, how the artist responded, and how the artist and city grew up together during ten years unfolds in the "Stories of the Streets and of the Town." Fortunately for the literary history of Chicago, George Ade has himself related the story of those early days. Said Mr. Ade to the writer in September, 1940, at Hazelden:

"My ambition, like McCutcheon's, was to report people as they really were, as I saw them in their everyday life, and as I knew them to be. Consequently, I avoided exaggeration, burlesque, and crude caricature; and I did not try to fictionize or to embroider fancy situations, as was common in the fiction of that day. In the 'Stories' there was not much emphasis upon plot, but instead carefully sketched, detailed incidents in the delineation of real characters in real life, depicting various episodes in their lives as related through the medium of their own *talk*.

"Talk, conversation, what people say when they come together on the street, their peculiar use of words, their 'slang,' their rhythms of speech—that's what I mean by '*vernacular*.' These are the things that have always interested me most; there is nothing more native than speech.

"But by 'slang' I did not intend the 'flash' talk of thieves or people of the underworld. When I used the word 'slang' I meant the 'vernacular,' as I said before. Indeed, my slang was selected for Mother and the Girls. I tried to make playful use of the vernacular—which is really another way of saying 'unconventional Americanisms'—rather than out-and-out slang. Of course, the extremes of slang change rapidly; yet, if you will look back through my 'Stories of the Streets and of the Town' the language will not seem frightfully antiquated. It isn't flagrantly dated, and it seems more natural than one might suppose, because it is written in the common, everyday vernacular.

"Writing conversation and dialogue day after day, and year after year, in the 'Stories of the Streets and of the Town' proved to be of great help to me later in writing plays. The art of conversation and of making 'talk' sound natural came from listening intently to all kinds of talk and getting it translated quickly into the printed word, thus carrying over onto the printed page the naturalness that goes with the spoken word. Many of the 'Stories' were, in fact, cast in dramatic form, some more deliberately than others; still others were only sketchy tableaux. But throughout there was that economy of situation which is the essence of the dramatic; and, too, the subject matter was something that everybody could understand and enjoy, because there was that same faithful realism. It was natural.

"The vernacular played an important part in the fable too; like the dramatic form it also carried over the peculiarities and rhythms of speech. When I wrote my first fables in slang I thought I had discovered something new. I thought I had created a new variety, using the archaic fable form as a base, but introducing vernacular speech and using capital letters. But to my great surprise I was accused of adapting a technique used by Ambrose Bierce. The only thing wrong with that claim was that I had never known anything of Bierce's fables (or of anybody else's for that matter). I had never seen them, or heard of them.

"My column the 'Stories of the Streets and of the Town' was contemporary with Eugene Field's column 'Sharps and

Flats' during 1893 and 1894; and at about the same time Pete Dunne was writing his 'Mr. Dooley' stories for the *Journal*. Field was positively brilliant, ranging from the highly sentimental to the rarest things that man ever wrote, but his technique was always faultless. Field wrote all his copy in that fine copperplate hand; he filled his entire column himself, often writing twenty-six hundred words a day. Pete Dunne was a highbrow—an intellectual. He got his education by reading; he didn't have a formal schooling, but he read voraciously. He wrote beautiful English. His 'Mr. Dooley' papers were really editorials in dialect; as a matter of fact, Dunne was an editorial writer. Dunne was a vindictive person, often caustic, but always witty.

"I knew Field and Dunne rather intimately. We were all members of the old Chicago Press Club, but in the Nineties a number of us purely professional newspapermen pulled out and started an independent Newspaper Club of our own. The old Press Club had become a 'free-lunch outfit,' extending its membership to all kinds and classes, many of whom had nothing to do with journalism. Another meeting place was the Whitechapel Club, just back of the old Daily News building (Wells and Madison), with its entrance from the alley between Wells and LaSalle, east of the News building and to the north, where the newsboys got their papers. The Whitechapel Club was a rip-roaring place, not the quiet, dignified spot that some writers have pictured it. The main feature was a spacious bar thrown across the front room, and built in the shape of a coffin. The chorus of the drinking song usually heard around this famous bar ran,

> 'Then stand to your glasses steady
> And drink to your comrades' eyes.
> Here's a toast to the dead already
> And Hurrah for the next who dies!'

"At these various clubs I picked up many leads, for their stories were the stories of the streets and the town, stories of Chicago life."

* * *

Ade caught the spirit of Chicago, the Chicago of the Gay

Nineties, in his compact, fable style, his daily episodes of
city life phrased in the vernacular. His 1001 tales of the
throbbing city had this basic element: they were motivated
by the *push* in Chicago life. They appealed to the contemporary Chicagoan who knew what they were all about. One
of those contemporaries, Albert Nicholas Hosking, recognized Ade's significance and his role in the life and literature
of Chicago, when in October, 1898, as editor and publisher
of a monthly chapbook called *Pickwick, The Town Crier*,[13]
he devoted a special issue to Ade, crying the wares of his
fellow-townsman:

"A person starting out in Chicago to make a name in
literature has an up-hill piece of work. Not because Chicago
has such a galaxy of literary men that it is hard to obtain a
place in this line—no, far from that; but, because Chicago
and its population are seeking means and schemes for making
the Almighty Dollar, and take little heed for art in any
form—in this I am speaking generally.

"And so, this being the case, when a person decides to
follow a literary pursuit, he must needs be wary. The average
Chicago reader wants something that appeals to him; something that treats of the atmosphere he walks in; something that
he knows of. He wants, if he reads fiction, the language that
he hears every day; he wants the local spirit and color portrayed of the city he lives in; he wants conciseness of speech.
Instead of saying: 'I think this project, if rightly handled,
would prove successful,' the Chicagoan does away with all
this and says 'It's a cinch.' He does not want a thousand-page
novel, but about one-tenth of this. He is willing to listen to
a love story if the thing is told quickly, and has the right kind
of a swing to it.

"And so there has been one man in Chicago's limited field
of literature who has realized this, and this man is George
Ade. Coming from an Indiana town some eight years ago,
Ade secured a position on *The Chicago Record*. In the field of
the reporter, seeing all sides of city life in the smoky atmosphere of the day and glare of electric lights at night, he soon
gathered the material that was to make for him the strain
of many tales—some more interesting than others, to be sure,
but all containing the *push* of Chicago life.

"Ade was an observer, not a dreamer. He realized that the city into which he had come had a certain personality to it. It had a certain 'something' that seemed to make up a part of every one of its separate inhabitants; and studying this 'something,' he started in to write—and write in a vein that would catch the people. I do not mean to convey the idea that he wrote in this manner for mere mercenary profit, but as a literary study. He realized that no matter what phase of life a writer took up, so long as he drew the pictures perfectly and truthfully he was carrying out his art.

"When talking with Mr. Ade some few days ago, concerning his 'Stories of the Streets and of the Town' in *The Chicago Record*, and about their beginning, he remarked, 'I thought some freakish stuff in this line would take better than two columns of jokes. Things about town, you know, that a man can pick up and put into a story.' And sure enough his 'freakish stuff' did take. These two columns, which appear on the editorial page, are read as eagerly as the editorials.

"Ade's pen has crystallized noticeable characteristics of the middle walks of life. He has taken a type like 'Artie,' and there are many of 'Artie's' kind, and portrayed the slangy, good-hearted, whole-souled character of his class, and not overdrawn him, as many would have done. He has put language in 'Artie's' mouth that is spoken by the majority of the young men of this class, locally. All in all, 'Artie' appeals to the average Chicagoan, and therefore he is liked. The love affair which 'Artie' gets into is commonplace; but, Ade handles it with such a grace that it cannot but appeal to the reader.

"And insomuch as Ade has drawn his many characters truthfully, insomuch he is an artist. His portrayal of 'Pink Marsh,' a type of the Chicago Negro, or 'Afro-American,' is as clever as Mr. Cable's Creole characters. From his 'politician' to his 'newsboy,' there runs that freshness of local color which is ever amusing, ever readable. Ade is a story-teller to the many, not the few."

* * *

Critical evaluation of George Ade as a literary figure has barely begun. William Dean Howells, novelist and editor, "discovered" George Ade, and continued his ardent admirer. Both were realists of a kind, Ade inclining to the realism approved by Howells: that is, fidelity to life itself, expressed simply, honestly, naturally. It was as the realistic interpreter of the American scene, particularly of the Midwest and of Chicago, that Howells hailed the accomplishments of George Ade.

When Henry B. Fuller and Robert Herrick were novelizing, and George Ade was still conducting his column, Howells commented on the Chicago scene in 1898:[14]

"Mr. Fuller's Chicago novels, like that of Mr. Herrick, take his city on the society side, but with rather more of a slant towards what may be called the humaner side. On the humaner side, with no slant at all towards the society side, is a book by Mr. George Ade, called 'Artie: A Story of the Streets and Town.'

"On the level which it consciously seeks I do not believe there is a better study of American town life in the West. It treats of American town life without the foreign admixture which is so characteristic in the East; its persons are types which one cannot fail to recognize who knows our better sort of hard-working people. The author of 'Artie' has not over-done them in any way; he has neither caricatured nor flattered them."

In a further consideration of the "Chicago School of Fiction"[15] Howells emphasized Ade's adroit directness, his lack of literary pose, "his perfect control in dealing with the American as he knows himself.

"In Mr. George Ade the American spirit arrives: arrives, puts down its grip, looks around, takes a chair and makes itself at home. It has no questions to ask and none to answer. There it is, with its hat pushed back, its hands in its pockets, and at its outstretched feet that whole, vast, droll American world, essentially alike in Maine and Oregon and all the hustling regions between: speaking one slang, living one life, meaning one thing.

"The level struck is low: the level of the street, which seems not depressed in the basement barber-shop where Pink Marsh polishes shoes, or lifted in the office where Artie talks to his friend and evolves himself and his simple love story. It is the same level in the entrance floor of the Alfalfa, where Doc Horne sits with his fortuitous companions and harmlessly romances. You are not asked to be interested in any one because he is any way out of the common, but because he is every way in the common. Mr. Ade would not think of explaining or apologizing or at all accounting for the company he invites you to keep. He knows too well how good it is, and he cheerfully takes the chance of your not yourself being better.

"But our life, our good, kind, droll, ridiculous American life, is really inexhaustible, and Mr. Ade, who knows its breadths and depths as few others have known them, drops his net into it anywhere, and pulls it up full of the queer fish which abound in it.

"Each fable is really a little satire, expressing itself in the richest and freshest slang, but of a keenness which no most polished satire has surpassed, and of a candid complicity with the thing satirized—our common American civilization, namely—which satire has never confessed before. I am trying to get round to saying a thing I find difficult: that is, how the author posits his varying people in their varying situations without a word of excuse or palliation for either, in the full confidence that so far as you are truly American you will know them, and as far as you are truly honest you will own yourself of their breed and more or less of their experience."

As an interpreter of the American scene, Ade has also been accorded high praise by Henry L. Mencken,[16] critic and author of *The American Language*:

". . . the whole body of his [Ade's] work . . . is as thoroughly American, in cut and color, in tang and savor, in structure and point of view, as the work of Howells, E. W. Howe or Mark Twain. . . . there is a vivid and accurate evocation of the American scene. Here . . . there are brilliant flashlight pictures of the American people, and American ways of thinking, and the whole American *Kultur*. Here the veritable Americano stands forth, lacking not a waggery, a superstition, a snuffle or a wen.

"Ade himself, for all his story-teller's pretense of remoteness, is as absolutely American as any of his prairie-town traders and pushers, Shylocks and Dogberries, beaux and belles. No other writer of our generation, save perhaps Howe, is more unescapably national in his every gesture and trick of mind. He is as American as buckwheat cakes."

*   *   *

"They Simply Wouldn't Let Me Be a Highbrow" wrote George Ade. But Ade was much more of a high-brow than he realized, at the same time achieving an art of *hofbrau* literary phrasing that appealed to millions of Americans—one of the qualities of true genius shared alike by Abe Lincoln and George Ade.

His fables in slang are *sugar-coated* social history capsules. His character sketches, his fables, his stories, and his plays are all cut from the same cloth—realistic reporting of the American scene, illumined by his sly Hoosier humor.

The "Stories of the Streets and of the Town" are a part of that tradition. They are cross sections of Chicago life in the Gay Nineties drawn by a master artist, cameos of Chicago culture when the "Lake Shore Drive put on its evening clothes in the afternoon."

Franklin J. Meine

Chicago, Illinois
September 1, 1941

Stories of Chicago

A Young Man in Upper Life

THIS is a story of a young man in upper life. He was honorably connected with a real-estate firm. By years of service he had risen from "the boy" to "our Mr. Ponsby." His salary had gone up in the same ratio. He had a desk of his own. His hopes and prospects had risen as various marks of favor were shown him by the two speculative subdividers.

The firm had gone up also—gone up literally. At first it held forth on the third floor of a dark and smoky old building, a relic of the '70s with a mansard roof, but no elevator. Then it vaulted upward to the sixteenth floor of a tower built from steel and glass, so that "our Mr. Ponsby," when he ascended to his daily work, was lifted in the quick, decisive way of a man holding to a rocket.

He liked the hush and quiet and the immense suggestion of space in this upper air. From his window he commanded a limitless view of atmosphere and he found this view very restful when he was bending his mind to something which required deep and prolonged thought. The members of the firm could sell lots if they had their man cornered, but they could

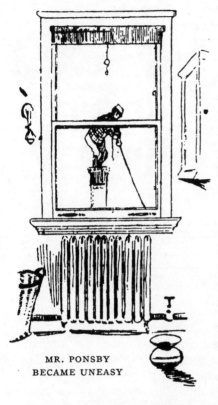

MR. PONSBY
BECAME UNEASY

not write the alluring descriptions which rolled so readily from their tongues. They had the mesmeric power which shows itself in personal contact, but they lacked the peculiar genius of getting up a display advertisement. This work fell to "our Mr. Ponsby." It was he who prepared the thirty-two-page prospectus setting forth the beauties and advantages of Hazel Glen, the future manufacturing and residence suburb of Chicago. When it is learned that Hazel Glen is still a primeval forest with a barbed-wire fence along the principal boulevard, it will be appreciated that Mr. Ponsby needed very favorable conditions under which to do his word painting. Perhaps the most formidable task to which he ever set himself was to think out and tabulate twenty-five reasons why Hazel Glen would in five years' time witness a general advance in values of from 1,000 to 2,000 per cent. When engaged in work of this kind he would gaze steadfastly out of the window opposite his desk and bend his whole intellect to the problem of getting gas, water works, public schools and quick suburban service for the future manufacturing and residence center of Cook County.

When he looked out of the window he saw nothing to distract his attention. He could think all the more intently. He saw simply a picture of smoke-laden air set in a hardwood frame. Back through this sooty air were the vague outlines of buildings almost as tall as that under whose roof he sat, but they were so far away that only by straining the eyes could they be seen at all.

One day standing at the window and glancing down the sheer precipice Mr. Ponsby saw that workingmen were tearing holes in the roof of the squatty building underneath. Four days later, as he was going to lunch, he was surprised to see that the squatty building had disappeared and that in its place was a hole in the ground with men and horses scrambling around the bottom of it. After that, as he went in and out of his own tall structure, he became accustomed to the sight of derricks and the sound of hammering.

One morning, with an unusual weight of responsibility on his shoulders, he sat at his desk and wondered what could be the matter. He had a slight headache, which was partly remorse and partly actual pain, but he knew this did not account for his lack of concentration. Mr. Ponsby was one of those self-willed young men who can watch a sunrise through an alcoholic mist and then, after three hours in a Turkish bath, can appear at the office and add up long columns of figures. As a rule he could fall into his chair and get the swing of his day's work within five minutes. On this particular morning he seemed turned around, or rather the premises were turned around. He wondered if any one had been moving the furniture. As he wondered he gazed out of the window, and it gradually dawned upon him that something new had come into the picture.

There, in the smoke-tinted atmosphere, alone and apparently unsupported, stood a steel column. At first sight it gave him a shock. He could not realize that the skeleton structure had been pieced together, high-

THEY WERE
EATING DINNER

er and higher into the air, until the topmost bough in that tangle of steel had reached his sky window and was standing there in offensive boldness to spoil his view and break the peaceful course of his business meditations. Often that day he found himself turning his eyes to the window for a few minutes of profound and abstracted thought, only to be confronted by that bar of steel and to feel himself annoyed by the presence of the stiff, immovable specter.

The next day was worse than ever. He had forgotten the specter and came cheerfully to his work. He sat at his desk, opened a few letters, whistled cheerfully, and then, from force of habit, looked out of the window, expecting, also by force of habit, to see what he had usually seen—nothing, and that faintly diluted by smoke.

What he saw was the solitary column showing itself above the ledge, and perched on the top of this column a man, the two making a very black silhouette against the midair.

"Great Scott!" said young Mr. Ponsby. "That man will certainly fall if he isn't careful."

The man didn't seem to think so. He was a muscular person, with very square shoulders. He wore a Scotch cap and a heavy suit with a tight pea-jacket. He held a rope which trailed off in the depths below him. As he sat on the cap of the lone column he chewed tobacco with much vigor and occasionally spat out into indefinite space. Mr. Ponsby, forgetting all about Hazel Glen and the advantages of shade trees in a suburb, held to his armchair in blank horror and amazement and watched the man with the pea-jacket untwine his legs from around the column and slowly come to a standing position, like a statue on a slim pedestal. Putting his hands up to his mouth, he shouted something, and there came faint answers from somewhere below.

Mr. Ponsby could not work. He tried for half an hour, but each time he put his eyes to his desk he began to wonder what the man on the pedestal was doing or whether he had fallen off. After two hours passed under these distracting circumstances he began to hope the man would fall off, and he even decided to quit trying to work until he saw it happen. Accordingly he tilted himself back and waited.

The man perched at the top of the pedestal grinned at him through the window and swung his arms to keep warm. At such times he maintained his equilibrium by hooking his toes behind the column and hugging it with his knees, a proceeding which made young Mr. Ponsby ache with a sort of chilling expectation.

But the man did not fall off. He crawled down the column and disappeared from view about 11 o'clock, only to reappear at 11:30. And about this time the restless arm of a steam crane threw its first diagonal shadow across Mr. Ponsby's window and helped to make his nervous condition more pitiable. What this steam crane was resting upon and how it suddenly came into this upper region young Mr. Pons-

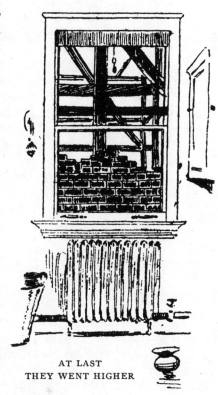

AT LAST
THEY WENT HIGHER

by knew not. He only knew that with it came other men in pea-jackets, and they all shinned up the solitary column and helped fasten on transverse straps of steel, which reached out in either direction and laid hold on other columns.

Then before his once peaceful window men sat on narrow girders, with their legs dangling over, and ate frugal lunches from tin buckets. After that they would lower the buckets by means of the rope belonging to the steam hoist, and when the buckets came back they would foam at the brim and would be not buckets but "growlers."

Young Mr. Ponsby found himself under a strain as the workingmen climbed or trotted back and forth in front of his window. He did not want to watch them, but he found that he had to, for he felt that some day one of them would make a misstep and go plunging down some sixteen stories to the pavement. So he sat at his desk day after day and suffered the nervous strain.

The skeleton structure had gone farther skyward, leaving a sharp-jointed network in front of his window, but the men continued to go up and down this like so many squirrels.

It was a glad morning when he saw above the rim of his window-sill the white cap of the mason who was putting a shell of terra-cotta around the steel limbs and joints. For three days he watched the masons with a show of interest which he could not explain. Then the terra-cotta wall went up to greater heights, and Mr. Ponsby, finding some relief in a bare wall, went back to his neglected work.

Since the Frenchman Came

ALL the homeless people who love comfort and cheer; all the women who wish to peer into Bohemia without being really a part of it; all the lonesome souls who remember Paris but cannot get back to it; all the free-born men who hold it as their privilege to smoke at the table; all the inquiring young men who wish to cultivate a taste for Brie cheese, and all the transient professionals who have wearied of the hotel sirloin, may be found sooner or later at one of the table d'hôte restaurants. These places have sprung up in Chicago during the last few years. They are owned by Frenchmen. Each bill of fare is a compromise between French and English, and the waiter may properly be called a "garçon."

*   *   *

All day the place is dull and quiet. At noontime there is an hour's awakening and a straggling dozen or two for luncheon, but not until 6 o'clock, when all the lights are blazing, do the tables fill up and the waiters rise to the frenzy of the occasion. The price is anywhere from 50 to 75 cents, never more than the latter, and this includes a bottle of wine. Sometimes it is a pint and sometimes a half pint. The waiter calls it "claret," and perhaps it is. The liquid is dark red and vinegary, and everyone drinks it copiously for the edge it gives to the appetite.

The Chicago restaurant man, with his strong liking for large slices of meat and dangerous sections of pie, has never made a success of a table d'hôte. It requires the close attention of a Frenchman—the genius born of enforced economy and the nice calculation which overlooks no detail—to give a dinner and a bottle of wine for 75 cents and make money. The dinner—one of two or three kinds of soup, fish, an entrée to be selected from a list of three or four, one or two vegetables, a roast, salad, dessert and coffee. Six courses, wine, "a bit of Roquefort, please," and a small coffee—why, the man with 75 cents becomes an epicure. If the entire feast were tipped before him in one job lot, as it is in a railway dining station, it would not be formidable. But when it comes to six instalments scattered through an hour, the liberality of the Frenchman becomes astounding.

There are certain old-timers whom you will see any evening. They have no other retreat and want none. They have a certain foreign way of bowing to the cashier. Their overcoats have capes. Some have pointed beards and others are bald, but fiercely mustached. They seek corner tables to themselves and there talk in French. The discussions are endless and never lacking in vigor. One is always in doubt whether they are artists, musicians or language teachers, but one cannot doubt their Parisian origin. They pour their claret into large glasses and order the water bottle taken away. The fish grows cold while they gesticulate at one another. To them dinner means a blissful two hours, the last half-hour being spent in a blue fog of tobacco-smoke.

* * *

At another table sit a young man and a young woman, well-dressed, well-behaved and undeniably modest. They seem too unconcerned and placid for a newly-married couple, and they are too young to have been married very many years. Their conduct is so correct that one is not justified in being inquisitive, and why should one be inquisitive? This is Chicago, and so let every table take care of itself. And yet one cannot but wonder who all of them are and where they came from.

Regarding the girls from the opera company there is not

much room for question. They are sweetly oblivious of all other persons in the room and talk "shop" with abandon.

"Say, tell that waiter to hurry up. We go on in an hour and twenty minutes."

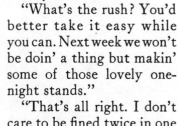

"What's the rush? You'd better take it easy while you can. Next week we won't be doin' a thing but makin' some of those lovely one-night stands."

"That's all right. I don't care to be fined twice in one month."

"You ought to stand in."

"I suppose I had, but I'm not saying a word. I got a letter today, and if things turn out all right you'll lose me."

"What is it?"

REGULAR PATRONS

"Oh, you'll find out in time. It's a speaking part, I'll tell you that much, and a good old line in the cast."

*   *   *

Sometimes the devotees of winter racing come with the evening rush, and they leave no doubt as to their identity. As soon as they have tucked their napkins:

"That settles it, Steve; it's the last time I'll ever play that dog. I've followed him a dozen times and it was always a cinch, and I never win but once. I pass him up, I tell you that."

"You're right. He's an in-and-outer. I wouldn't lay a cent on him and never would since he threw me down at Latonia. I had that race dead. Where was you?"

"I put my stuff on early and then went away with Mose to get a drink. How's that? Yes, gi' me some of that first kind of soup. Did you say you had it?"

"Nailed down. I got it right, too, but like a great, big geeser I only puts on ten. Well, I win twenty-five. That ain't bad, eh?"

"I guess it's some better than burnin' up fifty cold bucks."
"Well, a few."
And so on.

* * *

The Chicago young man who wants to try his French on some one gives the waiters much trouble. He insists on calling his orders in French and engaging the waiter in conversation. The waiter, who expects a tip of at least 15 cents, is too considerate to misunderstand, and so he says: "You have the true Parisian accent." This generally insures an increase of the tip to 25 cents.

The blasé youth is here—the blasé youth who would be a man of the world and begins by learning to drink a pousse café and smoke a black cigar, so that when he goes down the stairway and into the street the electric lamps have rainbows around them and the cable cars turn the wrong corners.

The French are not the only foreigners. On some evenings there are three or four languages mixed up in the polite babel. The people at the table d'hôte

OF THE OPERA COMPANY

talk under the cheering influence of claret, tobacco and strong coffee; the conversation grows bolder toward 8 o'clock, and a group at a table has been known to sing a song without giving particular offense to any one else.

* * *

If Chicago was backward in patronizing French table d'hôte restaurants it seems to be making amends now. Long after

New York and San Francisco had many such places, all prosperous, there was not one restaurant in Chicago where a man could get a course dinner properly cooked and well served for a reasonable price. One attempt after another was made by enterprising Frenchmen and Italians who thought they had found a rich field. They opened their restaurants, prepared their tempting bills and put the waiters at the tables. A few hopeful patrons came around each evening, but the general public continued to pass by and search out the quick-service oyster house and the rapid-firing lunch counter. There must have been a dozen abject failures in the ten years preceding the World's Fair. It was during the Fair that the tide turned. Who will ever know the full effect these visiting foreigners had on Chicago?

THEIR FIRST POUSSE CAFÉ

At any rate, the French table d'hôte restaurant is now a prosperous institution. The number of down-town people who can and will give an hour to their dinner is increasing. There seem to be more persons who prefer a dozen dainty bits to one huge piece of steak, accompanied by a windrow of potatoes. The powerful cheese of foreign manufacture has supplanted, to some extent, plain American pie as an after-dinner luxury. Coffee cups have become smaller, and the man who lights a cigar is not thrown out by a policeman.

*   *   *

The Frenchmen with the pointed beards and cape coats feel encouraged, and say Chicago is becoming civilized.

The Mystery of the Back-Roomer

THERE went the front doorbell again! Mrs. Morgane's hopes rose accordingly.

The bell gave forth a hollow gong-like sound. It was required to make a good deal of noise, as Mrs. Morgane's furnished apartments were on the second and third floors of the red-brick building, a tailoring and cleansing establishment having the first floor.

When the door-bell rang Mrs. Morgane at once said: "Some one for the top back room." She had been trying for over a month to rent it. All sorts and conditions of men had climbed the stairs and followed her into the room. She always pulled the curtain away up and began by telling that the last young man who occupied it—a very nice young man, by the way—had gone out on the road as a salesman and of course he couldn't keep a room in the city.

"It is small but comfortable," she would say. "We get steam heat from the building next to us. The bed has a lovely set of springs. The bath-room is on the floor below, but of course you have your pitcher here. I did get $3 for this room, but you may have it for $2.50.

They made all sorts of excuses to get out of the house. One would say the room was too small. Another insisted on running water. In some instances the room was too far up or too far back. An occasional caller would promise to "look around," and perhaps come back. Only a week before an elderly man with a shawl-strap full of books, after pointing out the danger of living on a third floor without a fire escape had said in a roundabout way that he "guessed" he would move in. But he didn't come.

Now Mrs. Morgane, having primped a little before her glass, hurried down-stairs to welcome another. Much depended on renting the top back room. With the other rooms taken her profits were but slight. All revenues from the back room would be so much clear gain.

She found at the door a rather pale man, apparently between 30 and 35 years of age. He was smooth-shaven and had an aquiline nose and melancholy eyes. The closely buttoned Prince Albert told in his favor, although it did seem to go badly with the striped shirt. Mrs. Morgane had ceased to be a stickler as to attire. The only man who had ever defrauded her of a full month's rent dressed beautifully.

The stranger was quiet and attentive as she told him the old story of the peculiar advantages of the top back room. She was more than surprised when he thrust a cameoed finger into his vest pocket and produced a $5 bill in payment for two weeks' rent.

No questions were asked.

*   *   *

Mrs. Morgane did not require the usual exchange of references. Like a court of exact justice, she regarded every person as respectable and trustworthy until he or she was shown to be something else and then she acted with great firmness. Her furnished apartments were for people more or less restricted as to finances and she didn't object if, instead of getting their refreshments outside, they sent out a pitcher and a dime. When she found a steady and reliable roomer she did all she could to keep him and for a year there had not been a change, except in the top back room. The furniture man had moved out a year before when an increase of salary changed his notions of life, and the first to succeed him was a very blonde young woman who asked a great many questions about the other people in the house and remarked that one couldn't be too particular. Her husband was out of town most of the time and during his absence she employed herself in reading woodcut weeklies and going to the theaters. The tickets came to her with some regularity and were always in plain envelopes. As for the husband, he proved to be a man of the most variable habits, calling sometimes twice a day and sometimes once in two weeks. Finally Mrs. Morgane grew weary at these eccentricities and so the blonde young woman was requested to go elsewhere.

The next one was a whistling young man, whose personal effects seemed to consist largely of photographs and Indian

"IT WAS NO WONDER THAT THEY BEGAN TO PEER AROUND
CORNERS AT HIM"

clubs. This young man, who professed an ardent admiration
of pugilism and the dramatic art, was employed in the pack-
ing department of a wholesale hardware house. He had a disturbing habit of dropping his Indian clubs during practice, and
one day while attempting an entirely new juggle he smashed
two panes of glass from the window. There was a difference of
opinion as to whether or not he should pay for the glass and
it was compromised by his moving away.

What need to tell of the three who came after him?

The last was a heavily mustached person who sang when
he felt like it, and felt like it when he came home along after
midnight. Mrs. Morgane couldn't stand that.

She now felt overjoyed to have in the room a man who moved in so quietly that morning that he did not disturb her at her work in the front room. He remained in the room all day and that evening went out carrying what appeared to be a small tin cash-box. She learned that he had been in bed all day and she observed, with some apprehension, that he and his tin box returned at 7 o'clock the next morning. The second day he remained in his room and on the second evening he departed in the same mysterious manner.

*   *   *

Mrs. Morgane was at the head of a strangely assorted community. Two steady men, given to early hours, had the large front rooms on the second floor. Behind them was the old book-keeper, who had been in that room ever since the furniture was carried in. At the rear was the woman who had separated from her husband. The exact trouble was not known to the other people in the house, but they agreed that the husband must be a brute. Mrs. Morgane and the girl who helped her had the top front rooms. The young woman stenographer, who was distantly related to Mrs. Morgane, had the next room back and then came the department-store young man, who performed wonders in the way he managed to get along on a small salary. He had two good suits and was saving up to buy a wheel. Farther to the rear of his little pocket apartment was a young man who worked in a book-bindery and employed his evenings in writing long letters. Then came the unlucky room, which had been taken by the stranger with the tin box. Mrs. Morgane had not so much as asked his name, and he had such a retiring way of turning the key in the lock as he went in that no one ventured to break in upon him or to try to scrape an acquaintance.

*   *   *

For a week he kept up his routine. In the afternoon or early evening, as the others would be going to their rooms or preparing for a cheerful reunion in Mrs. Morgane's parlor, they would see him stealthily going down-stairs. In the morning they would sometimes meet him coming back. It was no wonder that they began to peer around corners at him and that Mrs. Morgane tried to learn something from a study of his personal property.

There was but little to study. The wardrobe was limited, the trunk was always locked and the linen was marked "X9." No letters were left lying about and no mail came.

One morning when she met him on the stairway she said: "You're getting in late."

He smiled rather sadly and said: "A man in my profession can't sleep when other people do."

And before she could press further inquiries he paid another $5, which action she construed to mean that he did not choose to talk about himself.

*   *   *

That evening she found a pretext, however, for when he was about to depart she pounced out upon him and said: "I started to make out your receipt, but do you know I haven't learned your name yet?"

Three persons were waiting behind doors and at key-holes to catch his answer, which was most disappointing. He gave a name which may be found duplicated twenty times in the city directory and then he slipped away.

*   *   *

That evening there was an animated discussion of the stranger by Mrs. Morgane, the stenographer, the department-store young man and the woman who had experienced trouble with her husband.

"Now, what does he do?"

"May be he's a doctor."

"No; doctors have people send for them."

"But he said he was a professional man."

"He can't be a lawyer. They don't go around at night with tin boxes."

"Oh, I'll tell you, he might be a burglar and have his tools in that box."

"Get out! You can see that he is a gentleman. He doesn't look as though he drank."

"How about a gambler?"

"No; gamblers don't carry boxes, either."

All agreed that he should be questioned. The good name of the house demanded it.

The next Sunday afternoon the stenographer and the young man were present in the parlor as witnesses, when Mrs. Morgane by the most urgent methods lured him thither, and, after the commonplace remarks, asked: "By the way, what is your profession?"

He looked at her reproachfully as he answered: "I am a chiropodist in a Turkish bath."

"A what?"

"He removes corns," explained the department-store young man.

"And bunions," added the professional man.

*   *   *

They were interested and he told them of the work he did for the night customers. He was a professional man, after all. He became a favored member of the Morgane community and was afterward best man at the wedding of the stenographer and the department-store young man. It was in the morning, and he came around a trifle sleepy, for it had been a busy night.

In Chicago But Not of It

EVEN the entrance to the Art Institute is not at all like Chicago. It has too many broad landings and too little regard for space. The great terraced front is spread over enough ground to make the site of a sky-scraper. Then when the door is opened, instead of stepping into a corridor behind whose grated walls the elevator cages rise and fall, the visitor finds himself tip-toeing over the polished tiles, afraid to make any noise.

Any place as quiet as the Art Institute is a relief. The walls are dark-hued and restful, and there can be no more deadly silence than that made by a roomful of heroic casts and bronzes. The people who move along, usually two and two, fingering their catalogues and reading the unpoetic sticker labels, converse in whispers or a mumble. An occasional bell or whistle on the Illinois Central tracks interrupts for a moment, but the rattle of wheels on Michigan Avenue seems a long distance away.

The Art Institute is beginning to realize all hopes. During the summer of 1893 there was no room in it for the muses. It was in the possession of the busy delegate. Numberless typewriters were rattling away in the side rooms, the halls echoed with addresses of welcome which could not be easily located. There were many rooms and some kind of a "congress" in each that was large enough for a stage and a row of chairs. Morning, noon and night came the crushing at the doorways. Men and women with badges, catalogues and manuscripts elbowed one another. Policemen stood guard at every corner and told people to "take it easy." The place became littered with tracts and appeals and stray lace mitts and plain parasols.

Those were busy days—the days of the congresses when everything had to be discussed by some one—everything from esoteric Buddhism down to chop-feed. The delegates were for putting in as many hours as possible, so they ate at a café in a basement. Imagine the smell of cooking in a temple of art! The place certainly did not satisfy any artistic cravings. At the east were two huge temporary sheds made of wood and leaning in pitiful contrast against the classic pile. But even the stonework had a disturbing appearance. Some of it was white from the chisel and some blackened by the vandal influence of the smoke nuisance. Until November the so-called Art Institute was more like a swarming museum, with all sorts of "isms" and theories exhibited on the pedestals.

LOOKING AT THE OLD MASTERS

*   *   *

And now the change! The sheds have disappeared. The last blackboard chart and orator's glass pitcher were carted away many weeks ago. The kindly soot has made the whole exterior one unvaried shade of dinginess, suggesting an age equal to that of the pyramids. The committee-rooms and lecture halls have been given over to sculpture and architecture. Every bust, print or painting has found its niche. The whole interior glistens with cleanliness. In place of the congress orator you find the girl with the apron.

She is certainly more interesting, as a study, than a learned man with a passion for alpaca coats and white neckties. She is a student of art. As she would doubtless put it, she "is going in for art, and it's perfectly lovely." She has an easel and a boxful of rattling implements and a large square of paper marked with some strange beginnings, and a pair of coldly poised eye-glasses and the big gingham apron. Thus equipped she rambles, searching for that which she may make her own.

When you see her, you will say she is a refreshing sight. She spreads her easel in front of some plaster god, studies it in rapt admiration for a few moments and then begins making marks. She holds the pencil out at arm's length and, sliding her finger back and forth, gauges the distances and proportions. Such industry and such painstaking are surprising in one who would be expected to waste her time on chocolates and matinées. Almost any day there are a score of the aproned young women at the Art Institute. When they become weary of sketching they huddle together on the big soft divans and take turn about in raving over the Bonheurs, Geromes and Chases on the lower row of paintings.

A GROUP OF CRITICS

The institute policeman is different from those you meet in the outer world. His gloves are spotless white, his clothes are without a speck and he stands with his shoulders back. He doesn't know much about Phidias, but in a general way he is loyal to the "show." If a man asks the way to the oil paintings, this clever policeman not only points him the way up the shiny stairway and then to the north, but he goes ahead and gives the visitor some notion of the delights in store for him.

"It's up at the head of the stairs, sir, and you'll be mighty well pleased," he says. "They have some of

HE DIDN'T
LIKE THAT REMBRANDT

the greatest pictures up there you ever put your eyes on. I heard a man say here the other day it was one of the best collections in the world. I'd like to have what just one of them cost. I wouldn't kick."

* * *

Chicago isn't old enough to have very many artists who dare to affect long hair and it has no quarter where the art students flock, but the institute seems destined to become the home of the enthusiasts. They avoid the Sunday crowds and come around on quiet afternoons to look and gloat. The average visitor passes along a row of pictures, giving about thirty seconds to each. If any one picture is unusually bold as to size, color or execution he pauses to nod his head and say: "Pretty good."

This is the visitor who does the place simply as one of the sights of the town. He may be following a guide-book programme such as: "In the morning go to the Art Institute on the lake front; in the afternoon visit the stockyards; at night attend a meeting at the Pacific Garden mission." The enthusiast does not walk up and down the room. He plants himself before the "work" to be admired and begins a critical analysis of color, shade, technique, feeling and all the other things which critics find in a painting. He looks at it as though he were trying to count the buttons on the coat of the man in the far background.

Take one of Rembrandt's, for instance. The ordinary visitor would call it a man wearing his hat. The enthusiast would not call it anything. He would only lift his eyes in unspeakable thankfulness that he had lived to stand before it.

* * *

The people who don't know sometimes criticize Rembrandt very harshly. The other day a young man and a quiet old gentleman, perhaps his father, stood before "The Accountant" and made fun of it.

"I believe I could do that well myself," said the old one.

"I should say so. One-half of his face seems to be too dark."

"It's too dark all the way through. Why didn't he make a picture that looked like something?"

Only the enthusiast may appreciate the faded work of some "old master."

Mr. Pensley
Has a Quiet Day "Off"

THE persons introduced in these local incidents, which might be grouped under the title of "A Day of Complete Rest," are:

Mr. Arthur Pensley, a young married man.
Mr. Joseph Marshton, who travels in Arthur's class.
Mrs. Arthur Pensley, a devoted wife.
Various attachés of the club.

ACT I.

(*Scene—The bowling alley at the Athletic Club. Time 10 a.m. Mr. Pensley and Mr. Marshton, coats off and sleeves rolled up, have ceased playing for a moment in order to pick something off a tray carried in by a waiter. The blackboard is marked with the scores of two games, and the pins are set for a third. Mr. Pensley touches his right hand to the sponge.*)

Mr. Pensley—"Now, Joe, my boy, I'm going to give you some points on bowling."

Mr. Marshton—"You'll have to do better than you did last time."

Pensley—"You just watch me."

(*He selects a ball about ten inches in diameter, gets his hand well under it, takes a staggering run and sends the ball thundering down the alley.*)

Marshton—"By George, that's going to be good."

(*The ball strikes the pins and there is a sound like that made by a crew of house-wreckers.*)

P.—"Hot stuff! Set 'em up again, and I'll repeat the dose."

M.—"Don't get excited. Accidents will happen."

P.—"Is that so? Just keep an eye on your Uncle Hadley."

(*He selects another huge ball and starts it, but it rolls into the trough ten feet from the start.*)

M. (*laughing derisively*)—"Now you're getting down to your proper form."

(*Pensley grabs one of the smaller balls and sends it whizzing.*)

It describes a long curve down the alley and picks off two pins at the corner.)

P. (*in a tone of deep disappointment*)—"Only twelve. S-s-t! Boy! Same as the last time."

(*He goes to the blackboard, panting loudly, and marks up his score.*)

M. (*picking out a ball of medium size*)—"I think I shall have to hit that thing right in the middle."

P.—"The cigars that you don't."

M.—"Done."

(*He takes a long running start, the ball rolls somewhat to one side, but nine pins go down.*) "That's just my luck."

(*The boy with the tray enters again.*)

M.—"Now I'm going to get that other one."

(*He rolls twice. On the second ball the pin falls.*)

"Only ten! Well, it might be worse. It's yours, Artie, but I guess you'd better wait till we get what's on me."

ACT II.

(*Scene—The gymnasium of the Athletic Club. Time 11 a.m. Mr. Pensley and Mr. Marshton are in fighting jerseys and have begun to put on two pairs of big white gloves.*)

Mr. Marshton—"You want to make it kind of easy at the start, old man; I haven't done much with the gloves for a year or two."

Mr. Pensley—"Look here, don't give me anything like that. I've heard about you getting new men in here and putting them out."

Marshton—"Oh, pshaw."

Pensley—"How long shall we keep at it?"

M.—"Till we get tired, I guess."

P.—"Hold on, I'm going to have a brandy-and-soda before I go into anything as hard as this."

M.—"I'll just take one myself."

(*They wait for the brandy-and-soda and then get out on the floor and begin to spar quietly, laughing all the time.*)

P.—"I think I can reach that nose in a minute."

M.—"All right; go ahead and try it."

(*Pensley leads desperately with his right and Marshton coun-*

ters with his left, ducking at the same time. He lands on Pensley's wind and Pensley rushes upon him and staggers him with a blow in the neck. They mix it viciously for a minute or two, at the end of which time Marshton has a bleeding nose and Pensley is gasping violently for breath.)

P.—"Let's—whew—rest for—a minute—or two."

M.—"I don't object. It's pretty hard work."

(*They wait two minutes and recover sufficiently to get out and "mix things" again.*)

ACT III.

(*Scene—The café in the Athletic Club. Time 1:30 p.m. Mr. Pensley and his friend Mr. Marshton are facing each other at a small table on which are certain remnants and two tall, slender bottles, apparently empty. The waiter stands in a respectful and listening attitude.*)

Mr. Pensley—"Don't you want any dessert, Joe?"

Mr. Marshton — "No, I don't believe I do — just a small coffee."

Pensley—"Well, then, I'll take the same. I think I'll have a pony of brandy, too. Will you join me, Joe?"

Marshton—"Um—m—m, yes, I suppose so. I very seldom drink it, though, except after dinner."

P.—"Make it two."

(*The waiter retires.*)

M.—"How's Mrs. Pensley?"

P.—"Oh, she's fine as a fiddle. You must come up some evening, Joe."

M.—"Yes, I'll do that."

(*Presently the waiter arrives with the coffee and brandy.*)

P.—"John, do you know that Perfecto that I always get here? I forget the name, but it's a 25-cent cigar. (*The waiter bows.*) Bring us two of those, and, John, you bring the check to me."

M.—"Here, Artie, I object to that. Didn't I —"

P.—"Never mind; what's the use of having a day off if you can't have your own way? How much is this—$10.50? All right."

(*They sit and smoke for awhile.*)

ACT IV.

(*Scene—The billiard-room at the Athletic Club. Time 4:30 p.m. Mr. Pensley and his friend Mr. Marshton have started upon their third 100-point game. Since 2 o'clock each has walked around the table about 500 times. They have removed their coats, and are somewhat mussed up and streaked with chalk. Mr. Marshton is about to attempt a phenomenal masse. He is seated on one side of the table, and has his cue poised upright in the air.*)

Mr. Pensley—"Now, Mr. Ives, we will see one of your celebrated shots."

Mr. Marshton (*balancing himself with one toe on the floor and jabbing his cue slowly up and down in preparation for a quick stroke*)—"I don't make this every time."

Pensley (*with sarcastic emphasis*)—"No?"

Marshton (*suddenly giving a fierce lunge with his cue and making a white dent in the cloth*)—"Ugh!"

(*The cue ball buzzes around in a semi-circle and then spins like a top, about eighteen inches from the ball it was intended to strike.*)

P.—"That's a very fine shot."

M.—"Yes, I think we had better take something on that."

P.—"I don't care for a thing except another small bottle of beer."

M.—"Give me the same. I believe I'll have a sandwich with mine. We can stop this game long enough to eat something, can't we? What do you want, Artie?"

P.—"Oh, I'm not hungry, but I can eat a Swiss cheese sandwich."

M.—"Make mine caviare. Now, take that shot."

P.—"Why, that's easy for me. If I get them down in the corner I think I can run out on you."

(*He makes one point, then the balls roll badly, all three lining up against the rail. Mr. Marshton lies back in his chair and chuckles, while Mr. Pensley leans against the table, slowly chalking his cue and regarding the balls with a puzzled expression on his face. Several times he makes ready and then pauses to meditate. Finally he lets go a terrific drive, sending his ball around the table. It strikes a large number of cushions and then comes to*)

A DAY OF COMPLETE REST

a rest in a far corner. It is now Mr. Pensley's time to laugh, while Mr. Marshton begins to worry.)

M.—"By George, I never saw balls roll so badly."

P.—"Don't kick; don't kick. You have a very easy shot there."

(*Mr. Marshton makes the shot and immediately breaks into song. He makes a run of 6. Then the refreshments arrive and they take a recess.*)

ACT V.

(*Scene—The home of Mr. Arthur Pensley. Time 7 p.m. Mr. and Mrs. Pensley at dinner. Mr. Pensley is neglecting the dishes. Mrs. Pensley is radiant. Mr. Pensley is inclined to slouch down in his chair and close his eyes.*)

Mrs. Pensley—"Arthur, you are not eating at all."

Mr. Pensley—"Yes I am, my dear. I'm doing first rate."

Mrs. P.—"You've eaten hardly a thing, and you know it. Aren't you well?"

Mr. P.—"Oh, I'm well enough, but when a man takes a day off and lounges around he doesn't have much of an appetite."

Mrs. P.—"Where did you have luncheon?"

Mr. P.—"I had a bite with Joe Marshton at the club."

Mrs. P.—"What have you been doing all day?"

Mr. P.—"I just loafed around the club."

Mrs. P.—"You look as though you had a headache, Arthur."

Mr. P.—"I believe I have a slight headache. It's nothing serious."

Mrs. P.—"I'm glad of that. I hope you haven't forgotten that we are going up to the Thompsons' dancing party for a little while to-night."

Mr. P.—"Oh, thunder!"

Mrs. P.—"Arthur! Didn't I tell you all about it the other day, and you said you'd go? It's going to be a small affair, and Mrs. Thompson simply begged me to come and I promised."

Mr. P. (*in fine irony*)—"I feel like dancing. I think a Virginia reel would about strike me."

Mrs. P.—"What's the matter with you?"

Mr. P.—"My dear, this is just the matter with me: On a day off I like to keep quiet and rest up. If not, why take any days off? If I go up to the Thompsons' to-night and jump around there for two or three hours I know I'd feel rocky in the morning. Besides, my health hasn't been very good of late. You can see for yourself that I can't eat any dinner."

Mrs. P.—"What will you do, then?"

Mr. P.—"I think I'd better retire early. But you go to the dance."

Mrs. P.—"No, Arthur, I'd rather stay here with you. Can't I do something for you—a plaster or a cup of tea?"

Mr. P.—(*in evident disgust*)—"Tea!"

Mrs. P.—"Isn't there something else that you want?"

Mr. P.—"Yes, I want to take a good nap. I'm more used up than if I had been working all day." (*Exit.*)

Mrs. P.—"I'm worried about him. He can't get his mind off his business."

"Stumpy" and Other Interesting People

THE cars do not run very often in West 12th Street. During the wait for one, an opportunity was given to study the boy who ruled the neighborhood. He must have been 15 years old and large for his age. Although he stooped somewhat, evidently from long practice, he had broad shoulders and big-knuckled hands. The other boys were smaller and stood in awe of him. He was leaning against the sunny side of the meat market, addressing his henchmen. It was not an easy thing for him to talk, as one side of his face was horribly swollen with a gigantic quid of chewing tobacco. At intervals he relieved himself and the other boys had to jump to get out of the way. By looking at him, one would know instinctively that he carried a pair of "knucks" in his hip-pocket and a 5-cent book next his heart.

"Aw, chee," he was saying, "why didn't youse kids tell me

'bout t'e Morgan Street push bein' over here? I ain't a goin' to do a t'ing but trun de boots into dat skinny guy wat broke up d' game dat day last summer w'en we plays de O'Brien juniors."

"He says he kin do you," ventured a very small boy with a flannel around his neck.

"So-a-y, mebbe you'd like ter take it up fer him. I'll beat t'e face right off ye."

He started slowly for the small boy, who ran wildly across the street and disappeared into an alley.

"I guess none of you blokies wants to take dat up fer him?"

" 'STUMPY' LEANED AGAINST
THE DOORWAY"

No one answered and the boy who managed the neighborhood leaned against the building once more and scowled in contempt at his admirers.

"Daniel!"

A woman suddenly appeared from around the meat market corner. She was a very small woman, weighing perhaps 110, with a thin face and a wisp of hair caught together in a small knot. She wore an old calico dress and a splattered apron. Her sleeves were rolled up and her arms were "sudsy." Daniel heard her.

"Wha'je want?"

"Come here to me."

"Aw, chee!"

He started away with her and when she had him well in hand she drew back and gave him a resounding whack across the side of his head. Daniel emitted a yelp and ran on ahead of her. As for the small boys, being certain of protection, they shouted derisively at the fallen chieftain and the boy with the red flannel came back to join in the general glee.

* * *

The justice of the peace was a gray old gentleman with a

long, white beard. He always looked at a witness through a pair of old-fashioned spectacles, which added much to his expression of mild inquiry. In fact, he was such a gentle character that the shysters and constables managed the business of the court, as a rule, and kept him in good humor by addressing him as "judge." Very few justices of the peace can resist the blandishment of being addressed as "judge."

The justice was not a man of quick decision. In almost every case where the testimony was at all conflicting, he remained in doubt for several moments. However, he had laid down a rule of conduct for just such an emergency. It was, "In case of doubt, decide in favor of the plaintiff and order the defendant to pay the costs." This rule, consistently followed, had brought him a large revenue, as well as making him popular with a large following of constables. His sincerity was sometimes questioned, but the fact remained that he was an innocent old person who was firmly opposed to all manner of worldly vice and folly.

One day a complicated trial was dragging along. The charge was assault and battery. About half the witnesses had perjured themselves and now an attempt was being made to impeach the character of the plaintiff, a small man who sat by the stove, his face wrapped in bandages.

The principal impeaching witness was "Stumpy" Carroll, a young man who had been leaning in the doorway, tucking up his trousers with his thumbs and clucking at an invisible horse. Luckily the judge did not understand the significance of this sound or he might have fined "Stumpy" for contempt of court.

When the oath was administered, "Stumpy" raised his hand almost as high as his shoulder and answered in a firm voice: "Sure." He was then taken in hand by the attorney for the defense, who addressed him as "Mr. Carroll."

* * *

Attorney—"Mr. Carroll, are you acquainted with the plaintiff in this case?"

Witness—"Do you mean his rabs that's got his face tied up?"

Attorney—"Yes, sir."

Witness—"I know him easy."

Court—"How's that?"

Witness—"I know him wit' both eyes shut, see?"

Attorney—"He means that he knows him intimately. Are you acquainted with the circumstances of this alleged assault?"

Witness—"D'ye mean de scrap?"

Attorney—"Exactly, Mr. Carroll; the fight, to couch it in more familiar language."

Witness—"It's just this way: He was huntin' for it and he got it."

Attorney—"You mean that he provoked the assault?"

Witness—"He went up agin it and was faded; now he wants to beef and you can bet y'r natural that's the size of it."

Court—"What do you mean by all that?"

Attorney—"He means, your honor, that this plaintiff, after instigating the trouble and compelling the defendant to strike him in self-defense, now seeks to show that the defendant was the guilty party. Am I not right, Mr. Carroll?"

Witness—"Sure enough."

Court—"That's no evidence. Let him tell what he saw, and let him talk so that the court may understand what he means."

Witness—"If I asked him to come out and t'row in a blow I kind o' guess he'd drop."

The court rapped loudly and said, "No impertinence, sir; no impertinence!" while the plaintiff's attorney muttered so it could be heard all over the room: "An outrage!" There was no need of his saying this, for he had the case already won by virtue of the fact that he represented the plaintiff. The examination then continued.

Attorney—"Did you see the altercation?"

Witness—"You mean was I there when Billy smashed 'im?"

Attorney—"Exactly."

Witness—"Naw, and it's a good t'ing I wasn't. I'd a' been in it; I'll never see no friend o' mine trun——"

Attorney—"Yes, certainly, but you were not there. Now, Mr. Carroll, I wish to ask you if you are acquainted with the reputation of the plaintiff in the neighborhood in which he resides?"

Witness—"You'll have to come again, Cap."

Attorney—"Do you know this plaintiff? What is his reputation; what do people say about him?"

Witness—"Everybody that's on to him says he's a fink."

Court—"A wh-a-a-at?"

Attorney—"Be somewhat more explicit, Mr. Carroll."

Witness—"You know what I mean; he's a stiff, a skate. He drinks and never comes up. He's always layin' to make a touch, too. I know that boy like a book."

*   *   *

Attorney—"You say he is a disreputable character; that he waits around saloons so as to be invited to drink, and that he borrows money and does not repay it?"

Witness—"Put it to suit yourself; only remember he's an all-round gazabo."

Court—"Gazabo? Gazabo? What language is this?"

Attorney—"He means, your honor, that this plaintiff is thoroughly unreliable."

Court—"Humph! What did you ever see wrong about him?"

Witness—"Well, it's this way; he always got sore when any of the gang joshed him."

Court—"What's that last word?"

Attorney—"He says the man became angry at the slightest provocation."

Court—"Anything else the matter with him?"

Witness—"Well, I never thought he was right. He always acted to me kind o' nutty."

Court—"Nutty? Nutty?"

Witness—"That's what I said, you know—wheels. I don't say he's gone, but I guess some of his lamps is out, all right."

Attorney—"Sort of crazy, eh?"

Witness—"That's what he is. I got so I ducked every time I see him. It's a common sayin' around the corner: 'His trolley's off.' They're all onto him."

Court—"You say his trolley is off and some of his lamps have gone out?"

Witness—"That's what they are."

Court—"Do you know the defendant?"

Witness—"Who? Billy, here? Well, I guess yes. Me and

him challenge together at the nint' precinct. I'll say this: If you soak him it's dead wrong."

Court—"There is no necessity of you making any suggestion to the court."

Witness—"Let it go at that, uncle."

Attorney for the Plaintiff—"Your honor, I must object to the continued disrespect on the part of the witness. It is bad enough for him to slander this plaintiff, a man who is here bearing upon his person the marks of that devilish assault, but he also insults the court in the most brazen manner. It is disgraceful."

Having thus delivered himself, he glared wildly around the court-room to note the effect of his words. "Stumpy" looked at him calmly with one of those oh-if-I-had-you-outside expressions on his face, then he clucked a couple of times and said: "Back up."

"I repeat it," said the counsel for the man in bandages.

"What you say cuts no ice with me," remarked the witness.

*   *   *

He was not cross-examined, and the case was at once submitted without argument, "Stumpy's" friend being assessed the usual amount "and costs."

Small Shops of the City

ON THE west side is a cobbler's shop which is so small that the customers must wait their turns and go in one at a time.

Compared with this shop a bath-room is a reckless waste of space.

The pigmy structure has crawled in between two two-story buildings, and they seem, by contrast, to be skyscrapers.

It has a floor and a roof.

The walls are those of the adjacent buildings.

The shop is, therefore, a small tunnel plugged at both ends.

It is just as wide as the street door, but it is fully twenty feet long. The only clear space is the four feet next the front door.

Then comes the cobbler's bench. There would be no room sidewise, and so the bench is against one of the walls.

When the cobbler leans over to pound the heavy tacks in a shoe strapped to his knee his head almost touches the other wall.

A pound of coal blazes merrily in a toy stove. From the stove extending to the dusty window at the rear are shelves loaded with paper boxes and old shoes.

There are pairs of boots hanging from the ceiling and rolls of leather lying along the floor.

The passageway to the back window is so narrow that only a small man like the cobbler could travel it.

The cobbler is a short man with a saffron complexion and snow-white hair. His bared arms are the color of his face, a bronzed yellow, and his hair, which begins far back on his head, is worn in a bristling pompadour. If he were to put on evening dress and appear at a dinner every one would think him a foreign diplomat instead of a West Madison Street cobbler. His beard and mustache, also white, are worn quite short.

When a visitor enters, the cobbler must stop work, because his light is shut off. He answers questions with a quiet dignity and waits for the caller to go away. It is no place for neighborhood loafers. This is one case where the room must be more valuable than the company.

A SIX-FOOT FRONTAGE

The shop is but one of many in West Madison Street, between Western Avenue and the river. It is perhaps narrower and more crowded than some of the others, although there are plenty which fill in between larger buildings. They are as snug as fo'castles and as picturesque as mountain châlets. What is more they are where one may see them any day.

"Why should I have a larger place?" said the old cobbler. "I have room here to do my work and keep what little stock I need. Rents are high and a man who does work at a low price must find a cheap location. This is better than a basement."

* * *

This busy street, the artery of the west division, has a certain character which is lacking in those thoroughfares that were swept by the great fire.

Here is an older portion of the town, for it must be remembered that Halsted Street was the western border of the city limits, when 12th Street was the southern boundary.

FILLING IN ONE OF THE CHINKS

Some of the landmarks remain. Houses that were once outlying cottages have been furnished with store fronts and blazing signs.

There are buildings in West Madison Street not much larger than dove-cotes and there are others each as large as a pyramid.

If the hand of improvement can be stayed for fifty years some of the west side streets will be museums of antiquity. As a rule, however, the hand of progress does not hold back because of any regard for landmarks. As an instance:

Until a few years ago there stood at the corner of Jefferson and West Monroe streets an old-fashioned white house.

It was kept white only by constant painting, for the smoky factories had hemmed it in and pushed their high, ugly walls up to the very flower-beds of the front yard.

They were old-fashioned flowers—nasturtiums, hollyhocks and sweet peas. Over the trellised porch climbed the honeysuckles.

Every day an old man attired in the fashions of fifty years ago, could be seen sprinkling the flowers and plucking away the dead leaves.

The sight of this old white house with its frame of green and blossoms was like a moment's liberty to the men who toiled in that noise-ridden and smoke-laden part of the town. People pointed out the place and told how this old man with the swallow-tail coat and brass buttons had clung to his house after all his

A LANDMARK AND ITS NEW FRONT

former neighbors had fled before the advance of big buildings.

One day there was a streamer of crape on the door, and next day the best old families came into the factory district in their carriages and gave the old gentleman a correct burying.

The next week some drays backed up and hauled away the hair-cloth chairs and black-walnut book-cases.

Then a crowd of workmen swarmed to the place, tramping down the flowers. Within an hour after they arrived the house stood open and windowless. One man climbed out on the roof and began to chop away a gable. In four days the landmark was a strewn heap of rubbish.

One would not recognize the corner now. It is occupied by a tall, box-like building of brick.

It has been so and must be so with many old buildings of the west side as the frontage becomes more valuable. The pressure of business is already felt when the small stores begin to fill in the chinks.

There are some very small places, with a frontage of three or four feet each, which pay an average rental of $10 a month.

Then there are larger establishments, say ten feet frontage or slightly less, which pay at least $25 a month each.

*   *   *

Near Center Avenue and on the north side of the street are a bakery and a laundry office, both of which get along comfortably in a room less than ten feet wide. When it comes to

JUST AS WIDE AS THE DOORWAY

doing business in a place of that size everything must be kept ship-shape and a great many articles must be hung on nails or put on high shelves. Only a few doors away is a tailor-shop of about the same proportions. A few bolts of cloth are tucked behind the little show window. Like many of these dwarf stores the tailor-shop has pushed up a bulletin board from the roof, so as to make room for a sign large enough to attract attention.

Only a little farther east are two very small cobbler-shops, one of which has already been described. The other is perhaps an inch or two wider and the occupant is a young man who works at a bench near the door so as to catch all the light that falls into his cubby hole. This second place is near May Street and fits tightly in between a grocery and a steam laundry.

The smallest tailoring establishment of the lot is near Carpenter Street. It has a frontage of six feet, yet the proprietor manages to have a neat window display. His bolts of cloth are stacked closely against the wall, so as to give visitors a chance to get back to the stove and the working part of the shop. In spite of the cramp, three friends of the proprietor manage to wedge in near the stove and talk politics to him while he sits cross-legged, with his glasses on the end of his nose, and stitches on a pair of trousers.

*   *   *

Near this shop are two places which equally divide between them a small and low addition built out to the street from a venerable frame building with a peaked roof. One-half of the addition is a laundry office and the other half is a tailor-shop. Over the narrow cornice the old building rises abruptly, as though built upon the flat roof. Just to the west is the sheer wall of a high brick structure. As though it could find no draught for its chimneys in such a pocket, the small building has long metallic pipes which reach over and connect with the flues of the tall building.

* * *

Near Green Street there is an undersized candy store. The window is large enough to show a dozen dishes of candy. The little showcase set outside takes all the frontage not given to the door. The single counter is narrow and only one side is shelved. Not far from Union Street is a yellow-front restaurant, very aptly called "The Hole in the Wall." The capacity is apparently anywhere from seven to twelve, and the cook has a back room larger than a telephone booth. Windows at each end admit plenty of light and the place is quite clean. The frontage cannot be more than ten feet.

* * *

It would be a long story to tell of all the places, each of which selfishly takes up as much as fourteen feet of the street. This chapter has dealt only with the stores that are actually small.

The Intellectual Awakening in Burton's Row

BURTON'S ROW was, in some respects, a little world to itself. It was the nucleus of a new suburb, sprung up at the end of a narrow wooden sidewalk which spanned the prairie to the south. In winter the sidewalk was sometimes hopelessly lost in the snow. In the early spring sections of it were either submerged or else floated about as rafts for the Hanrahan boys.

The implement factory, where all but one of the men were

employed, was half a mile distant, and the school was three-quarters of a mile in another direction. The man who didn't work at the implement factory was Mr. Dawson, who was a photographer with two small rooms near the factory. The neighborhood was not much addicted to the folly of posing before a camera, and Mr. Dawson depended largely on the tin-type habit among the younger people, with a sprinkling of babies and brides to be done in cabinet size.

Mr. Dawson could properly be called the prominent man of Burton's Row, not only because of his superior attainments, but also because of his wife. It was understood that she had been a school-teacher out in the country somewhere before she became Mrs. Dawson.

Mr. and Mrs. Dawson were responsible for the literary movement in Burton's Row.

The owner of the six houses was a hopeful speculator of the name of Burton. It was his policy to go out into the country and begin a town and then permit the city to "build out to it," buying the lots from him. In this instance the city had been backward in filling up the gap. By some calculation Burton had discovered that his six houses had numbers and were on an extension of some city street. The numbers were quite large and the figures many; so it was easier to speak of the six houses as Burton's Row and to number them from 1 to 6, beginning at the east.

The Swanson's lived at No. 1. Mr. Swanson was a sober, industrious young man and the father of a flaxen-haired girl. Mr. and Mrs. Hanrahan and their two children were in the next house. The Williams couple, lately married, were in No. 3 with a lot of new furniture. The Dawsons were in No. 4. Old Mr. McClatchey, day watchman at the factory, was a widower. His youngest daughter, 15 years old, attended to the household affairs. They lived at No. 5. At No. 6 resided the Neinbergers, he and she and the three children. Therefore the little world had eighteen persons.

* * *

The row was built after a socialistic pattern. Each house was exactly like every other. They were all the same height and width. One fence reached the length of the row. The only differences were trivial. The Dawsons had a door-mat on the low front stoop. Mrs. Swanson always kept flowers in the window. In the McClatchey front yard was a stake, to which the goat was usually tied. Mrs. Neinberger's curtains had scenery painted on them. A drunken man would have had some trouble in picking out the right place, but Mr. Williams, who was the only one addicted to strong drink, never made a mistake. He would pick out the two middle houses and enter the one that had no door-mat in front.

The women, being left to themselves all day, soon became fast friends. They found material for gossip in the routine of their daily life, and when nothing else could be done they compared husbands.

It was during these talks with the other women that Mrs. Dawson became impressed with the idea that she should be an instrument for lifting Burton's Row to something above the dull consideration of eating, working and sleeping. In the outside world great things were transpiring. They, as wage-workers, were affected and they should know the truth and be guided by it. So she spoke to her husband.

"Let us organize a neighborhood club," said she. "We will meet once a week to discuss matters of current interest. The men will be encouraged to read the newspapers, and the exchange of opinions cannot help but broaden their views."

"I think it's a good plan, Luella. It'll give me a chance to buckle McClatchey and Hanrahan on this tariff business. They're free-traders, but they don't know why. I can show them why they've been working half-time all winter."

"Yes, but you must be careful and not antagonize them too much. We want to discuss everything fairly and without passion. Now, what shall we call it?"

He left it all to her, and she selected "The Circle of Inquiry."

* * *

The first meeting was called for the following Monday evening. The cards of invitation caused such a commotion as had not been known since the day the Hanrahan boy had been knocked senseless by the McClatchey goat. Mrs. Dawson followed up the cards with calls along the row, and she secured the coöperation of all the women, except the McClatchey girl, who, she said, was hardly old enough to grasp the subjects to be taken up. Having the women, she was sure of the men, although Mrs. Swanson experienced great difficulty in convincing her husband that he should attend.

This was to be the first formal gathering of the residents of Burton's Row. As announced by word of mouth, the programme was to consist of a paper on "Immigration," read by Mrs. Dawson, after which the members of the circle would be expected to join in a general discussion.

* * *

The Dawson front room was dusted and tidied on Monday evening. In the dining-room a cocoanut cake, a bowl of apples and several pies were in readiness for the "lap supper," which was to be served as soon as the immigration problem had been solved.

Never before, it is safe to say, had there been so much scrubbing, button-hunting and shoe-polishing all at one time as on this Monday evening. Mrs. Dawson was amazed at the change in her neighbors as they arrived in twos, all except old Mr. McClatchey, who came alone with a clean shave, a long black coat and a huge black cravat. They sat timidly around the wall. Under the restraining influence of their best clothes and the impending solemnity they appeared to forget that they knew one another.

"Well, Mr. Hanrahan, it is quite a nice night outside," remarked Mr. Williams.

"It is that, the finest I ever see," said Mr. Hanrahan.

"I think we'll have some good weather now," joined in Mr. Swanson, shifting his feet uneasily.

Old Mr. McClatchey, who had been gazing thoughtfully at the floor, nodded his head in assent.

Just then there was a rustling of manuscript. Mrs. Dawson had taken her place at the center-table and unrolled her "paper." A most profound silence was given her. She began to read.

* * *

It appeared that she regarded the United States as an asylum for the poor and downtrodden of the earth, but she was bitterly opposed to the importation of the criminal and pauper elements of Europe. She was also against anarchy, and believed that unless immigrants were willing to accept our institutions, abide by our laws and become good American citizens they should at once return to their native lands.

These highly original views were indorsed by Mr. McClatchey, who not only nodded his head, but said aloud several times "Y'r right."

Mrs. Dawson concluded with a brief extract from Emerson and then said: "We shall be glad to hear from any one on the subject."

* * *

After a few moments of awkward silence McClatchey began.

He said, in opening, that we are all foreigners. Because some one got here twenty years ahead of somebody else was no reason why the second man should be shut out of the game. He was in favor of letting in everybody except the Chinese. These, however, were not his exact words.

"I'll just tell you what's the trouble," broke in Mrs. Williams. "The foreigners come in here and take all the offices. I

"MRS. DAWSON HAD TAKEN HER PLACE AT THE CENTER TABLE"

don't object to them coming here, but they ought to wait awhile before they run everything."

"Who runs everything?" asked Mr. Hanrahan, who was becoming agitated.

"The Irish!" she answered, sharply.

"Y'r right," he said, smiting the table. "And why?"

He told them. The Irishman got out and hustled. He always voted, he attended the primaries and he stood up for his rights. What did the American do? Staid at home and kicked. He finished by telling Mrs. Williams that she talked like a "female depaty."

"Hold on, Terry," broke in Mr. Williams. "Don't talk like that. You know that I don't care a continental where a man was born, but I do say we don't want no cheap labor piled in on us."

Hanrahan arose. "I'm a mimber of the union. No man can iver saay I worked cheap. Can they, McClatchey?"

Mr. McClatchey shook his head.

Mr. Williams hastened to apologize. Mr. Hanrahan still had the floor. "I do move," said he, "that immigration is all right except for crooks."

The American-born vote was disconcerted and saw itself beaten. "All in favor," said Mr. Hanrahan. It was carried unanimously. He sat down.

Another painful pause and Mrs. Neinberger came in. She asked Mr. McClatchey about the goat. He chuckled at the suggestion and began to talk. When he concluded it was time for the lap supper.

On the following Monday evening the meeting was at the Hanrahan house, the host entertaining his guests by playing the flute.

* * *

Mr. Neinberger, when it came his time to receive on Monday evening, had a German supper. The men played seven-up in the front room and the women got together in the back room. Thus it was that the Circle of Inquiry became a popular institution in Burton's Row.

Some Instances
of Political Devotion

ELECTION day was near at hand and the Monica lodging house was full every night.

"Tommy," the proprietor, had all the men listed and tabbed. He was under contract to deliver them early on Tuesday morning at so much per head and he was largely depending on "Cinch" to help him. "Cinch" was the "scrapper" of the house. He was a tall, broad-shouldered man with a frowsy head and a rough beard somewhat bleached from long marches in the sun. His enormous capacity for liquor, his ability as a fighter and his supreme antipathy to work made him a natural leader among the bleary guests of the Monica, who had been gathered together that they might exercise their rights as free-born citizens. When a man came home raving full of stale beer it was the duty of "Cinch" to choke him until he was quiet and then jam him into one of the bunks. If a member of the colony went astray and threatened to desert before election day it was "Cinch" who went out among the barrelhouses until he caught the offender and brought him home in disgrace.

It was clear that "Cinch" had in him the making of a practical politician of great value. He proved this by selling out at the right time.

The news reached "Tommy" on the eve of election. The proprietor did not live at the Monica. He had rooms in another building farther to the north, on the dead line between the business houses and the lava beds. At least once a day, however, he came to his hotel to look after his business affairs and the herd of voters. It was a wearing responsibility, for he knew very well that, as the voting hour drew near, the agents of the corrupt opposition would be among his followers, attempting to lure them away with drinks and bribes. There can be no greater disgrace for a working politician than to lodge a man for two weeks before election and then lose his vote on election morning. He becomes an object of contempt,

45

and in the next fight no money is "placed" with him. "Tommy" believed that his forces were true to him. Here, on the night before election, most of the men were in the house, the others were almost sure to turn up before morning, and "Cinch" was full of hopeful promises.

"Tommy" sat apart from the others, smoking a long cigar vigorously, so as to kill the other odors, when he felt a hand laid on his shoulder. Turning about, he saw the small red face of "Bumpers."

"Tommy, they're givin' y' the double-cross," said "Bumpers," in a stage whisper.

"Is that so?" said "Tommy," sarcastically. He was accustomed to get such reports.

"Yes, it's so. 'Cinch' is t'e hull 'ting in it, too. I see him talkin' to Fatty, de fly-cop, a long time to-day, and to-night he passes each o' de boys a buck an says, 'stay wit' me an' t'ere's another one in it.' " In proof of his assertions, "Bumpers" produced a dollar from a rat's nest, which had once been a pocket. The sight of the dollar was enough for "Tommy." He handed "Bumpers" another dollar and said: "Keep your face closed."

*　　*　　*

It was the predicament of a statesman's life. He knew that the lodgers feared "Cinch" and looked upon him as a leader. "Cinch" had money, too, and was evidently in a deep conspiracy to steal the entire vote of the house. What could be done? "Tommy" made up his mind after some deep thought.

Ten minutes later he and "Cinch" were leaning against a polished bar. "Tommy" was buying drinks, and "Cinch" was gulping them down with evident enjoyment. It was a first-class place and "Cinch" recognized a difference in the whisky. After remaining there long enough "Tommy" carefully steered the traitor south toward the hotel and pulled him into a 5-cent place. "Cinch" had reached a condition in which the drinks are thrown in mechanically and without calculation of probable effect.

When they reached the lodging house the office was swarming with colonists, and "Cinch" was deeply under the influence of the two kinds of red liquor. Every one knew that when he was in that state he would insist on fighting. They waited in terror.

This was the time for "Tommy." He went behind the high pine desk and removed his hat, coat, collar and cuffs. "Cinch" was declaiming loudly and threatening death to all about him.

"Tommy" walked up to him and gave him a push. "Shut up, you big stiff, and go to bed."

The little company of "hobos" was amazed. So was "Cinch." He started in to kill "Tommy" but "Tommy" had put the drinks in the right place. "Tommy" butted him, upper-cut him, knocked him down, jumped on him, beat his head against the floor and finally sat on him slowly pummeling his face until "Cinch" cried "Enough." Then he arose and said:

TOOK HIM TO THE LODGING HOUSE

"Is there any other bum that wants to throw me down?"

No one answered.

"To-morrow morning," said "Tommy," "I want every one of you to go with me and vote. You needn't be afraid of that guy I just licked. To-day I give him some money for you boys and I hear he was tellin' around that it came from the other side. Are you boys with me? [Loud shouts of "Yes!" and "You bet!"] All right."

When "Cinch" arose next morning he was weak, sore and humiliated. His prestige was gone. He fell in line with the others and marched over to the polling place. The precinct did more than was promised and "Tommy" handled "soft money" that evening. Next day the lodgers were thrown out into the street and the regular rate of 15 cents a night was restored.

* * *

On the morning of the day last December when voters were choosing between Hopkins and Swift a very prominent republican politician, who was a member of the campaign committee, went into the 1st ward to quietly look for frauds. He pulled up his coat-collar, drew his hat forward and loafed around the polling places just to see what was happening and not to attract attention. In the "Hinky Dink" precinct he was standing apart watching the barrel-house delegation put in enough ballots to offset the entire school-teacher vote. A man with a badge noticed him and called him aside.

"Have you voted yet?" he asked.

"No, not yet."

"Come on over and have a drink."

"TOMMY" IMPROVED THE OPPORTUNITY

They went into the headquarters conducted by "Hinky Dink" McKenna and the man wearing the badge stood treat. The two talked for a minute or two about the weather and the probable size of the vote, and then the prominent republican began to edge toward the door. But the other man followed him.

"Here," said he, pushing a half dollar into his hand. "Don't put it off any longer, but go and vote for Hopkins."

The prominent republican was too much amazed to return the money. He began to wonder if he resembled a tramp. It was a good joke, but perhaps the joke was on him. At any rate he didn't tell the story until some time afterward.

* * *

Under the old wide-open system the "floater" was paid to vote a certain ticket which was placed in his hand and which was put into the ballot-box under the eye of the purchaser. Nowadays the only thing to do is to hire him to vote and to depend on his promise that he will vote a certain ticket. At one of the late elections a precinct boss had been guaranteed $100 if he could get a majority of fifty for the ticket. The precinct had been well canvassed and at 3 o'clock in the afternoon, having checked off the voters, he began to fear that he needed a few more ballots. Imagine his joy when he saw an even dozen members of his party lounging down toward the polls. He had been sending around for these fellows all day, but they had eluded him. And now, instead of marching up to the polling place, they halted in front of a saloon and began to sun themselves. The "boss" went over to speak to them.

"Boys, you'd better hurry up and vote. Polls close purty soon."

"Aw, we ain't in any hurry," remarked the spokesman.

"You're not goin' back on us, are you?"

"We'll vote your ticket if we vote any, but we don't care much to vote."

"How much do you want?"

"Five apiece, and there's twelve of us."

"You'll not get it. I'll give you a dollar apiece."

"That's all right. We won't vote."

For a quarter of an hour they wrangled, each declaring he would not give in. At the end of that time the "boss" gave $25 and it was divided among them, $3 to the spokesman and $2 to each of the others. Then they marked up and did their duty to the party, and the "boss" saved his $100.

* * *

It is a curious fact in municipal politics that the man who must be paid before he will vote always seeks an office in case his party is victorious. At the latest important city election the democrats expended over $10,000 in the 1st ward in order to capture the "floaters," the "bums," the "lodgers" and the shoulder-hitters. They captured them by outbidding and outgeneraling the republicans, who were just as anxious to organize what Michael McDonald calls "the better element." The democrats expended considerably over $2 for each vote obtained in the ward. It was a "fair" price. As the daughter of the Texas congressman says in the play: "Thank goodness every voter was paid and father is under obligations to no one." Yet the story around the city hall is that after the 1st ward has been bought with hard money it demands other favors. It wishes to run all-night saloons, opium dens, crap games, gambling houses and prize-fighting clubs, all because it gave a majority! It wants to be paid twice. As for the voters themselves, each one tramps the dim hallways of the city hall looking for some kind of an easy, restful job with a large salary attached.

*   *   *

Where these patient applicants are gathered together you may hear the tales of political ingratitude.

One man had his head laid open while attempting to kill a Swede in the "ate" precinct, and yet nothing had been done for him.

Another marched every night and carried a flag, but they hadn't noticed him since election.

The most pathetic story was by a young man who held up two battered hands for inspection. The twisted fingers had evidently been broken, as they were stiff and big at the joints.

TOLD HIM TO GO AND VOTE

"See them mits?" said he. "I got 'em that way playing ball for John P. Hopkins. Out there in Pullman he got up a ball team to go out and represent the town. I went out and played all summer and used up my hands. Now he throws me down. That shows how much a man cares for you after he gets in. I always thought John would do the right thing by me. I played good ball, if I do say it myself."

Old Days on the Canal

IN THE good old days, before the town lay under a pall of
smoke and the rushing trains bore down their victims at
every crossing, life was happy along the "levee." The
"levee" in question is not that part of State Street taken up
by cheap theaters, saloons and pawn-shops, but it is and was
the row of houses fronting on the Illinois and Michigan Canal
just as it joins the south branch of the Chicago River. The
"levee" lies just east from Ashland Avenue and would be on a
line with 29th Street if the latter could only be extended
through the diagonal streets and crowded dock buildings of
old Bridgeport.

When the canalboats loaded with grain, came crowding one
another up to the stone lock, when money was plenty and
profits were big and an army of men found employment along
the old Illinois and Michigan, the Canal House was crowded
every night. It was the long, frame hotel at the west end of
the row and was called a pretentious hotel in its day. Some
big card games were played inside its walls, and the old captains still remember some of the fine dinners spread there.
Along the row were saloons and groceries, the two being much
the same in those days, where high revels, with some rough-
and-tumble fighting, were of nightly occurrence. The "levee,"
the like of which is to be found in every canal or river town,
had its rise and fall with the canal.

It began in 1848, when the canal was completed and the first boat came in tow from Lockport. That year Chicago spent over $400,000 in constructing canalboats. The "levee" grew with the traffic until 1866, which was the most prosperous year ever known. But the epidemic of railroad-building which began just after the close of the war sent branch roads whip-sawing all through the canal's territory. The roads began a persistent fight against the boats. The passenger business thay had captured long before, and the war on freights is still waging. The tolls decreased steadily from 1866, yet the canal is to-day an important waterway of which the late-comers to Chicago know very little and of which the older citizens have forgotten much. Yet this is the same town that turned out men, women and children on Independence Day in the '30s to celebrate the first excavating. Hundreds of persons marched down the old Archer's Road to Bridgeport. Others rode in boats which were pulled up the Chicago River by horses. Speeches were made and a spirit of intense jollification marked the beginning of an enterprise which was amply fulfilled and which is now forgotten and neglected, as are the pathetic old buildings along the "levee."

ONE END OF THE LOCK

* * *

The Canal House leans wearily forward on its supports. Its windows have been torn out and the front doors are nailed over with boards. The warped clapboards have been worn black by wind and weather. Nothing is needed to complete the ruin. Only a few years ago a man reopened the front room as a saloon. The old canalboats creeping by were surprised to find a new gilt sign on the dingy front, but they were not surprised when one day it disappeared and the boards were again nailed over the front. Every square-fronted building in the row stands vacant, with rough boards nailed against the doors and windows. The open ground in front, once a busy street, has sparse bunches of grass overgrowing it. Sometimes for half a day at a time no living thing is seen along the deserted water front. A stone abutment spotted with moss marks the location of the old lock. The greatness of the "levee" lives only in memory.

The Illinois and Michigan Canal divides like a letter Y just before it joins the south branch. On the northern arm of the canal is the lock through which the boats must pass in and out. On the other arm are the Bridgeport pumps, which make an earnest although somewhat futile effort to lift into the canal from the south branch enough water to cause the river to flow in from Lake Michigan, instead of sending its slow and filthy current out into the city's water supply. The pumps have never succeeded in purifying the river, but they empty enough black water into the canal to give it a current of four or more miles an hour and give it a level of several feet above the south branch.

*   *   *

There are about sixty canalboats now plying between Chicago and various points on the canal and the Illinois River. Of these about thirty handle coal from the quarries. The others are grain-boats, which, on the down trips, carry coal, lumber and various other supplies for which there is a country demand. Until last year the ice-boats did a big business, but the drainage canal along the Des Plaines valley crowded some of the ice houses out of the way and the railroads competed so strongly that they captured the business of those remaining. The ice-boats are floating idly along the canal and a half-dozen big delivery wagons are lined up near the dock, showing all

COMING OUT OF THE LOCK

degrees of weather-beaten neglect. One of the fleets which went down the canal recently consisted of a tug, a heavy stonebarge and one of the veteran ice-boats, roofed over and having little windows along the sides, so that it very closely resembled the pictures of Noah's ark.

Inspector Mulcahy opened the gates at the east and the water ran out. The tug and the stonebarge crept into the lock and the gates closed behind them. The side gate was opened and the rush of water lifted them to the new level.

"What are you goin' to do with the old hulk?" asked the inspector.

"I s'pose we'll knock her into kindlin' wood," replied the mate, or bos'n, or something of the stonebarge.

An elderly man, very short and with iron-gray whiskers, explained that the Iceland was one of the oldest tows on the canal.

"All the old ones are going," he said. "The business is nothing like it used to be, when we traveled with mules and lived, right with our families, on the boats. We could make money in those days. I've seen as many as 300 boats waiting at LaSalle, and this country right around here used to be pretty lively, too. This spring I've made two trips to Henry for grain, but there wasn't any money in it. The railroads cut rates at every point we can touch with boats. But they can't kill the canal, because the state takes care of it and keeps it dredged out."

*   *   *

There was evidence of the state's care, for two dredges were waving their wet arms just a few hundred yards below the lock and bringing up huge bucketfuls of the black and mushy sediment that had been pumped in from the river. When a barge was full a towline was thrown ashore and two mules, a boy riding the one behind, pulled the unspeakable cargo away. In the language of canal mariners, any two boats lashed together make a "fleet," and even the mud-scows are given that resounding title when they travel more than one at a time.

*   *   *

West from the lock and hugging one another along the south shore are canalboats of all descriptions, some moldy with age, some kept bright with paint and having potted flowers in the windows. One flatboat has a house built on it. Here dwells a large and happy family. The ancient captain who had been seen at the lock lives on one of his boats, and there were several where women could be seen through the cabin windows, busily setting the table for the noon-day meal. The cloth was white and the butter yellow, so that one rather envied them this continual camping-out kind of life.

* * *

Just across from the "levee" a pug-nosed boat lay at rest and two men were lazily scrubbing her deck. The sunshine was bright and warm and the dull old row of houses seemed to sleep in the genial warmth. All the open ground was sprinkled with yellow dandelions. Far to the left stood a brick building, once the home of the lock-keeper when he was a man of importance. The trees around the old house had filled out with light-green leaves. This scene was almost rural in its suggestion of modest quietude.

Then a tug came around the point to the east, lashing the water into suds and shrieking like a crazy thing.

With the Market-Gardeners

ALL afternoon the Gruber family had been gathering the garden truck and washing it.

There was a bushel of spinach pulled from a patch that had simply leaped out of the ground under the influence of a heavy rain followed by two days of sunshine. As for the young onions, they were so white below and so rich in color above that they were as handsome as bouquets after being tied into bunches and packed away into crates. The rhubarb stalks came in bigger bunches. A bushel basket was filled with lettuce. There were also some horse-radish roots.

When the feed-bag had been filled the wagon was ready to go, but it was then only 6 o'clock in the evening, not a seasonable hour for starting to market. Mr. Gruber and the oldest boy, Herman, went to bed at once. They needed no alarm-

clock to arouse them at midnight, as Mrs. Gruber claimed to
have the extraordinary power of awakening herself at any
hour of the night, if she would only make a strong determina-
tion just before retiring.

The Gruber family "worked" a ten-acre truck farm near
Jefferson. It was a part of the great vegetable fringe lying inside the city limits. The Gruber cottage was on the continua-
tion of a city street and it probably had a number somewhere
up in the thousands, but no one had ever been able to calculate
what it was. This family combined the tax-paying privileges
of city life with all the charm and freedom of a residence in
the country. They could see very little of the town, but they
had the satisfaction of knowing they were a part of it.

*   *   *

At 12 o'clock, almost to the minute, Mrs. Gruber rapped
on the door of Herman's room. Five minutes later a man carrying a lantern came out of the kitchen door and started to
the small shed known as the stable. The son lagged behind a
little, but he was in time to assist in hitching up. Before they
started they ate a bite in the kitchen and drank some of the
steaming coffee hastily prepared by Mrs. Gruber. Then they
climbed into the front seat and the wagon creaked away into
the darkness.

It was a long drive, but one that was never dull. The cool
night breezes made the men wonderfully wide-awake and
they had that adventurous feeling of one who travels deserted
thoroughfares and knows that the darkened houses are full of
sleeping people. At first they passed small farms and open
stretches of prairie, then a few straggling suburbs, and finally
they came into a closely built street with a half-filled night
car bowling slowly along it. The street lamps were not so far
apart and there were occasional restaurants, wide open and
brilliantly lighted, and any number of open drinking places,
with curtains drawn half way up, as a mild compromise with
the law. The horses jogged through residence districts and at
last turned into one of the thoroughfares that never sleeps,
one of those streets where vice and commerce begin one day
before another is ended. Other wagons had fallen in ahead
and behind. It was a short procession that turned into Hay-

market Square, which was already noisy and busy in its preparation for another day of traffic.

* * *

Some of the wagons holding the more favored positions next to Desplaines Street had been backed in as early as 8 o'clock on the previous evening. Those coming a little later had taken the next best stands so that when the Grubers arrived at about 2 o'clock the rows of wagons were forming to the west and they had to take the best location they could get, which was in a row next the pavement on the north side of the square and near Union Street. It must be known that Haymarket Square is a broadening of Randolph Street and extends from Desplaines Street to Halsted Street. Two parallel street-car lines slice it down the center. At the east end the car lines spread from each other and encircle a small inclosure within which is a pedestal. On top of the pedestal is a policeman made of stone. He stands with one hand uplifted and in the name of the state of Illinois he "commands peace" of the honest German gardeners who lounge in their wagons below. About 200 feet to the north, where an alley opens into Desplaines Street, the first dynamite bomb ever thrown in the United States did its destructive work. That was May 4, 1886. The Desplaines Street riot passed into history as the Haymarket riot, and the vegetable mart was given a bloodthirsty notoriety which it does not at all deserve.

* * *

The first marketers came soon after daybreak, some with baskets and some with grocery wagons, to get the pick of the produce. Then came the commission-house wagons, which lined up close to the sidewalk, with some of the teams swung sidewise to economize space. From one end of the square to the other three narrow passageways are left open. The one in the middle permits the passage of cars, which run a gantlet of horses for two long blocks. The perspective of two rows of horses standing in military lines facing the car tracks, the animals almost nose to nose the entire distance, is something very nearly spectacular. In all the jumble at either side there is one cleared road large enough to allow the passage of a wagon, and this holds a moving line of trucks and delivery wagons the whole day.

Perhaps at 8 o'clock the big market has its largest business. Within two hours after that many of the wagons are sold out and have begun to push their way through the scramble in an effort to escape.

* * *

Who are the truck farmers? Germans almost to a man, or woman, either, for that matter, for there are plenty of women who are independent producers and plenty of others who ride in on the wagons.

What do they sell? Every fruit or vegetable that grows in this climate, but in early May principally lettuce, radishes, spinach, onions, horseradish and the like. They sun themselves in the wagons until sold out, or, if trade drags and darkness is coming, they close a profitless bargain with one of the dealers along the street. Between them and the dealers the big western and northwestern sections of town are supplied with green stuff.

Haymarket Square is almost strictly vegetarian. There are no such displays of fish, wild game and poultry as will be found in South Water Street. Strewn before the open fronts and kept cool beneath the wide awning with its festoons of garlic are berries, potatoes, oranges, asparagus, radishes and cucumbers. The square is in possession of the fruit and produce dealers. There are a few stores and some saloons that came into notice during the anarchist excitement, when it was believed that many of the half-crazed conspirators lived in and about the square. The policemen who know the neighborhood say the old crowd of agitators who were associated with the men hanged in the county jail do not frequent the Haymarket saloons. These places depend on the teamsters and truck farmers. There is sand on the floor. Eight kinds of dark free lunch in bowls are on a table and the beer is served in large glasses known as "tubs."

Mr. Gruber and Herman had sold everything except the horseradish when the whistles over toward the river began tooting the noon hour.

"Horseradish is just as good one time as another," said Mr. Gruber as he put it back into the bucket and tucked the cloth around it. He and Herman had a lunch in a barroom restau-

"ONE CLEARED ROAD HOLDS A MOVING LINE OF DELIVERY WAGONS"

rant, spring onions and cheese being the principal courses. There was some buying to be done, but at 1 o'clock they were homeward bound. When they reached the quiet streets Herman was leaning heavily against his father and had passed into honest sleep, the result of fatigue and onions. A little farther on Mr. Gruber discovered, when the tongue jammed into a flour wagon ahead, that he, too, had been dozing. They always went home drowsy, and they were no exceptions to the rule, for out at suburban crossings one may often see, in the course of an afternoon, a dozen truck wagons with the driver of each nodding on his seat and allowing the lines to hang loose.

Fair-Minded Discussion in Dearborn Avenue

THIS thing of living in families is not calculated to brush up the intellect.

In families opinions range altogether too much in the same direction. The head of the family advances an opinion which is at once sanctioned by the other members, and should the solitary outsider choose to contradict this opinion he is almost smothered in the scrimmage.

Now, in a boarding-house it is different.

In the Dearborn Avenue boarding house it is notably different.

There never was a proposition, of any character whatsoever, that would receive the unanimous indorsement of the breakfast circle.

This was illustrated one morning when the patriotic boarder happened to say something about the curse of slavery. At the other end of the table sat a seedy man who couldn't hold a job, even though he claimed a Virginian ancestry. He flared up at once and denied that slavery was a "cuhse." With that the two of them figuratively "clinched" and fought it out, their debate covering the first slave-trade, the Missouri compromise, the Dred Scott decision, the emancipation proclamation, the fifteenth amendment and the civil rights bill. Of course the opinion of each remained unchanged, but the mere fact that such a question "Was Slavery Wrong?" should be debated with acrimonious vigor proves that truth was untrammeled in this Dearborn Avenue nest of intellectuality. Not a doubt of it.

Conditions always favored trouble. The boarders represented in their nativity half a dozen different states. Religious opinions ranged from ardent methodism to outspoken atheism. On the subject of alcoholic liquors, the women were a unit for teetotalism, while some of the men put their liberal views into practical demonstration and the morning afterward frankly told of their depravity.

* * *

One of the interesting characters was the patriot. He continually made references to the "flag" and to "our institutions." In his lapel was a red, white and blue button, which was generally supposed to be the insignia of some mysterious oath-bound organization. This man was trying to monopolize the love of country. He didn't want any one else to love it as he did. When he got a chance at the piano he would sing, "My Country, 'Tis of Thee," and "The Star-Spangled Banner." At times he would give weird "tips" about impending conspiracies to blow up all the little red schoolhouses and butcher the children. This excess of circus-day patriotism, coupled with the fact that he wore his hair pompadour, made the other boarders rather suspicious.

The baseball young man persisted in reading extracts at the breakfast table. He kept posted on averages and individual records and could tell how many base hits were made by Anson in 1883.

Next to him sat the elderly bachelor who had given up all hope of everything. It was difficult for him to acknowledge that any action was the result of an honorable motive. He had gloomy suspicions regarding the female sex. One of his particular boasts was that he had not voted for ten years. He evidently regarded this as a great accomplishment, as he spoke of it often.

"I don't vote at all any more," he would say, as though he were the injured person.

The man who was depended upon to defend the democratic party had lately weakened in his faith, although when the taunts of the two women republicans became unbearable he was still combative. The women were sisters and one was a widow.

There was one man who remained as neutral and indifferent as the landlady herself. She stood aloof from discussions for

UNBIASED AND LUMINOUS VIEWS ON MATTERS OF CURRENT INTEREST

obvious business reasons; but he really didn't care about silver, prizefighting, predestination or anything else outside of the wholesale grocery trade. When appealed to he would simply said, "Well, what's the difference?" or "I suppose you are both right."

The foregoing were the regulars at the places. When the ten chairs were filled the extra places were taken by such transients as the man with the Virginian ancestry.

One morning the endless debate turned upon the subject of the political situation.

"I see these Coxeyites are still marching around the country," said the grumpy old man. "They ought to call out the militia and kill every one of 'em."

"No, no," said the patriot. "As long as they abide by our institutions and carry the American flag they have a right to march. But the people ought to refuse them food, and then they'd starve and have to disband."

"You two fellows have got hearts too big for your bodies," remarked the ball crank. "I think these armies are all right. I see they're playing baseball."

"Yes, they'll do anything but work." This from the sour bachelor. "Why should we support them?"

"How many did you ever support?" This from the ball crank, who did not lift his eyes from the paper.

"Well, in a time like this these men become a burden on all of us. I'm glad I didn't vote to put into power an administration that brings such a condition."

"I should say so," remarked the republican sisters.

"It's my opinion that you don't vote for fear your candidate will be elected, and then you won't have a right to kick at him," said the democrat.

"I refrain from voting because one party is as bad as another."

"Oh-h-h!" said the sisters, in evident disapproval.

"I'm against this administration because it doesn't stand up for the flag," said the red, white and blue boarder. "It hasn't treated the veterans right."

"Bah!" remarked the grumpy man.

"Well, it hasn't," interrupted the widow. "Now I was reading in one of Mr. McKinley's speeches——"

"McKinley!" snapped the grumpy man. "A creature of corporations; a man traveling on his looks. Why, he's been making that speech for ten years."

"I should say so," added the democrat. "If he's elected president he'll stand on the front steps of the White House and have a man throw a calcium light on him. He's the professional beauty of his party."

"I don't care what you say," retorted the widow. "I think he's just as nice as he can be."

"He looks like a good man," said the widow's sister.

"One thing in his favor"—this from the patriot—"is that he seems devoted to our institutions. I believe he has a real affection for the flag."

"He has an affection for anything that will give votes," bluntly put in the cynic. "He's like all other politicians."

"I disagree with you there," said the lukewarm democrat. "Of course I don't like the way Cleveland has acted here lately, but you must admit that he does as he pleases, no matter whether it pleases people or not."

"I think he's horrid," this very timidly from the republican sister.

And the widow backed her up: "If he was so infatuated with that black queen, why didn't he elope with her?"

The landlady repressed a simpering laugh and the disagreeable bachelor seemed annoyed that some one else had borrowed his style of argument.

* * *

"Anse ought to go on first himself," interrupted the ball crank who had not been hearing the controversy. "He could brace up the team."

"Yes, I guess he can play pretty good ball," put in the indifferent man. This was the first time he had spoken, but he was evidently anxious to change the subject, even to baseball.

"I'm in favor of any candidate who is loyal to home interests," thoughtfully remarked the lover of the old flag.

"That's right, that's right." (A scornful interjection from the cynic.) "Unless the foreign-born citizen takes out a permit and wears an eagle in his hat, don't let him breathe without a permit. I suppose you are opposed to buying anything abroad if you can get it at home for two prices."

"Oh, now you're talking sense," triumphantly exclaimed the free-trade democrat. "You're an anti-protectionist. You're one of us."

"I'm not one of you," was the indignant reply. "You're just as bad as the other fellows. You don't know your own minds. Here you have been tinkering with the tariff for months. What have you done? Nothing."

"I don't know about that. You take sugar——"

That was where they entered the fog. The indifferent man and the ball crank escaped with the transients, and within two minutes only the democrat, the patriot and the elderly bachelor were left floundering in the tariff mire.

*   *   *

This morning was only one instance.

For clear, unbiased and luminous views on topics of current interest there never was such a place as the Dearborn Avenue boarding house.

Little Billy as a Committeeman

IT WAS a great day for "Little Billy" when, as a member of the arbitration committee of the Longshoremen's union, he went forth to represent the cause of labor.

For a man who works along the docks and who has known the tyranny of a mate on a Mississippi steamer, it is a strange experience to be lifted to sudden eminence and given large responsibilities. The longshoremen drew no lines on color and nationality. "Little Billy," as black as ebony, was a brother so long as he stood for union wages and the rights of the men. And he was just beginning to find out that he was a man. Two years before he had roustabouted on a Mississippi steamer for starvation pay. Finally he concluded it would be better to work in a freight house than carry barrels up-hill, so in company with other adventurous spirits he struck out for Chicago and big pay.

It was big pay compared with what he had been receiving, but, like every other dissatisfied man who finds that he is supported by numbers and organization, "Little Billy" fell in with the movement for higher wages. He wanted 25 cents an hour because all the other men wanted it and because he had become convinced that his work was worth that much. In the strike of 1893 he took part merely as a private in the ranks. He was one of the strikers that chased a transportation agent one night. This agent professed great contempt for the roughly dressed men who unloaded the vessels, and when the strike was declared he purchased two large revolvers and sent word to the strikers that they must not come around his premises. They came one evening, however, to argue with the non-union men and he advanced upon them with both "guns" drawn. The strikers, instead of being terrified, charged upon him, whereupon he threw away his weapons, in order to lighten himself, and ran for his life. They chased him around a freight house and over the railroad tracks. He would have been captured had he not in his desperation jumped into the Chicago River. When he jumped the strikers became frightened and proceeded to scatter. The agent was rescued by a policeman.

This episode was considered a victory for the strikers, and "Little Billy" was especially gratified, as it was the first time he had ever chased a white man. A few days later the men were given the wages they asked. It was a complete victory, and "Little Billy" from that time was a more rampant union man than ever before.

*   *   *

The longshoremen of Chicago lead a life different from that of any other workmen. Even in the busy season their work comes in odd jobs and in the winter they are necessarily idle. Time is money with a big iron steamer. When she comes to the dock she must be unloaded as rapidly as possible. The new cargo is hurried aboard and she is sent away. The longshoremen after ten days of idleness may suddenly be called upon to work eighteen hours or more at a stretch, the "shifts" changing until the vessel is unloaded and then reloaded. They must be strong and willing. It is downright hard labor, "breaking up" a cargo of barrels or big boxes and wheeling it into the freight house. The colored men are the only ones who find any comfort in it, for they sing at their work.

Although the men have an organization each summer, it always goes to pieces in the fall, for then the river "gangs" are dispersed. The married men find other employment and large numbers of the homeless ones find refuge during the winter in the hotels and lodging houses along the river. Even if they have no money they can find shelter, and the landlord will collect his pay after navigation opens. There are about 1,700 men who find employment along the docks in season, but it is a changing and floating population. When President Howard of the union began his organization in the spring of 1894, he found new men in large numbers. At the first meeting in the hall in Randolph Street over fifty men were present. He made a speech pointing out the necessity of organization, and asked the men to step up and sign their names. A short Irishman in a suit of blue overalls was suspicious. He declared that he would sign no papers until the men were organized.

"IT IS DOWNRIGHT HARD LABOR"

"How can we organize unless we get your names?" asked the president.

"I'll nawt sign me name."

"No, sah, 'n I doan' guess I will," added a colored man as he moved toward the door.

The president jumped to the door and put his back against it. "Nobody gets out o' here till he signs. You fellows sign that paper, and be quick about it."

By such endeavors was the union built up, and when the transportation lines proposed to change the wages from 25 cents an hour to 17 cents a ton the union revolted, and over 600 men went on a strike.

The men said they could make money unloading pig-iron at 17 cents a ton, but when it came to mattresses or any light merchandise they would starve to death. They stood out for the old scale of 25 cents an hour. Daily meetings were held at the hall. Missionaries were sent among the unconverted.

It was a stubborn strike. The longshoremen are good fighters.

"Little Billy" was in the forefront, rather hoping that there would be trouble. He was in favor of marching along the docks and wiping out every non-union man, but the others held him in check. This blocky young colored man with the gingham shirt and slouch hat made a speech or two at the meetings and was becoming so prominent that he couldn't be overlooked. That is how it happened he was appointed on the committee of twelve which was to call on the agents of the different lines and talk over the situation. He was the only colored citizen on the committee. There were two Irishmen, a Swede, a German and a few native-born longshoremen, and they wore their unloading clothes, but nevertheless they were a committee determined to meet the agents on equal grounds.

*   *   *

"Little Billy" knew that one of the lines had brought longshoremen from Buffalo, but he did not know that forty of these imported men had fighting records and had been put in the freight house to lie in wait for strikers. They pretended to do some work, but they all wanted to fight, and if there could have been any choice of victims they probably would have selected a colored man—a small one.

Around at the office in one corner of the freight house the committee was given an audience with the agent, but "Little Billy," the man of action, the dusky Napoleon of the long-shoremen, said: "No; you'ns go an' talk wif 'im. I'se got to see some o' these hyuh men."

So he walked right out into the freight house and watched the line of half-dressed men wheeling in the heavy casks. And all the time the knowledge throbbed within him that they were common laborers while he was a committeeman.

"Look hyuh," he said to a hairy man, whose red-flannel shirt was rolled open in front. "Whah doan' yo' boys come and jine d' union 'stead o' bein' a lot o' scabs?"

"Sa-a-ay," asked the man with a glad gleam in his sound eye, "are you one o' them strikers?"

"Yes, suh, an' you'ns had bettah stop this heah——"

That was as much as "Little Billy" could say. Two of the big kind were on top of him. They threw him back against a tier of barrels, and one kicked at him. They dragged him out and hammered at his head, which he was trying to duck under his shoulder. They threw him down and dragged him across the floor and gave him a clear throw-out into the street.

*   *   *

The meeting was still in progress half an hour later when something with bandages on it and smelling strongly of arnica came up the middle aisle and stood before the chairman. It waved the arm that wasn't crippled and said: "Heah I am."

"Why, it's 'Little Billy,'" exclaimed the chairman.

"Yes, suh, an' I been to dem Transit docks."

"Billy, didn't I tell you not to pick quarrels?"

"No, suh; I didn't pick no qua'el. You doan' have to. Jes' show yo'se'f an' yo' get it. I'se resigned."

"Why so?"

"You'se got to get heavy men for dis committee. Dis boy's too small fo' de work."

At the Green Tree Inn

JUST suppose that one of the army officers who lounged around the taverns at the river fork away back in the '30s should be set down on the Lake Street bridge today. Would he recognize Wolf Point?

Would he know that the black dock, with its crowded buildings, swinging derricks and heaps of block stone had once been the wooded promontory where stood the Wolf Tavern?

Could he pick out, on the west shore of the north branch, the exact spot where Samuel Miller built his cabin and opened it as a public house?

Would the bridge policeman be able to tell him where the Sauganash Hotel had stood?

Probably not, although the Sauganash Hotel was in its day a greater wonder than the Auditorium.

Would the soldier, returned from Fort Dearborn, find anything to recall the days when Chicago was a straggling hamlet?

*   *   *

If he looked for the Green Tree Inn he would find a tall building of red brick with "Railway Supplies" across the front of it. But if he were to stand on the corner and accost all the gray-headed men who passed he might find some one who would tell him that the Green Tree Inn had escaped the fires and improvements of sixty years and was still standing as a lonesome relic of the great old pioneer days. Then, after he had got his bearings, he would find the old tavern crowded in between other wooden houses in a thoroughfare leading to the northwest from where the old tavern had stood. He would find that it had been moved a few hundred feet from its original site and was beginning to show signs of decrepitude. He would find the same old roof, the same square-paned little windows and the clapboarded walls growing rusty in spite of repeated paintings.

*   *   *

The Green Tree Inn, which was built on the river bank at the northeast corner of North Canal and West Lake streets in

1833, is now at 33, 35 and 37 Milwaukee Avenue. It would
have no claim to distinction were it not the oldest building
in Chicago. The histories have casually mentioned this fact
and it is a matter of vivid knowledge to the older settlers,
but of the hundreds of persons who pass it daily very few
know its history.

The authorities are prone to disagree on the incidents of
early Chicago history, but there is a mutual agreement that
the Green Tree Inn was built by James Kinzie in 1833, and

THE OLD GREEN TREE INN

received its name from a solitary oak tree which stood near
the building. One historian asserts that David Hall, half-
brother to James Kinzie, was a partner in the building. In the
summer of that year Silas B. Cobb, a builder, then less than
21 years old, came to Chicago and assisted in constructing
the Green Tree Inn. Mr. Cobb is still living and has an office
in Dearborn Street. Only a few weeks ago the veteran architect
visited the old building, went up into the loft and tapped the
hickory rafters. He said the structure was good for many more
years of hard service.

* * *

The old frame house has often changed its name. First
opened as an inn by David Clock, it was soon sold to Edward

Parsons, who called it the Chicago Hotel. In 1848 it became known as the Noyes Hotel, and in 1849 the name was again changed to the Railroad House. In 1851 it was the Atlantic Hotel, in 1854 the West Lake Street House, and in 1859, when it was cheapened into a lodging house with a saloon downstairs, it lost the dignity of a name. It changed hands again, and at the time of the fire was the property of an Englishman, whose widow still occupies part of the first story. She owns the building and is proud of it, not because it is so old, but because she helped pay for it and has made it a source of small revenue.

* * *

She is a little woman, with a black cap and a pair of steel spectacles and a black shawl about her shoulders. She says her memory is failing her, but she remembers distinctly how she became matron of the establishment.

"My sister said to me that the man at the Lake Street Tavern wanted a house-keeper, because his wife was dead. I went there on a Friday and went to work. I shan't ever forget it. That night I said to him that I must go and see my sister in Green Street and he asked if he could go along. I said, 'I s'pose you can if you want to.' So he went along. My sister was making over a dress for me. It was a lovely thing, violet silk. We went in and my sister said to him, 'Sarah was married in this dress once.' He spoke up and said, 'She's been married once and I've been married once; now why shouldn't she be married in it again?' Well, we laughed of course. I was 52 years old then. On a Saturday the dress was finished and on Sunday we were married. I don't regret it either, though he did spend lots of money and left me to pay for the house. I've stuck to the old place ever since. I came with it when they moved it from the old corner. Three times I've saved it from burning, and I'll tell you it's a good old house now."

* * *

It was in 1880 that the house was moved from the corner of West Lake and Canal streets to find company with other old and squatty frame structures at the entrance to Milwaukee Avenue. There it stands to-day among the junk stores, one-story saloons and blacksmith-shops, and it still attempts to preserve a battered dignity. At 33 lives Mrs. Sarah Barrington, the owner, the housekeeper who married the landlord. She has the curtains drawn and the door chained. The visitor must pull vigorously at the bell-knob and she will inspect him through an inch or two of opened door before admitting him. She has one big room and a little kitchen. A portrait of the duke of Wellington hangs over her arm-chair. The furniture has been in the room for twenty years. Sometimes there are visitors to see the old house. Mrs. Barrington has their cards neatly tied together with black thread. She also has thirteen prints which she bought at the international exhibition in London in 1862. One shows the Crystal Palace, another Westminster Abbey, a third Trafalgar Square, and so on. She can show just where she stood at each place and she affirms that by means of a telescope she once read the time on the big clock of the parliament tower, and it was just fourteen minutes of 2 o'clock. On these

A VIEW FROM THE BACK YARD

matters she is positive, but she is not so full of recollections regarding the Green Tree Inn. She can only tell that the cigar store in the middle has been paying rent for seventeen years, and that there has been a saloon in the other end ever since she can remember.

When she was suddenly promoted from housekeeper to proprietress the up-stairs had beds for lodgers, and it has been a lodging house ever since.

The sign at the foot of the stairs now reads:

> ## OLD LAKE STREET HOUSE

In the saloon and cigar store, as well as in Mrs. Barrington's private apartments, the floor is hilly and the windows have warped to an angle, the ceilings are low, the wainscoting narrow and the doorways cramped. Some new counters and shelves make a strange contrast with the old-fashioned outlines of the room. A dormer window looks over the black shingles into the back yard and there are small square windows under the gables, but in its general aspect the oldest building in Chicago is not sufficiently picturesque to attract attention on its merits. The signs and awnings in front help to disguise it and there is no placard to tell the public of its historic importance. The Scandinavian who owns the saloon said it would do no good to advertise his place as the oldest in Chicago. He said his customers didn't care for such things. They would go where they could get the largest glass of beer.

Mrs. Barrington didn't believe there was much interest in the old tavern, as the visitors came about a year apart. She only hoped she could sell the place for enough money to take her back to England and keep her there. She wanted to see the Nelson monument again, and although she got Nelson mixed up with the battle of Waterloo, she meant well.

The Advantage of Being "Middle Class"

WHY IS IT that the middle class has a monopoly of the real enjoyment in Chicago? The term "middle class" is used in the English sense.

Theoretically, at least, there are no classes in Chicago. But the "middle class" means all those persons who are respectably in the background, who work either with hand or brain, who are neither poverty-stricken nor offensively rich, and who are not held down by the arbitrary laws governing that mysterious part of the community known as society.

The middle class people wouldn't scourge a man simply because he wore a morning coat in the afternoon. Again, if his private life were redolent of scandals they would not tolerate him as a companion, no matter how often he changed his clothes.

It is quite a privilege to belong to the middle class, especially during the warm weather in June. A middle-class family may sit on the front stoop all evening and watch the society people go to the weddings in their closed carriages. Father doesn't have to wear a tight dress coat all evening and have a collar choking him. He may take off coat or vest, or both, and smoke either pipe or cigar without scandalizing any one. If he and mother wish to get some ice-cream they go around the corner to get it, or else they may send one of the children with a pitcher. If they were above the middle class, of course, it would never do for them to be seen in a

READY FOR THE LAKE TRIP

common ice-cream place, and the idea of sending a pitcher would be shocking.

*   *   *

At the Clark Street bridge a double-decked steamer, with electric lights and a resounding orchestra, was preparing to start on its nightly trip, so far out on the broad, cool lake that the town would be only a long fringe of intermingling lights.

A HOT EVENING
IN DEARBORN AVENUE

The passengers were streaming aboard—young workingmen and their tittering girls, clerks in new straw hats and unmistakably summer clothes, tired husbands and smiling wives.

They were ranging themselves about on the upper deck, placing their chairs so that they could have something to lean against. The orchestra had bounded into a popular air, and the bass horn was repeating over and over:

Pum, pum, pum-pum-pum.

One impatient couple had begun to waltz. A hundred or more persons, gathered on the bridge and the approach, looked on with silent envy, feeling like the plowboy who stands at the rail fence and sees the rest of the family start for the county fair. Some of them could not resist the temptation to go down the platform and aboard.

All the passengers belonged to the fortunate "middle class." Society, you must understand, could not patronize cheap excursions on the lake. Therefore "the upper class," except for the small portion that can afford private yachts, never enjoys a breezy moonlight ride on a steamer, and Lake Michigan, except for its commercial uses, might as well be a thousand miles to the east.

* * *

There were many pictures of contentment along the boarding-house belt of Dearborn Avenue. The slope of stairway leading up to each house had become an amphitheater where men and women in lightest and cheeriest of summer attire were listening to the concerts of the street musicians. In front of one large house an Italian, with a street piano on wheels, was grinding out "Trovatore" for the benefit of a family which cuts a wide social swath. The Italian was rather to be pitied. He

"LIGHTS AND SHADOWS AND COOL DEPTHS OF LINCOLN PARK"

did not know that the family was debarred from coming out on the front porch to hear his music. The family was supposed to close its ears against all street pianos. Although the rooms were lighted, no one came to the windows and the music was wasted upon some appreciative children who marched and danced, keeping time with it.

Suppose the members of a well-known family should be grouped on a front porch listening to a street orchestra, and that just as the collection was being taken up some one who knew them should pass by!

* * *

Dearborn Avenue leads to the lights and shadows and cool depths of Lincoln Park. First there is a broad, smooth roadway, which shows boldly in the electric glare, and then there is a deeply shaded drive between solid walls of trees. It widens and brings into dim outline a dark statue with a massive pedestal. Each wheelman coursing the drives is marked by a speck of lantern, and the illusion is that of racing fireflies. No carriages disturb the night with a clatter of hoofs. Under the trees, right and left, the shade is so deep that sometimes voices may be heard where no one can be seen. Only a few feet away a flood of light shows every blade of grass and every pebble. All roads into the park lead to some circling pathway which is laced with the black shadows of trembling leaves, while misshapen blotches of the blending light fall on the figures and the benches.

There are at least two figures on a bench and one has a light dress. Both are silent and immovable until the intruder has passed on. The girl, who can be seen only in small pieces here and there where the patches of light have fallen, is always handsome, just as a half-finished picture is always sure to be beautiful in its fancied completion. Out in the clearing possibly it would be different.

* * *

Two young men had wandered into the park and had sought the paths less beaten, where the grass is rank and the breeze has a woody flavor pleasant to the nostrils. Neither could sing, but both of them did sing about "nights in June" and "lovely maidens," and they even went so far as to talk about the effect of moonlight on a distant ridge of trees.

Coming back to earth, they saw that the man on a bench ahead undoubtedly had his arm around the woman. As they drew nearer it became a shocking fact. The woman had pillowed her head on the man's shoulder and was either asleep or contented. The young men laughed and made remarks which were loud enough to be overheard, but the man was complacent.

"He has nerve," remarked one. "I suppose he doesn't care."

"She doesn't care, either."

Then they passed close by the bench and saw, cuddled up against the woman, a tousle-haired little girl fast asleep, with a doll in her arms. After which they passed on very quietly, and one of them said: "We ought to go back and apologize to that man."

In Lincoln Park a wide avenue for pedestrians leads straight north to the small lake. The pavilion, with its swinging lamps, lies directly ahead, and these lamps throw bands of fiery reflection across the water, so that from a distance the pavilion seems mounted upon flaming piles which glow and burn even under the rippling waves. Against these glaring pillars the small, darting boats appear in distinct silhouette, but away from the lights and with banks of heavy vegetation as a background they become a ghostly gray. The guitars and voices always sound more sweetly across the water, while the splashing and the laughter have the happy effect of turning thoughts away from hot weather.

On the shores of these lakes, which are linked by quiet waters lying under stone arches, the young man who drives the delivery wagon sits of an evening and holds the hand of the young woman who addresses letters. They are very happy, as well they may be, for no Chicago millionaire has such a magnificent front yard, with such a large lake and so many stately trees around it. They must feel sorry for the millionaire, who cannot go to a public park in the evening to stroll or sit for the reason that so many other persons go there. It doesn't trouble the delivery boy to have other people present and enjoying themselves.

The Junk-Shops of Canal Street

SOME one has asked the question: "What becomes of all the pins?"

The question has never been well answered, because there are no dealers in second-hand pins.

What becomes of the empty bottles, the tin cans, the rags, the broken stove-lids and worn-out copper boilers? They go to Canal Street, sooner or later.

That which is rubbish in a backyard becomes merchandise in Canal Street and some lean-fingered speculator converts it into bright money.

Canal Street is an object lesson in economy, a practical sermon on the value of looking after the pennies. A 3-cent bottle is not worth saving, but 100 of these bottles gathered up by a shaggy gentleman carrying a gunny-sack pouch means a clear profit of $3, which sum counts very largely along Canal Street.

The junk-shop region of Canal Street lies south from Taylor Street and is being slowly pushed still farther to the south by new brick buildings. For a block south from Van Buren Street the business front is most imposing, yet the site of these tall handsome buildings with their big windows and gilded signs was occupied only a few years ago by the same sort of tottering, aged and unpainted little structures which may still be found between 12th and 16th streets. Even in this backward region an occasional brick building is showing itself, making the contrast with its neighbors something painful.

* * *

In this second-hand strip and along the overcrowded streets leading off to the west reside many Russian Jews, new to American privileges, but half-recovered from the persecution which held them down for generations and compelled, by force

"TOTTERING, AGED AND UNPAINTED LITTLE STRUCTURES"

of circumstances, to exercise their commercial instincts in a modest way. If frugality and untiring industry count for anything this district will work out its own salvation. The second generation will do business in tall brick buildings like those up toward Van Buren Street. In the very heart of this populous settlement stands the magnificent Jewish manual training school, a voluntary contribution by the representative Jews of Chicago to the children of their less favored brethren. It combines the common-school features with the modern methods of manual training for both boys and girls. Over 800 children attend regularly.

*　　*　　*

After passing 12th Street one could well imagine himself out of Chicago. Every shop sign is painted in the angular characters of the Hebrew alphabet, and even the play-bills in the windows are in Hebrew. The queer little cheap stores, the comfortable manner in which whole families take possession of the sidewalk, the strange language of bargain and sale at the front of every grocery, and the heaps of faded merchandise exposed for sale, give to Junktown a character all its own. The bottle dealer, the rag dealer, the scrap-iron man, the grocer, the butcher, the cheap store man and the saloon-keeper are the business magnates. There are also basement shoe-shops and a few blacksmithing places, one of them having Jewish workmen, certainly a hopeful sign. One purpose of the training school is to encourage the poorer Jews to adopt trades and learn to work with their hands rather than become street peddlers and small dealers in junk.

*　　*　　*

Canal Street and its western outlets swarm with children, most of them streaked from playing in the street and, in warm weather, lightly clad with not more than one garment. Happy children they are, most of them plump and healthy, in the bargain. They are always playing in the sun, for Canal Street is so wide and the houses are so low that there is seldom any shade. A bale of rags or a mound of scrap-iron is a famous playhouse, and there is always a prospect of hanging on behind some slow rag-wagon. The horses on Canal Street are too deliberate to run down any children.

There are thousands of bottles packed in barrels and boxes, which lean against the dingy fronts. A nervous man who dreads contagion will surely hold his breath when he passes one of the rag warehouses. It is a musty and mothy odor that hangs around the ramshackle place, and one doesn't like to

"DECREPIT WAGONS ARE LINED UP BETWEEN THE HOUSES"

stop and think where all of those soiled and tattered things came from.

It seems that all the "played-out" and worthless odds and ends of the town have been dumped on Canal Street. The rusty scrap-iron lies around in tangled masses. Decrepit wagons are lined up between the houses. Burned-out boilers are strewn on the vacant lots. The crockery exposed for sale at the cheap stores is dusty and cracked, the suits of clothes are ready to fall to pieces from shoddiness. As for the vegetables, they seem to keep away from Canal Street until they are withered and spotted and consequently cheap.

* * *

The buildings themselves do not stand erect on their foundations. At one corner saloon the bareheaded children go down-hill to get their buckets filled, as the venerable structure seems to have settled back on its haunches. The fences around the scrap-iron yards are propped up from outside.

It is a terribly second-handed neighborhood, and it is no wonder that the eye longs for something new—a new coat of paint on a house, a new dress on a woman, a new "Rags Bought" sign. But everything is picturesquely dull and smoke stained. At every breath of wind the dust is gathered in clouds and blown into the stuffy little second-story bedrooms, from the windows of which the heads are always sticking out.

* * *

It may be found, upon investigation, that, considering what these poor people get in the way of home comforts, they pay more dearly than the families on a boulevard.

A Breathing-Place and Play-Ground

COMPARISONS between the three divisions of the city are always odious.

One cannot rhapsodize too much over the advantages of the south side without rousing the wrath of the numerous west-siders, while the statement that either the south side or the west side affords a pleasanter location for a residence than the north side simply moves every north-sider to a broad smile of contempt.

Each division has something to be proud of, and after hurrying the visitor through a fringe of slums can show him certain "views" intended to excite his admiration. On the west side it will be a view south on Ashland Avenue, a majestic thoroughfare which always seems ready to be put in a picture-

"A FOUNTAIN SPLASHES INTO A ROCKY BASIN"

book, or a glance at Union Park and the delightful panorama of Washington Boulevard.

On the south side Michigan Avenue and the branching boulevards to the south, the flowery gateway to Washington Park and the imposing pile of buildings overshadowing the lake front will be submitted as about the best things that the town can show a stranger.

The north side has Lincoln Park, the Lake Shore Drive and those exclusive residence thoroughfares, the "places" and "courts" running east to meet the lake. It also has Washington Square, and to many people this is the most picturesque bit in all the great division, because it is a green spot standing in a framework of noble architecture and bearing a certain dignity which comes only with age.

Washington Square is bounded by Clark Street, Walton Place, Dearborn Avenue and Washington Place. At the west the bright-colored cable cars chase back and forth all day. On the east is the smooth, white boulevard, alive at every hour with flying wheelmen and handsome carriages. Between these thoroughfares lies a patch of nature almost undisturbed. The two diagonal pathways meet in the center where a fountain splashes into a rocky basin. The trees are high and gnarled, throwing great irregular areas of shade on the ground.

The landscape gardener has done but little for the square. It stands as nature decreed it and as the great fire mercifully spared it.

This square was given to the city when Bushnell's addition to the city of Chicago was surveyed. It was offered as an attraction to an outlying residence district. Now that the city has encompassed it and moved on miles beyond, it remains as a breathing-place and playground in a waste of buildings.

It was donated at a time when ground was cheap and now its value is greater than all of the original addition. What is more, it can never fall victim to the greed of "improvement." It will be the poor man's country place and the children's romping ground for all time to come.

* * *

The fire of 1871 scorched to death nearly all the large trees on the north side. It happened, luckily, that there were few houses immediately west or southwest from the square. The Unity Church, of which the Rev. Robert Collyer was pastor, stood, as it now stands, at the corner of Dearborn Avenue and Walton Place. North from the square stood the Ogden house, one of the two houses in the burned district that escaped destruction. It was sheltered by the trees. As soon as the fire crossed the river many people hurried north to Washington Square with such goods as they could convey and put them in the square, thinking they would be safe there. Later, when the fire rushed northward with such rapidity, these people were compelled to fly for their lives, leaving their property behind. It was soon ignited by flying sparks and burned up. In a few hours the scorched trees of the square and the Ogden house, which they had sheltered, stood alone in a desert of strewn ashes.

* * *

Just across Walton Place from the square is the Newberry Library, its massive stone front of Spanish renaissance rising even above the highest trees. Unity Church and the New England Congregational Church face the square on the east. Each has a broad Gothic front, which is beginning to show respectable signs of age. Facing the square from the south and standing at the corner of Dearborn Avenue is the Union club house, with its dark and heavy stone front. West of it is a row of tall, prim and freshly painted apartment houses.

"ITS MASSIVE FRONT
RISING ABOVE THE TREES"

With the venerable trees and the prospect of fortress walls and ponderous stone doorways to north, south and east, Washington Square has a charm peculiarly its own.

It is what one might expect to find in a city of a few centuries' growth, but in Chicago it is always supposed that the trees are to be set out in straight rows and the houses are to smell of fresh plaster and have the litter of the builders scattered around the front door.

* * *

This particular portion of the north side, especially from Dearborn Avenue to the lake, is said to have had a more stable population during the last twenty-five years than any other region in Chicago. The men whose homes were burned in the great fire rebuilt on the same sites and assisted in rebuilding the churches. The congregations remained almost intact, while those in other parts of the city had to be reorganized. The neighborhood, not being subject to violent changes, settled down to eminent respectability and fixed habits of life, and these seem to find expression in the shady old-fashioned square.

In pleasant weather the square is crowded. The children come from a mile around to roll in the shade and dip their bare feet in the basin where the water falls. The nurse-maids wheel baby-carriages by day and the housemaids come with their young men at night. Men in working clothes sleep under the trees. Other men squat against the trees reading newspapers. The employe who picks up scraps of paper with a long sharp stick has to go around every hour or so.

It is a meeting place of all classes. The boys hauling their brother in a soap-box mounted on two wheels march ahead of a lavender-canopied baby-carriage. The dressed-up children from Dearborn Avenue, who dare not take off their shoes, are the only unhappy youngsters ever seen in the square. They suffer for awhile and then disobey the parental orders, just as they might be expected to do.

Vehicles Out of the Ordinary

ANY one who keeps his eyes open can find a number of strange vehicles in Chicago, but he must go out into the districts where the people live, and not confine his observations to the down-town district. In the crowded business streets the trucks, delivery wagons and hansom cabs are about the only types to be seen.

At a corner in the southwestern part of the city the evangelist's wagon was drawn up alongside the board walk and a small crowd had collected to listen to the music and read the inscriptions. The vehicle was something like a fancy farm wagon with a canopy top to it, except that the sideboards were not so high. It was drawn by two horses, and the driver sat in a broad seat at the front. Behind him was

THE ORGANIST
IS IN THE PORTABLE CHURCH

the organ, which was built as a part of the wagon, being joined to the floor and the sideboards. The scriptural quotations were painted on red cloth curtains concealing the back part of the wagon, where there were two or three chairs. When the

"THE WAFFLE MAN WITH HIS SQUATTY WAGON"

curtains were removed and the canopy moved out of the way the back part of the wagon became a rostrum, or pulpit.

The man at the organ played some introductory chords and sang a hymn in a robust voice loud enough for out-door use, and the evangelist made an exhortation.

Then the driver clucked at his horses and said "Getep" and the portable church was driven to another corner and the services were repeated.

*   *   *

On many of the less pretentious streets the waffle man with his squatty wagon is a familiar and welcome sight. His establishment on wheels is drawn by a patient horse, who is always more willing to stop than he is to start. The wagon, which is of a dull red color, is mounted on low wheels.

The waffle man does his own driving, for his gasoline stove is at the front of the wagon. His cooking utensils, batter, and the rest of the kitchen outfit are kept in shelves at the front, while at the back there is a flat counter where the customers may be served. Sometimes he rings a bell and again he will keep up a mournful, monotonous wail of "Wa-a-a-fles; wa-a-a-fles."

The waffle booth on the corner or the handcart of the "levee" district has been familiar for a long time, but the waffle wagon which supplies families is a thing of recent date.

The old cobbler and his traveling shop are known on many of the streets in the northwestern section of the city. He has a covered wagon, which is fitted up inside with all that is needed in a repair shop. The driver, who is as old and grizzled as the cobbler, labors to keep the horse going, and shouts "Old Shoes to mend!" The venerable cobbler saves rent and gets plenty of work, for the children know him and wait for him, a dozen or more gathering around his queer vehicle to watch him put on the half soles.

* * *

The sandwich wagon or "buffet car" is common enough, especially on the south side between Van Buren and 12th streets, and on the west along Halsted and Madison streets. There are a few along North Clark Street, and now and then one may be found even in the remote districts, especially around the parks or any resort where people congregate of an evening. It was the sandwich wagon that popularized the "ham and egg sandwich," an oily luxury which has been taken up by many of the restaurants.

At first the wagons served only sandwiches, but with growing competition they have introduced cold-meat lunches, baked beans, coffee, hot corn on the cob and other delicacies. If one is not troubled with a false pride one can get a good warm lunch at low prices and stand on the curbstone while he eats it. Occasionally there will be seen a buffet car with a little counter in the back end of it. At the counter are three stools, so that at least three customers may sit while they are being served.

THE OLD COBBLER AND HIS SHOP

The average sandwich car to be found in State Street has numerous windows decorated with tempting advertisements.

The oil or gasoline stove is banked about with loaves of bread, the carcasses of chickens and great knobs of ham. "Albert" or "Charley," or whatever may be the name on the illuminated sign, wears a white jacket and a white cap and takes a professional pride in turning a piece of ham without putting the fork to it.

As a rule, each of these wagons has a "stand" where it remains from an early hour in the evening until the last customers go home, sometimes the break of day. The horse is not kept "hitched up" all night, but is in shelter near at hand, and when there are no more 10-cent pieces in sight he and the "buffet car" disappear.

"A LUNCH AT CHEAP PRICES"

* * *

An intelligent Italian, whose "territory" covers the residence streets far up on the north side, owns a street piano. It is one of the large kind, mounted on a cart platform. Until quite lately he had to employ another Italian to go with him and help pull the thing. This was not always easy work, especially if the street happened to be rough or a trifle slippery. Therefore, to save himself labor and avoid paying an extra salary, he bought a small donkey, which now does all the hard work. This little animal soon became thoroughly acquainted with his duties. He stands perfectly still when commanded to do so, although the command is in Italian, a new language to him. His head hangs down, his eyes close and the ears droop in a melancholy way until the piano begins to pound out "The Blue Bells of Scotland." As soon as those familiar strains are heard he lifts his head and prepares to move, because he knows that is the last piece in the repertory.

* * *

The fish-peddler's vehicle is nothing more than a box

mounted on two wheels, with a pair of shafts in front and a place behind for the peddler to stand. The driver stands back of the box, in which the fish are packed in ice. When a customer calls him all he has to do is say "Whoa," lift up the lid, haul out a fish and weigh it with his spring scales.

*   *   *

Another strange peddler has a wagon with a hayrack on top and makes his living by selling sheaves of straw and sacks of corn-husks, which are used as bedding in many quarters where foreign laborers reside.

The lemonade wagon and the confectionery store on wheels were common enough in the World's Fair neighborhood last year, but there is an air of novelty about the tin-type "gallery" on wheels now jumping from one vacant lot to another.

Advertising agents are responsible for many of the weird vehicles on the streets. They send out Roman chariots to advertise a new chewing gum, and one of them rather overdid it by having a red-headed woman drive four white horses abreast.

Every one in Chicago must have seen at one time or another those two huge bill-boards, joined at the top, mounted on four small wheels and drawn by a team of shaggy donkeys not much larger than jack rabbits.

It will be conceded that the moving van is the most majestic vehicle to be seen, while from an artistic standpoint the gilded pie wagon has no rival. Then there is the fancy little steam boiler on wheels which is used in blowing out the stopped-up pipes.

Every summer the suburbs are visited by strolling gypsies who make homes in the big gaudy caravans. It would be an interesting procession—one made up of the queer vehicles in Chicago.

"Hobo" Wilson and
the Good Fairy

A CHILLY TOWN! A chilly town!" murmured Pemberton Wilson as he limped around to the sunny side of warehouse F and slowly let himself down to a recumbent position on the hot, tarry boards.

"A chilly town. That's what; even in the summer-time," said Pemberton Wilson as he threw a stray nail into the muddy slip and lazily watched the rings enlarge and lose themselves in faintest ripples. "You take any train and it lands you here, and the only comfort of bein' here is that there's so many trains out. I s'pose my stomach thinks I'm trying to go without anything for a week just on a bet. The country lanes must be sighing for me. I wonder if turnips are getting large enough."

To designate Pemberton Wilson as a "hobo" would simply corroborate his opinion of himself.

He had carved "Hobo Wilson" on many a section shanty and mile-post between Scranton, Pa., and Council Bluffs, Iowa, and there were friends who knew him as "Rooster."

On one Indiana trip he had earned the title of "Come-Again Wilson" because he had a persistent way of getting on a train after once being put off.

Like many another of his class, he was not devoid of sentiment or philosophy. He carried in his breast pocket a speckled volume of Burns' poems. He had forgotten to return it to a public library in southern Illinois. The book opened of itself to the lines: "A man's a man for a' that." "Hobo" Wilson read the poem as he lay with his back against the warm boards of warehouse F, and then he put the book back in the pocket of his coat, which he had thrown down beside him.

* * *

At the bend in the river a coal vessel was being unloaded. The click of the machinery and the noisy dumping of the big buckets at regular intervals became rather soothing when the rhythm was understood. "Hobo" Wilson tapped with his thumb, keeping time, and looked through the rigging of a lumber schooner in the second slip beyond at the coughing smokestack which reached up from a small planing-mill. The mill was buzzing in changeable tones, like a nest of discordant bumble-bees.

The smoke rolling from the stack drifted through the rigging, where the yards and netted lines seemed to cut it into irregular shapes. "Hobo" Wilson watched drowsily until to his blurred vision there were many fantastic forms floating in the foggy maze. And he was not greatly surprised when one of these forms took on the outline of a dwarfish human being and floated slowly toward him. It poised for a moment above a hawser timber and shook itself, a shower of soot falling from it. Then it settled into a comfortable sitting attitude and looked at him.

"Well, Rooster, how's everything?"

The voice was rather small and shrill. "Hobo" Wilson could not answer at once. He was marveling at the appearance of his strange visitor. The little man was hardly three feet high. Under the slouch hat was a good-natured and wrinkled face, decorated on the chin with a small tuft of beard, which might have been gray at one time, but which was now blackened and dusty, the same as his face and clothes. The latter were of rough quality—a hickory shirt, a shoddy pair of trousers, fringed at the bottoms and held up by one suspender, and a pair of worn shoes, much too large and laced with hemp twine.

"Are you down on your luck, Rooster?" asked the little man.

"I'm livin' on th' air," said Hobo. "But where did you come from?"

"I just dropped in with the smoke. Don't know me, eh?"

"That's what I don't."

"Listen, 'Hobo' Wilson. Do you remember last Saturday morning when you were at Hammond and divided your hand-out with a brother who alighted from a box-car, a day out from Louisville and very hungry?"

"I do. 'A man's a man for a' that.'"

"True enough, Rooster. That was a good deed. More than once I've seen you give a comrade a good place on the truck."

"Where was you?"

"I dare say you didn't look up into the rolling cloud of smoke to see the good fairy of the hoboes."

"Fairy!"

"Cert. You didn't expect the guardian fairy of the hoboes to tear around the country in all kinds of weather with a little white robe and some ostrich-feather wings?"

"I s'pose not."

* * *

"HOBO WILSON,
I'VE WATCHED YOU"

"'Hobo' Wilson, I've watched you. I never saw you do a pard any dirt. The good things of this world must not all be given to brakemen and farmers and people who work. Are you hungry?"

"Sure."

"Then feel in the pockets of that coat beside you and believe me when I tell you that every man must live before he dies."

"Sufferin' brake beams!" gasped "Rooster," as he drew from one pocket after another crumpled rolls of bank-bills. He heaped them up on the faded check cloth and his tears fell on them.

"No more drillin' in the snow; no soup houses; never again in a bucket. Pard, you've done——"

But when he looked up again the one-gallused fairy had disappeared and the smoke which pushed through the rigging and rolled away was blacker than ever.

* * *

He put all the money in his pockets, first throwing away the balls of twine, the old pocket knife and the needle and thread wound about a beer cork.

On the street car he could find no bill less than $5 and the conductor grumbled about the change.

"Give me the change, confound you," said Mr. Wilson, "or else I'll have that number off of your cap."

Thereupon the conductor quieted down and gave him his change. Mr. Wilson tossed 10 cents to a baby on a seat in front of him and then settled back to enjoy his ride. He had never known of a more beautiful day. He observed with much satisfaction that every one else seemed as happy as he. The women in the doorways were smiling and children romped along the sidewalks. He counted the money from one pocket and found that it amounted to $65, or 1,300 glasses of beer. The other passengers watched him curiously.

He alighted at Polk Street and walked over to "Dinny's" place. The old crowd was there.

"Come up, you fellows," said Mr. Wilson, "and drink all you can hold. I mean it," he added, as they did not seem willing to stand up and take chances. "Here's the stuff."

"DRINK TILL YOU BUST"

He dribbled out on the bar the silver which the conductor had given him.

There was a rush and Dinny began setting out rows of schooners.

"Drink up that money!" shouted Mr. Wilson, "and say, Dinny, give me a good cigar."

* * *

While the boys were taking away the "scuttles" as fast as they could be passed up Mr. Wilson went out to purchase a wardrobe. He knew the place to go, because he had stood before it many a time looking at the brilliant neckties and white collars. The proprietor met him gruffly, but melted into smiles when he saw the roll of money.

"Fix me up from the skin out," said Mr. Wilson. "Give me the best stuff you've got and hand it out quick. Have you got a back room?"

Certainly he had a back room. Mr. Wilson was shown to that apartment and was treated with every courtesy. One by one the necessary articles were pushed into the room. At the end of ten minutes he was a new man. His neck felt the dignified embrace of a collar for the first time in years. The stiff shirt had straightened him up. He put his money into his new clothes and strolled out. The big officer who had once kicked him moved respectfully aside to allow him to pass.

"I'll hire some one to lick that fellow," said Mr. Wilson as he directed his steps toward a fancy bar-room.

* * *

He drank cocktail after cocktail, and their only effect was to increase his general cheerfulness and make every one around him more attentive to his wishes.

"Where's the best restaurant in town?" he asked, leaning over the bar and familiarly addressing the man in the white garments.

"It's two blocks down."

"I'll show you where it is," said a man who wore clothes almost as good as those of Mr. Wilson, "come with me."

Mr. Wilson locked arms with the gentleman, who introduced himself as president of a bank and said he was proud to be allowed to walk along the street with Mr. Wilson. They met several distinguished citizens whose names Mr. Wilson had read in scraps of newspaper around the lodging house.

They met the mayor, the postmaster, Mr. Armour, Mr. Field, Mr. Pullman and others. Every time Mr. Wilson was introduced the whole crowd went and had a drink. Mr. Wilson showed them how much money he had and they slapped him on the back and said he was a good fellow.

At last Mr. Wilson and the banker sat down to dine. They had lobster and pie and champagne and all kinds of drinks, and Mr. Wilson gave the waiter a dollar to fan him while he was eating.

Mr. Wilson ate two lobsters, for they were the first he had

tasted in ten years, and every one in the house watched him when he pulled out such a lot of money and demanded to know how much he owed the place.

After that he and the banker went riding in an open carriage and all the people along the street stopped to see them go by. They halted in front of a saloon and had the bartender bring three bottles of champagne out to the carriage—one for Mr. Wilson, one for the banker and one for the driver.

While they were drinking the champagne out of the bottles a crowd gathered around. Mr. Wilson ordered a policeman to disperse the crowd, and he did so promptly.

* * *

"Now, what shall we do next?" asked the banker, putting his arm around Mr. Wilson's neck.

"Oh, take a little ride and then have something more to drink. Drive up, there!" and he stood up in the seat and kicked the driver in the back.

So they drove up one street and down another, while the bands played and women at the windows waved handkerchiefs. Mr. Wilson leaned back in the cushions, thoroughly happy and counting his money, when he felt a sudden pain in his right foot.

The pain became more sharp.

He raised himself to his elbow.

* * *

He was getting the "hot-foot." A heavy policeman was pounding the sole of his shoe. The club was lifted again, but "Hobo" Wilson drew back his leg.

AT EACH STEP
THE TRUTH BECAME CLEARER

"Go wan now! Get a move!" said the policeman, giving him a kick with the broad of his foot.

"Well, I'm goin'," whined "Hobo" Wilson, whose head was all in a whirl as he came to his feet. He picked up his coat and limped around the corner of warehouse F and at each step the cruel truth became clearer to him.

"Thank goodness for one thing," said he, "I can still taste the lobster."

*   *   *

There was one remarkable circumstance in connection with this adventure, and it is a puzzle to Pemberton Wilson, alias "Hobo" Wilson, alias "Come Again" Wilson, alias "Rooster." He remembered throwing away the pocket-knife, thread and needle and string when he found the money.

Sure enough, when he searched his coat afterward he found that of his personal property only the copy of Burns remained.

How "Pink" Was Reformed

IT WAS very difficult to tell whether "Pink" had been drinking or not. The only signs were a slight reddening of the eyeballs and an increased violence of laughter.

There was no such thing as detecting an alcoholic flush in a face which had the dull brown-black color of chocolate. It was generally known around the building, however, that "Pink" was addicted to spirituous, vinous, malt and other intoxicating liquors, with a racial preference for gin. He had other worldly habits, which he gladly confessed. These were "craps" and "policy." Even to the customers who could have no possible interest in such lowly speculation he confided stories about "passin' de bones," "Little Joe" and "gettin' ole eight," whatever he may have meant. One day when he appeared with a new suit of checked garments he announced that he had hit the "Kentucky row" on a "gig," or something of that kind. This was conclusive evidence that he gambled at times and was a person of bad habits.

However, he was so obliging, so ready to laugh at jokes and

so conscientious in his work of polishing shoes that his faults were overlooked. His chair was in the main corridor of the building near the elevator. Those who were well acquainted with him knew that his name was William Pinckney Marvin, and that he had aspirations to leave the lowly occupation of cleaning shoes and get a job at one of the race-tracks.

* * *

It has already been intimated that "Pink" sometimes drank, but seldom to the neglect of business.

From the story afterward told by him it would appear that on the day of misfortunes "Wilse" Johnson, who worked in the hotel, approached the boot-blacking stand and asked: "Are you strong?"

Pink gave him the white of his eyes and said: "Man, I'm too strong for any hotel colo'ed person."

Wilse suggested that he had some "bones" in his pocket and "Pink" said: "I ain't got no strength to run; mus' stay here and get action."

They began rolling at 10 cents a crap, but too many people stopped to watch them, and "Pink," who had been "got into" for 30 cents, advised an adjournment to the alley, where he knew of a good place. They sought the quiet alley, "Pink" leaving his business interests to go to rack, and for the next hour there was a rattle of dry "bones," accompanied by a chanting duet of such expressions: "Come on, seven" and "I mus' have fo'." At the end of that time Mr. "Wilse" Johnson was bankrupted, for "Pink" had "faded" him to the extent of $3.50.

In the flush of success "Pink" offered to buy, and the two sought a neighboring saloon which fronted on the alley. "Pink" met some white men in there and called up the house. The white gentlemen waived all prejudice as to color and accepted his hospitality. After that there were other drinks, and he was introduced to a number of colored men, who were apparently friends of "Wilse" Johnson.

* * *

"Pink" remembered distinctly next day that he made speeches on several topics, feeling that he had a right to do so, because he had done most of the buying. "Wilse" Johnson was gloomy and unsociable. It was during a discussion of the freedman's condition that they fell into an argument over the question: "Isn't a colored man as good as anybody else?" While "Pink" was addressing himself to the question "Wilse" Johnson made some disparaging remark, which the speaker properly resented. It was all a misty recollection, but "Pink" knew that some one pushed him from behind, while some one else struck him over the head with what felt to be a billiard cue. Something landed in his eye, and he felt himself lying on the floor being jumped on.

At about 6 o'clock that evening he reached his "stand" in the lobby, his legs describing strange curves, his garments torn and bloody and his face an awful picture of dark, rare meat.

A sympathetic man sent for the janitor and the latter dragged "Pink" into a wash-room and with the aid of cotton and arnica dressed his wounds. The injured and betrayed man could give no account of what had happened, although he constantly mumbled an intention to cut out several important parts from some one's anatomy. Shortly after 7 o'clock he was able to walk around and the janitor had him put on a State Street car, with instructions to the conductor to dump him off at the right corner.

*   *   *

At the very hour when "Pink" Marvin and "Wilse" Johnson got into a dispute over the civil rights of the colored man, a murder was done in a "levee" saloon about ten blocks distant. Two colored men engaged in a fight. One stabbed the other and escaped through the back door. The wounded man died within an hour and that evening every policeman in uniform and every "fly" man was on the lookout for a murderer, a colored man of whom there was but a vague description.

*   *   *

"Pink," slightly repaired, and with his head tied up, leaned heavily back in the corner and dozed as the car moved southward. He did not see the two officers in plain clothes studying him from the back platform, and was considerably surprised when awakened by a rough shake.

"We want you," said one of the men.

"Wha' fo'," asked "Pink."

"Aw, come on and don't talk. You're the guy that had the fight in that saloon."

"Yes, sah, but——"

"Aw, come on," and they had him between them running him toward a patrol box. There was the usual crowd and a great many people pushed around and wanted to know what he had done. "Pink" was too thoroughly sick and miserable to care what happened to him. He was thrown into the wagon, the bell went ding-ding-ding, and he rode to the station in a hurry. The moment they pushed him into a cell he collapsed and did not waken until broad daylight.

Then, with a racking headache, a burning throat and a dull ache wherever he had been struck or kicked, he tried to figure why he should be in the police station. It was the first time he had ever been arrested and he remembered that when taken into custody he was riding peaceably in a cable car. After breakfast a turnkey unlocked the cell door and said: "Come

HE WAS TAKEN TO THE STATION

out here, Marvin, the captain wants to talk with you." So
he had told his right name.

Sore and limping he followed upstairs and was pushed into
a small room, bare of carpet and with no furniture save a small
desk and several chairs. The captain was a large man with a
small mustache and a uniform very new and bright. He spoke
rather kindly to the prisoner.

"You were out drinking a little yesterday."

"Tha's right, boss; I don't deny it."

"Got purty full, eh?"

"I had too much, fo' a fac'."

"Got into a little fight?"

"They jumped on me, seh; I didn't do nothin'."

"How did you happen to go in there?"

"Well, seh, me and a frien' o' mine goes in to take a drink.
We meets some mo' fellows."

"I see. What started the fight?"

"I don' 'zactly remembeh."

"What became of your knife?"

"I didn' have no knife at all."

"Is that so?" There was a sudden change in the tone. "Do
you know that you got into a fight in there and killed a man?"

"Wha's dat—wha' you say!" He was staring at the captain
and trembling like a leaf. Then, with a cry like that of a frightened child, he fell across the arm of his chair in a dead faint.
The captain threw open the door and motioned to an officer,
who roused "Pink" and half dragged him back to the cell.

"He's the man all right," said the captain.

"He just the same as admitted it last night," remarked the
desk sergeant.

* * *

"Pink" lay crouched in his cell for two hours, crying in terror, before he thought to send for his friend the janitor. He
was a murderer and entitled to special privileges. The janitor
was summoned. He stood at the bars and listened to "Pink's"
choking narrative.

"That's funny," said he. "Larry was up this morning and
said you broke a looking glass in his place, but he didn't say
you stabbed any one. Did you have two fights?"

"Pink" gave it up. He was ready to give up everything. But the janitor sent for "Larry," who came and told a straight story and the captain, much puzzled, sent for the colored bartender, who had seen the stabbing. He took one look at "Pink" and that settled it. He said the guilty man was a light yellow. "Git out," said the captain, giving "Pink" a shove, and "Pink" ran.

Each Sunday morning at the African Methodist Episcopal Church the minister says: "The offering will now be taken" and Brother William Pinckney Marvin marches up in front and starts around with the basket. When the hymns are sung his voice rises loudly and joyously above all others. Since that morning when he rushed from the station he has shunned the "bones" and the "gigs" and if any one dares to suggest drinking he quotes scripture, his favorite passage being: "De way of de transgressor's hard, and no mistake."

SHANTIES

After the Sky-Scrapers, What?

EVERY time the down-town confusion of roofs, chimneys and towers is viewed from some eminence there must come to the mind a query: "When will Chicago reach the era of stability?"

Over there to the northwest a cluster of men no larger than flies are hacking away at a roof from which arises dry clouds of dust. The first blow is struck at the cornice, and the destruction is not to cease until the last foundation stone has been rooted out of the clay.

To the northeast is a right-angled web of steel towering above black roofs and showing like the skeleton of a great monument.

There has not been a time in years when the destruction and construction were not to be seen from this same window, and even the old residents who have watched the ceaseless and marvelous changes of the business district say it is apparently as much unfinished as it was fifty years ago. They may come back in spirit a few centuries hence to view the same old tearing down and building up.

* * *

Chicago need not complain because the critics are not satisfied with this town. The town is never satisfied with itself. A man builds a six-story brick building with a stone front, across the top of which is a tablet bearing his name. It fills with tenants, the foundation settles into place and is ready for permanency. The man snaps his fingers and says: "Pshaw, this will never do! I must have been an idiot—building for a village!" Out go the tenants, bag and baggage; in goes the wrecking crew, and behold! there remain only a hole in the ground and a barricade of rubbish, and the pedestrians have to walk in the street to avoid the horrors of improvement.

This business region is like a household which never settles down—where the "cleaning" goes ahead the year round.

To-day the drawing-room is full of ladders and buckets.

To-morrow the dining-room is having doors hacked through its walls and a new floor is being put down.

The day after, carpets are being laid. The man of the house knows that after the work is finished, after every article of furniture is in place, the pictures hung, the rugs spread and the lamps lighted, it will be a snug and beautiful home, but no sooner is one spasm over than another begins and he can never settle down to a quiet enjoyment of the comforts he has purchased.

*   *   *

The down-town thoroughfare no sooner adopts a tidy front and an unbroken row of bright windows before a vandal army wrenches a building to pieces, puts a rough wooden shed over the sidewalk and begins the clamorous work of driving the earth full of enormous piles, on which is to rest the towering structure of bolted steel. Then the way is strewn with bricks, sand and riveted slabs of metal.

"It's an ugly locality while the work is in progress, but wait until the sky-scraper is completed and the litter taken away." That's the consolation. When the day comes the vandals rush upon a building next door, and once more—Babel.

After the sky-scraper, what?

The corner building lot on the busy corner held in the '30s a two-story frame with a peaked roof. It was a likely building, but the '40s wouldn't have it.

Then there came a three-story frame with a square front to the street and a double storeroom down-stairs. And the '50s sneered at it.

Nothing would do but brick. The new building was longer and had stone steps in front, with fancy work along the cornice and the inside doors were "grained." They called it a "block." But long before the fire wiped it away it stood abashed in a neighborhood of larger buildings and the tenants were third-class.

There came an opportunity after the fire to build a magnificent business structure which should anticipate the growth of the city rising from its ashes. What if the people did call the builder reckless when he made the entire front of heavy stone, which overhung in carved folds? Why not heed the lesson of the fire and build something to stand forever? It was a pride indeed—five stories high, finished inside with hardwood

SPRAWLING SHANTIES WHICH ARE IN LUCK TO HAVE
SURVIVED SO LONG

and a multiplicity of gas-jets. There was a passenger elevator
and the windows had plate glass. At last it deserved the name
of "block" and its offices were greedily taken.

* * *

Who would think that twenty years could bring about such
a change? The stonework was ink-black from ooze and smoke.
The gorgeous front looked as out of date as a fashion picture
which one occasionally finds in the files of the *Lady's Magazine.*
The good tenants had left the musty hallways, with their yellow gas-lights, and had gone to new buildings where the elevators flew, where the walls were of white marble and the
electric lights were turned on by the snap of a button. The
dark, clumsy hardwood doors and arches were not to be com-

pared with the later styles of cheerful oak and maple. The slivered wooden floors were cheap and commonplace beside the new surfaces of inlaid tile. The palace which was to endure for all time had become the habitation of doubtful detective agencies, high-sounding publishing concerns, obscure lawyers and struggling little corporations trying to float stock.

Around the building loomed the giant office buildings of the new era and they had set an increased value on ground space. They had demonstrated that a lot with fifty feet frontage may draw revenues from 500 inmates instead of the former 150. The ground under the old building had become so valuable that it could not be wasted in holding up an antiquated five-story ramshackle.

So the wreckers battered the old thing to pieces and some of the men who had admired it twenty years before said: "There goes an old landmark, and it's a good thing. Now we'll get a nice fourteen-story building on that corner."

In a matter of a very few weeks the gaunt triumph of new methods was completed. It had the architectural proportions of a hitching-post and it had been reduced in rank from a "block" to a "building." But it was a great success. Men passengers clung to the bars and women shrieked in hysteria when one of the lightning elevators made a rocket leap for the roof. There was a restaurant in the basement, a cigar-stand in the main lobby and a barber-shop on the eleventh floor, to say nothing of mail-chutes, a telegraph office and a bureau of clean towels.

The owner was satisfied. He had reached the climax once more and was just as certain of it as his predecessors had been back in the '30s, '40s, '50s and '70s. But after the sky-scraper, what?

Every writer dealing with Chicago has said much about the remarkable condensation of the business activity of the city into that small area bounded on the east by the lake, on the north by the Chicago River, on the west by the south branch and on the south by no fixed line or street. It is a case of going either south or up into the air. Those who have preferred to remain in the thick of the business turmoil built and are building into the air. There is nothing new in the prophecy that some day, and it will not do to postpone it too long, every building in the business region will be at least twelve stories high, the streets will be so many cañons and the sunshine will filter down through crevices in that vast area of flat roofs.

* * *

Some day, also, it may be necessary to begin tearing down these rows of sky-scrapers, just as the perfected buildings of the '70s are now being demolished. In this town are certain "wrecking" companies which tear down buildings for a consideration. Happily for them, they will be out of business before the trussed and interlocked mountains of structural iron have to be razed.

"It will be a fearful task to pull down one of those buildings," said a manager of a wrecking company. "Think of the thousands of rusted rivets holding the framework together. Around this framework is the shell of mortar and brick, locking the joints. You can batter down a brick or stone wall, and it is easy enough to chop away wood, but if the Masonic Temple is ever to be pulled down and carted away some man will have a beautiful job on his hands."

* * *

The builders block the sidewalks and the pavers have torn the street until it resembles a strip of the Bad Lands. The paving of ten years ago, which was to remain forever, is no longer satisfactory and accordingly there is to be a new kind, which is to last forever.

The newly paved streets meet badly paved streets, which must soon be disemboweled. The amazing sky-scrapers have as next-door neighbors sprawling shanties which are lucky to have survived so long. Therefore it behooves the patient citizen to accustom himself to walking through dark sheds and climbing the heaps of granite blocks. Not for many years at least will this great business center of Chicago be improved to its limit and thoroughly satisfied with itself.

Sidewalk Merchants and
Their Wares

HE WAS a beautiful example of patience and long suf-
fering. There under the shelter of the corner and free
from the currents of humanity which met at right
angles he stood all day long, holding out his merchandise for
the inspection of an indifferent public and chanting, "Shoe-
strings—5 cents a pair."

From the ninety and nine he received not so much as a
glance.

Perhaps one in a hundred turned his head at sound of the
appealing voice, but did not slacken his speed.

About one of a thousand stopped to look at the strings or
perhaps to chaff the mournful dealer.

And let it be supposed that one in 10,000, either moved by
charity or suddenly reminded of a need, bought a pair of shoe-
strings and tucked them away in a back pocket.

The dealer always met the buyer with rare self-possession,
as if a customer were not a novelty.

He gave no evidence of excitement when a man bought two
pairs, and there was no change in his hopeful attitude when a
prospective customer broke away without buying. He had the
quality of equipoise, so rare in business men.

The bunch of shoe-strings was always the same size and the
greasy cap was always set at the same vagabond angle on his
gray head. The coat and vest had once been of gay check and
were of juvenile design. The coat, for instance, was short behind and slashed away from the third button in front.

At one time there had been silk facing on the lapels, but it
had worn down to a few threads. The vest was double-breasted,
and there were pins to mark the former location of buttons.
The baggy and stained trousers had once been braided down
the sides. These wrecks of cheap gentility were in harmony
with the narrow, bony face, which was stubbled with gray
beard, while the eyes seemed to have lost all expression except
that of tired indifference. The flesh had a dead pallor, for it is

POPCORN BALLS A CENT APIECE

a curious fact that whereas whisky will cause one man to puff and redden it will draw the blood from another and eat him from within until there seems to remain only an ashy parchment over the skeleton.

* * *

"Shoe-strings—5 cents a pair."

This quavering cry seemed to have become a habit with him, for sometimes he repeated it over and over when the corner was quiet in the lull of an afternoon and there wasn't a possible customer within hearing distance.

Where did he live and how did he live? Suppose he sold as many as five pairs of shoe-strings in a day (large estimate). His total receipts would be 25 cents, but not more than half of that would be profit. How could he live for 12½ cents a day? Did he ever eat?

What had been his life? A man who begins early to be a "bum" and drunkard does not live to be 60 years old.

Another thing: Any man of 60 can remember well-dressed days of prosperity. Did the shoe-string man remember such days, and if so what must have been his reflections as he stood on the corner all day, starving for liquor?

It would seem that one who has the patience to stand and offer goods could find something more salable than shoe-strings. But the sidewalk merchants do not think so, for one sells the 5-cent strings, another cheap handkerchiefs, another collar-buttons and another pocket combs.

Did you ever see any one buy of them?

* * *

Not all of these penny speculators are old and physically disabled.

In a city where manual labor has always commanded a fair remuneration the broad-shouldered immigrant prefers to take his chances hawking collar-buttons. He would rather make 25 cents a day and be in "business" than work for $1.50 a day.

The rush of immigration is responsible for the unloading in the streets of Chicago of the cheap and picturesque ragamuffins to be found in the poverty districts of European cities. Five years ago the Italian children who played and sang on the street corners were regarded as novelties. Now the streets swarm with them and they are as bold and bothersome as English sparrows.

They tag at coat-tails and beg for pennies. With noisy concertinas and capering dances they infest saloons. The smallest girls have learned the vulgar dances of the day and the larger ones sing bad parodies on popular songs.

Most of the flower girls come from this same class. The flower girl is a thing of beauty on the stage, where she wears bangs and a pink dress and does a neat song and dance. The flower girl of Clark Street, at the hour of midnight, is a frowsy young creature, who goes from one basement drinking place to another. She fastens flowers in the button-holes, then says: "Give me whatever you please."

Saucy, forward, and with a frightful knowledge of the things which children should not know, she is interesting in her way, but it is not a promising way.

THE ARISTOCRAT OF HIS CLASS

*   *   *

In the alley where the newsboys gathered there is a ceaseless competition for pennies. The Italian at the end of the alley gives a spoonful of ice-cream on a piece of brown paper for 1 cent. His countryman near by sells hot sausage at 2 cents a link.

In a basement stairway is the waffle boy. Further along is the old woman who offers an enormous sweet cake and a mug of "pop" for 5 cents. Then there is the man who sells popcorn balls at 1 cent each, and if his receipts were all profits he couldn't become rich.

These alley establishments do a lively business at certain hours of the day.

* * *

HOKEY-POKEY PENNY ICE-CREAM

It is not to be supposed that all the street merchants belong to a class with the shoe-string man. Many a fruit stand does a business which would be creditable to a retail shop, and the young gentlemen with their showcases full of cut roses and sweet-peas come very near being public benefactors.

But the straying "barker" who jingles his collar buttons before you and the frayed mortal who holds out the speckled combs—these are the pitiable evidences that Chicago is becoming a metropolis. In order to sustain one feature of metropolitan life a large number of people must expose either their misery or their helplessness.

* * *

The arch-fiend of the sidewalk business men is he who sells the 50-cent umbrellas, and the only mitigating circumstance in his case is that the purchaser might have known that he couldn't get an umbrella for 50 cents.

The umbrella man comes out of hiding every rainy day and

you may find him at a down-town corner howling vociferously and holding a real umbrella over a grain sack stuffed full of the alleged umbrellas which he is offering for 50 cents apiece.

Happy is the man who goes home in the rain without yielding to the entreaties, for this is the story of one man who purchased.

The handle was made of varnished pine and the ribs of telegraph wire. It opened with a creak and assumed a dumpy shape, one side being much depressed; but the owner thought it would answer the purpose. It had the general appearance of an umbrella.

He started out in the heavy rain and the canopy of thin black stuff gathered water like a sponge.

He felt his hand getting wet and discovered that a dark stream was trickling down the pine stick. Then a drop of something fell on his arm and left a stain like a drop of ink.

It would have been bad enough if the umbrella had simply leaked.

But the rain which came through washed out the cheap dye and spattered it over the unhappy man underneath.

He should have thrown away the thing, but he hadn't the courage, because the rain was driving so hard. He kept the umbrella over him and endured the shower bath, but when he reached shelter he was polka-dotted from head to foot.

The umbrella had washed out to a dirty gray color, and the handle seemed covered with mucilage.

He tried to close the thing, but it bagged out fearfully, so he threw it out of the window, and some unsuspecting person stole it and was doubtless punished in due time.

Some of the Unfailing Signs

IF YOU were to be wrecked in the Pacific Ocean 2,000 miles off the mainland and driven by the storm to the coast of an unknown island; if you did not know your latitude, longitude or the direction of the wind; if you met on the beach a young man with two cigars in one upper vest pocket, while from the other upper pocket protruded three sharpened pencils and the white bone handle of a tooth-brush; if you didn't know the name of the island or the name of the young man, you could at least be certain of one thing—viz.: that the young man was a telegraph operator.

And you would know that he was not a city operator, but one of a suburban or country town.

Of course you can't give any good reason why the telegraph operator should balance his vest by putting cigars on one side and the pencils and tooth-brush on the other. Neither can you explain the tail-feathers of a peacock.

There are some things that must be accepted as universal truths.

WHAT IS HE?

Suppose a man is standing in front of a boarding house in Van Buren Street. He wears a close-fitting suit of black and the short sack coat flares out somewhat in a bell shape below. The coat has rather wide braid on it and the vest is slashed away from the lower button. The shirt is blue-striped and the soft black hat is flat on top and fits well down on the head, scraping the ears. With trousers of the spring bottom type and a cameo ring on the third finger of the left hand what more is needed to identify the man as a "railroader"? Not an engineer or a passenger conductor, but one of the freight "crew." Possibly he is the conductor, but probably he is the brakeman. The usual mark of distinction is the heavy gold chain which is worn by the "railroader" as soon as he is "given a train."

If there remains any doubt as to his identity it might do to count his fingers and thumbs, watch the "hunch" of his shoulders when he walks or ask him the time of day. If the watch is open-faced and the man says "Nine forty-three" —that settles it.

The railroad man could be picked from a procession of 100 men strung along in a row and there wouldn't be much risk of a mistake. If he had a look of worn patience in his eyes, affected an iron-gray mustache, had box-toed shoes and dangled a secret-society emblem set in jewels the odds would be several to one that he was a passenger conductor with a good "run."

THE BOARD OF TRADE YOUNG MAN

*   *   *

What person, unless he chooses to consider it undignified to do so, has not studied these trade-marks as shown in the apparel of the men who crowd by him in the street? After he acquires a certain amount of expert knowledge, based on observation, he classifies a man almost as soon as he sees him.

If he meets in Jackson Street a square-shouldered young man, with a small, soft hat pulled forward over one eye, a short office coat flapping in the wind and a general suggestion of good clothes worn in a "don't-care" fashion, isn't he satisfied at once that the young man belongs to the board of trade? He does not have to turn around and watch the young man go into the building.   *   *   *

Volumes might be written about the ready-made white bow, or the "dress" bow, as it figures in the every-day life of Chicago.

According to the set rules of fashion such a bow is to be worn with evening dress, but no less a personage than Mayor Hopkins has set this rule at defiance.

When *Harper's Weekly* asked for his photograph at the time of the railroad strike he sat before the camera wearing a ready-made white bow-tie with a cutaway suit.

The picture appeared in the paper, and was the cause of much talk. The "make-up" was that of a graduate from a preparatory school, but it served the purpose of causing the mayor to appear a peculiarly timid and guileless young man.

The white-lawn tie is a great favorite in the city hall.

It is easily adjusted, and does not interfere with the display of diamonds.

After it has been used for about a week and begins to curl up at the ends it is not an object of beauty, but fortunately it can be replaced for 10 cents.

ALDERMANIC

This same pattern of neckwear is very common among ministers of the gospel.

With them the use is allowable and the simple bow of pure white makes a chaste contrast with the somber black coat.

Pure white is emblematic of purity.

The girl graduate looks well in white.

But there is some difference between a girl graduate and "Tubby" Bite, sewer inspector and a handy man in a "mix-up."

* * *

Have you seen during the summer a strange girdle of leather or cloth with pockets and false buttons? It is called the "sash-vest," and the proposed penalty for wearing one is ninety days in the Bridewell or disfranchisement for life.

"NINETY DAYS"

The sash-vest, it will be remembered, was always worn by a willowy man who appeared to be either convalescent or on the decline. There was something the matter with him besides the "sash-vest." The man who wore one of these also had oil on his hair, carried a black silk handkerchief and wore low shoes and spotted stockings.

The summer was half wasted if you didn't see this young man. If you did see him, you will continue to meet him in your dreams and imagine him this winter with rabbit fur on his overcoat, a green muffler around his neck and his hands incased in yellow gloves.

There is no mistaking the "fly man" from the city hall,

CONCEALING THEIR IDENTITY

whether he is found at a charity ball, disguised as a guest, or standing on a well-known corner smoking a cigar and "shadowing" something. In the first place, his "partner" is with him and they are smoking. They appear too strong to be workingmen and they are too full of leisure to be business men. They wear their hats forward and speak to each other in subdued tones. The mustaches and the jewelry, the stealthy side glances and all the other symptoms are present. They simply couldn't be anything else than "fly men" and when they begin to hang around a corner all the neighboring children come out to see who's going to be detected or arrested.

* * *

During the time of the anarchist scare in Chicago a young man was told to disguise himself as a workingman and hang around a certain 18th Street saloon where anarchists were supposed to hold meetings. The young man at once attired himself in a checked pair of trousers of the "song and dance" kind, a red flannel shirt and a short coat.

Having completely disguised himself as a workingman he

entered the saloon, where the long-haired and beer-sodden revolutionists were sitting about the tables eating rye bread and organizing a new social condition. They looked up as he entered, and a moment later there was a concerted rush for him and a loud demand, in several foreign languages, for his life. He was chased for about a mile along the car tracks and was then headed off by the police, who took him in charge as a "suspect."

If this young man had made a preliminary trip to 18th Street he might have learned that the workingman did not wear a fireman's shirt or a tout's trousers.

*   *   *

A GREAT LAWYER

You can see him any day racing toward the entrance of the county building. His hair is altogether too long, his silk hat is too small and too frouzy and his Prince Albert coat is shrinking in the arms. But if he should cut his hair, exchange the tall hat for a derby and wear the ordinary tailor-made business suit how would people know that he was a lawyer?

He is the lawyer of theatrical methods who is going to succeed by reason of his eccentricities.

Once in his youth he heard a great criminal lawyer make a speech and move the jury to tears. That lawyer had long hair, which was never combed. Since then he had understood that if he grew long hair and never combed it he could be a great lawyer also. It is just as necessary for him to have long hair as it is for a physician to have whiskers and a white vest. If it were not for him and the brakeman, the "fly man," the board of trade man and the hundred others, what a monotonous task it would be to watch the street crowd!

A Plantation Dinner
at Aunt Mary's

D IDN'T you ever eat any 'chidlins'?" asked the man who had the party in tow. "Why, you've missed half your life. There's nothing finer."

The others listened but said nothing. They were not qualified to speak with any authority of "chidlins," and one or two of them confessed, almost with shame, that they had never partaken of pig-tail, which, the chaperon declared, was the best part of the animal excepting, always, the "chidlins."

If the "chidlins" were taken from a beef they would be called "tripe," but as they are derived from the autumnal hog they are "chidlins." The word, to be correct, is "chitterlings." In the old days when men wore ruffled shirt fronts the fluted and convoluted laces on the shirt bosom were "chitterlings." The name was afterward applied to the tripish parts of the hog because, when fried, they curl and ruffle in the skillet.

Down south the word has been abbreviated to "chidlins," and "Aunt Mary," who never heard them called anything else, has a sign above the whitewashed door:

CHIDLINS, 15 CENTS.

The man who discovered the place was in the party. He and the man who had been discoursing on the virtues of pig-tail had received their education in eating south of Mason and Dixon's line. When they said that "Aunt Mary" was the only woman in Chicago who could prepare a plantation dinner the others had to be silent.

Far south along slushy streets and into narrow, unfamiliar thoroughfares they led the way. The wet and drifting snow-flakes lost themselves as soon as they reached the black paste spread under foot.

HEADQUARTERS FOR "CHIDLINS"

Although the afternoon was but half spent there were lights in many of the houses. In one of the streets, where the low buildings were huddled in close rows, the man who had discovered the place called a sudden halt and said: "Here we are."

A steep stairway led to the white basement front, where a dim light showed against the panes. "Aunt Mary" was waiting and she went into a convulsion of laughter before any one said a word to her "Aunt Mary" was short and very fat. Her round figure was puckered in at the waist-line, or what should have been the waist-line, by tight apron-strings. She had a face of ebony, eyeballs as white as the outside snow and a close growth of kinky hair. She laughed so hard that she had to back through the side door into the kitchen before she could recover sufficiently to say "Ev'thing's ready."

* * *

At the rear of the low room was an old-fashioned bureau with a kerosene lamp on it. The tin reflector behind the lamp threw a full light on the table, which had been carefully "set." In the center was a glass cake-stand bearing a pyramid of "rusty-coat" apples and there were some tufts of celery and a deep glass dish floating full of radishes. "Aunt Mary," from the depths of the kitchen where the open front of the cook-stove showed a hot blaze, called out that she "couldn' git no 'possum."

"What! no 'possum?" exclaimed the man who had been dwelling on this feature of the dinner.

"No, seh. Ah see one yist'day hangin' up, but de man say

he done sol' it. Ah had ve'y strong tem'tation to grab dat 'possum. Man say too eahly fo' 'em. Gwine to git sev'al nex' week."

"What have you got?"

"Chidlins."

"That's good. Any pig-tails?"

"Yes, seh, and snouts, too."

Greatly cheered by this information the seven epicures took their places at the table. One chair had only a small remaining patch of cane seat, and the man to whom it fell spread himself to avoid going through to the floor. "Aunt Mary" and her accomplice, an older colored woman of solemn manner, who occasionally peeped out from the kitchen, had taken pains to have everything correct. Japa-nese napkins had been rolled up in the tumblers. When, just at the beginning, a very dark young man, with big pearl buttons on his overcoat, came in the front door, he was hurried into the kitchen and kept there.

* * *

"Chidlins," announced "Aunt Mary," as she waddled in from the kitchen bearing a platter, from which rose a cloud of grate-ful steam. While that platter was being passed around she reap-peared with the pig-tails. Then she brought in the "snouts" and the corn-cake.

She was laboring under great excitement. The compliments lavished upon the tempting

scramble of pig-tails, the chorus of "Ah-h-hs" which wel-comed the "chidlins" and the seraphic smile of the southern man when he beheld the "snouts" before him—all these worked on "Aunt Mary's" sensitive nature until she paddled around in pure happiness. She would have been in a flushed condition if there were such a thing as a charcoal "flush." As it was her large frame shook, jellylike, from emotion, and she chuckled incessantly.

"The way to eat chidlins," said the Tennessee man at the head of the table, "is to sprinkle them with salt and then pour on some vinegar. Talk about your honey-comb tripe! Give me a little of that corn-cake."

The corn-cake was in thin, hard slabs as yellow as gold. The men who knew said it was "genuine," and the others devoured it hungrily. They praised the "chidlins" also and declared they had never tasted anything better.

"Do you really like them?" asked the man at the head of the table, with the deep smile of one who feels that he is fully vindicated and upheld.

COULD TELL BY THEIR COLOR

"Certainly I do. I'll take some more."

"Buttahmilk," announced "Aunt Mary." The Tennessee man held out his tumbler and ventured the opinion that the colored lady at his left could give the Union League chef cards and spades and then beat him out. * * *

But she hadn't completed her triumph. When next she entered she carried a platter on which was spread a four-legged animal almost buried under the split sweet potatoes.

"Bre'r rabbit," said she as she moved the dishes and made room for the platter.

"Try some of the rabbit," suggested the man who had discovered the place to his neighbor at the left. But the latter refused rabbit and demanded more "chidlins," while "Aunt Mary" disappeared into the kitchen rocking with laughter.

"Maybe you think this doesn't carry me back," said the man at the head of the table as he looked at the array of corn-cake, rabbit, buttermilk, snouts, pig-tails, "chidlins" and sweet potatoes. "This is like it used to be at butchering time, when they couldn't keep me away from the cabins. As long as the snouts and ghost-stories lasted I didn't want to go home. Nobody on earth but a negro woman could cook this stuff so it would be any good. 'Aunt Mary's' been there. How about that?"

"'Deed I has," replied "Aunt Mary," from the doorway.

At this point in the dinner a most unfortunate thing happened. The corn-bread gave out. There was some white bread on the table, but white bread at a plantation dinner was simply out of the question. After a brief commotion around the kitchen stove "Aunt Mary" brought on some hot corn-cakes, the ingredients of which were meal and water, but they were done to such a delicate brown that every one declared them beyond criticism.

*   *   *

By this time the company was many miles away from Chicago and had been on one or two 'possum hunts. The chromos hanging around them, the homely wall paper with its up-and-down streaks, the batter-cake smoke, the purr of negro voices in the kitchen and the rich odor of pork helped the delusion.

The climax to the dinner was sweet potato pie with coffee. The Tennessee man said it was regular plantation coffee.

As they were putting on their coats they saw in the kitchen two young men of "Aunt Mary's" complexion sitting close to the stove and watching it with apparent interest.

"Any chidlins left for the boys?" asked the man who discovered the place.

"Dey ain't waitin' fo' nothin' else," said "Aunt Mary."

"Do they like them?"

"Who? Dem boys? Caint yo' tell by de coloh?"

Mr. Benson's Experience
with a Maniac

BENSON was very happy when given an opportunity to visit the county insane hospital at Dunning.

As a student in a medical college he had a professional interest in the various forms of insanity. He had read up on the subject, and, although he had searched only in books, he had an idea that he could tell by examining a brain whether the deceased had been responsible for his acts.

The long words which are juggled by experts on the witness stand he had fully mastered and he knew the theoretical distinction between "melancholia" and "kleptomania."

The visit to Dunning would give him an opportunity to study the actual symptoms of insanity. A county commissioner with whom he had lately become acquainted invited him to accompany some officials who were to make a business call at the institution. He accepted readily.

* * *

Arrived at the hospital, he asked more questions than all the other visitors put together. Upon having a case explained to him he would say, "H'm, suicidal intentions, etc.," or "Ah, yes; I understand; incipient paresis." The keepers couldn't contradict him. The keepers had one class into which they put all the inmates. They spoke of them as "nutty."

Benson was a trifle disappointed. He saw haggard men and women moping along the walls, mumbling to themselves or giggling in feeble good-nature at the little company of awed visitors, but he did not see the big men who beat down iron doors with their bare hands and tossed keepers into the air while being overpowered.

There was no particular pleasure in conversing with a trembling, pink-lipped man attired in the cheap hospital garb and with dark circles around his eyes, who had $175,000 in the First National Bank and wanted to be released right away in order to keep an engagement with Queen Victoria.

Benson had the student's natural curiosity to see some "good cases."

"I should like to visit the violent wards," he said to the assistant warden. They had strolled away from the rest of the party.

"You have already seen many inmates who are violent at times," replied the assistant warden.

"I know, but I want to see the padded cells and get a look at some of the noisy ones that have to be tied down."

"Well, now, let me see. I don't believe we're having trouble with any of them to-day, but if there are any contrary ones you will find them in that ward right over there. Shall we go in?"

"Certainly, I want to see everything."

"Very well, I'll take you in, but remember one thing. Don't pay any attention if one of them comes up and makes a motion as if to strike you. Just humor him and don't be scared."

* * *

A keeper opened the door for them, and as they stepped in the twenty or more inmates scattered down the corridor tunnel and looked at them with that sudden and curious interest which one always encounters in a place where men are locked up and cooped together. The opening of a door and the entrance of a visitor bring a moment of novelty and entertainment into the humdrum existence.

"Hello, Reub," said the assistant warden.

Benson saw leaning against the wall, near the first barred window, a man of prodigious build. He was several inches more than six feet tall, with broad shoulders, bulging chest and a stumpy, muscular neck. His heavy face was impassive until the assistant warden spoke, and then it relaxed into a stupid smile.

Benson studied him.

"Reub" returned the steadfast gaze.

Benson smiled in a friendly way.

"Reub" chuckled and made peculiar gestures, as if tickling some imaginary person.

Benson winked and with that "Reub" laughed aloud and made a rush at him.

The assistant warden was at the other end of the room. The keeper who had opened the door was not looking. Luckily the door was still open. Benson ran and "Reub" ran after him.

As Benson dashed through the door, closely pursued, he heard the keeper shout: "Stop, Reub!" The only answer was a yelp from the maniac.

*   *   *

Benson ran as one whose life was at stake. He was guided only by his terror. As he sped along the hallway he heard the heavy footfalls of the crazy giant, who seemed to be gaining at every step, and who, as he ran, kept up a hoarse gurgling which sometimes rose into a shriek of demoniacal laughter.

"Help! help!" gasped Benson, as he threw his whole weight against a door which suddenly appeared before him. He clutched the knob with both hands and wrenched it fiercely.

Thank heaven! It flew open. He dived half-way across the room.

Bang! He had upset a typewriting machine. He staggered and recovered himself just as the heavy frame of his pursuer collided with the door behind. A woman screamed.

Benson swung himself around the end of a desk railing and ran blindly toward a door which promised open air.

The maniac cleared the fallen table and typewriter with one bound. He screamed with exultation.

Benson could already feel those big knotty hands at his throat. If he gave up all would be over in a moment. An aroused maniac is like a wild beast hungry for blood.

These and a hundred other thoughts flashed through his mind as he bolted madly ahead. The door was ajar. He sprung through it, slammed it behind him and tore along a cinder path.

*   *   *

All this had happened within a very few seconds. Benson had no plan of escape. He was simply spurred on by a frenzy of fear, and as he reached the cinder path he heard the click of the latch and knew that crazy "Reub" was hardly fifteen feet behind him.

*   *   *

The path led straight up to a doorway through which he bounded, and there ahead of him was a stairway.

He had no time to look about him.

Up the stairway he went and still the gurgles and the shrieks seemed to come nearer and nearer. Horrors!

He ran blankly into a row of windows. It was ten feet to the ground below. Should he make a stand and fight? He had rushed straight ahead instead of making the turn to follow the stairway.

He hesitated the hundredth of a second but—crash! He was through the window and to the ground below, torn, bleeding, but running desperately for his life.

Then another crash and a shattering fall of glass! The maniac had jumped after him!

Benson staggered as he ran and the landscape reeled before his eyes. What was that? Again the demon shriek—a shriek of triumph; for Benson was running toward a high board fence.

He saw it and cried aloud in awful fear, but still he ran. He leaped for the fence and threw one arm over it. With all his remaining strength he attempted to scramble to the top.

Too late! Too late!

He felt a hand on his back and heard a voice close to his ear: "You're it! You're it! Now see if you can catch me."

Benson fell in a heap on the ground and looked with dazed eyes at "Reub," who was standing thirty feet away begging him by gestures to continue the game of "tag."

Artie Blanchard

ARTIE BLANCHARD went to the charity entertainment, and, as he said afterward, he had "no kick comin'," although it wasn't exactly his kind of a show.

Artie had started in at the general offices as messenger boy and had earned promotion on his merits. What he lacked in schooling he made up in good sense, industry and a knowledge of human nature.

He had the reputation of being worldly, even "tough," but he didn't deserve it. He was simply overmasculine. If he used slang it was because slang helped him to express his feelings with greater force and directness.

He was always interested in prize-fighting because he admired gameness and muscular power and had both of them pretty well developed in his own well-knit figure.

If he showed a disposition to "kid" on all sorts of topics it was because he took a cheerful and good-natured view of life and also gave his hearers credit for having enough perception to understand that he didn't mean all that he said.

Artie was well dressed, although he was inclined to follow his own notions as to personal adornment. He was jaunty rather than "swell," and like all hard-headed men he hated any sort of an extreme, such as a very high collar or a very low-cut vest. He had no evening dress, or "first-part clothes" as he called them, because he had a jovial contempt for "society" as he had caught glimpses of it, although he was on cordial terms with many young men who devoted all of their leisure time to it.

MRS. MORTON

On the other hand, he had the utmost respect for women. In fact, he held all good women in such deep and tender regard that he seldom attempted to express himself on the subject, holding that it was too sacred for the every-day fool intercourse of men in this world. Only to those who knew him well and had proved themselves worthy of such confidence did he reveal himself. Others, who were but partly acquainted with him, held him to be a person of rather low morals.

Not that he was a drunkard or a gambler or a rowdy, but he lacked reverence and repose. His language was that of the streets, and he was an anarchist regarding so-called "good form."

There is no excuse for telling so much about Artie except that there are so many young men of his kind in Chicago who combine good conduct of life and strict attention to business with a playful pretense to heathen depravity.

* * *

One day Mrs. Morton, wife of the city manager, came into the offices and "held up" the boys for 50 cents apiece, and then gave each of them a ticket to the charity entertainment to be given in the parlors of a certain south side church on the following Wednesday evening. Artie had to "cough up," and he did it with apparent willingness.

"I don't want you young men to think that I am robbing you of this money," said Mrs. Morton. "I want you to come to this entertainment. I know you'll enjoy it."

"Blanchard can go all right," suggested Miller, with a wink at the man next to him. "He lives only about three blocks from the church."

"Then he must come," said Mrs. Morton. "Won't you, Mr. Blanchard?"

"Sure," replied Artie, blushing deeply.

"Why, Mrs. Morton, he hasn't been in a church for three years," said Miller.

"I don't believe it," and she turned to Artie, who was making motions to "call off" Miller. "Now, Mr. Blanchard, I want you to promise me faithfully that you'll come."

"I'll be there all right," he replied, smiling feebly.

"Remember, you've promised," and as she went out she shook her finger at him as a final reminder.

"Well, are you going?" asked Miller.

"What's it to you?" asked Artie. "Didn't you hear what I said to her? Sure I'm goin'. I've got as much right to go out and do the heavy as any o' you pin-heads. If I like their show I'll help 'em out next time—get a couple o' handy boys from Harry Gilmore's and put on a six-round go for a finish. Them people never saw anything good."

"I'll bet the cigars you don't go," spoke up young Mr. Hall.

"You'd better make it chewin' gum," replied Artie. "Next thing you'll be bettin' real money. You guys must think I'm a quitter, to be scared out by any little old church show. I don't think it'll be any worse than a barn fight over in Indiana."

*   *   *

"Well, I goes," said Artie, the morning after the charity entertainment.

"Where?" asked Miller, who had forgotten.

"Where? Well, that's a good thing. To the church show—the charity graft. I didn't do a thing but push my face in there about 8 o'clock last night and I was it from the start. Say, I like that church, and if they'll put in a punchin' bag and a plunge they can have my game, I'll tell you that."

"Did you see Mrs. Morton?"

"How's that, boy? Did I see her? Say, she treated me out o' sight. She meets me at the door, puts out the glad hand and says: 'Hang up your dicer and come into the game.'"

"That's what she said, eh?"

"Well, that's what she meant. She's all right, too, and the only wonder to me is how she ever happened to tie herself up to that slob. It's like hitchin' up a four-time winner alongside of a dog. He ain't in her class, not for a minute, a part of a minute. What kills me off is how all these dubs make their star winnin's. Why, out there last night I saw the measliest lot of jays, regular Charleyboys, floatin' around with queens. I wish somebody'd tell me how they cop 'em out. Don't it kill you dead to see a swell girl, you know, a regular peach, holdin' on to some freak with side whiskers and thinkin' she's got a good thing? That's right. She thinks he's all right. Anyway, she acts the part, but you can't tell, because them

ARTIE

fly girls know how to make a good many bluff plays. And say, you know Percival, that works over in the bank—little Percy, the perfect lady. There's a guy that I've known for five years and so help me if he gets on a street car where I am I get off and walk. That's no lie. I pass him up. I say, 'You're all right, Percy, and you can take the car to yourself,' and then I duck."

"Was he there?"

"The whole thing! That's no kid. He was the real papa— the hit of the place. One on each arm, see?—and puttin' up the large, juicy con talk. They were beauts, too; you couldn't beat 'em, not in a thousand years. There they were, holdin' to this wart. Up goes my hands into the air and I says to myself: 'Percy, you're all right. I wouldn't live on the same street with you, but you're all right at that.' But he couldn't see me."

"Couldn't see you?"

"No, he lost his eyesight. He looked at me, but he was too busy to see me. No, he had on his saucy coat and that touch-me-not necktie, and oh, he was busy. He wasn't doin' a thing. I think I'll give the bank a line on Percy. Any man that wears that kind of a necktie hadn't ought to be allowed to handle money. But you ought to have seen the two he had. I'd like to know how he does it. I had a notion to go up to one of the girls and say: 'What's the matter? Haven't you ever seen any others?'"

*   *   *

"Did you like the show," asked Miller.

"It's this way. They liked it and so"—with a wave of the hand—"let 'em have it. If they put the same turns on at the Olymp the people'd tear down the buildin' tryin' to get their coin back. Mrs. Morton got me a good seat and then back-capped the show a little before it opened up, so I didn't expect to be pulled out of my chair—and I wasn't. If I'd been near the door I'd have sneaked early in the game, but, like a farmer, I let her put me way up in front. I saw I was up against it, so I lasted the best way I could. Two or three of the songs were purty fair, but the woman that trifled with the piano for about a half-hour was very much on the bummy bum. Then there was a guy called an entertainer that told some of the Billy Rice gags that I used to hear when my brother took me to the old Academy and held me on his lap. But he got 'em goin' just the same. Well, I says to myself, 'What'd Weber and Fields do to this push?' On the dead, I don't believe any of them people out there ever saw a good, hot variety show. It just goes to show that there are a lot of people with stuff who think they know what's goin' on in town, but they don't. I've got no kick comin', only it was a yellow show, and I'm waitin' for 45 cents change."

"I should think you would have got the worth of your money simply by seeing so many good-looking girls," said Miller.

"The girls are all right, only I think they're losin' their eyesight. If I had time I'd go over to that church and make a lot o' them Reubs look like 30-cent pieces. Not that I'm strong on the con talk, but I know I'd be in it with them fellows. I think it must be a case of nerve. That's all there is to 'em—is nerve. But the girls—wow!"

"Fine creatures, eh?"

"Lallypaloozers!"

A Story from the Back Streets

FRIENDSHIPS are formed in all sorts of ways. Here is the story told by Mr. James Meers, sometimes called "Foxy Jim," of the manner in which he became the best friend of Mr. Byron Foley, often called "Pinch" Foley by his intimate acquaintances:

"An' I sez to him, squarin' off an' bringin' my fis' down on the bar, I sez, 'You're a liar.' Them's the same i-dentical words.

"'You're a liar,' I sez, 'an' w'ats more you're nutty,' I sez.

"Wid that he backs off an' lams at me wid his bones.

"'I'm a liar, am I?' sez he. 'Will yuh eat it?' sez he.

"'No,' sez I, fer I wuz gettin' red headed.

"Bot' of us had been drinkin' some, but we w'an't loaded.

"Then he comes at me wid a drive in the neck.

"'Take that,' sez he.

"I sheers off, brings up me right an' lams 'im in his blinkers.

"'You're a liar,' sez I.

"Then he grabs me under me arms an' tries to do the grapevine. But I wuz onto 'im. I knuckles his t'roat an' lams 'im one in the ear.

"He sheers off an' feints at me wid his right.

"A feller grabs him.

"'Hol' up,' he sez.

"Anodder feller grabs me.

"'Let me git at 'im,' sez I. 'He's a liar,' sez I. 'An' nutty,' sez I.

"Wid that I breaks away an' lams 'im. The feller interferes.

"Then I wuz crazy.

"I sheers off an' comes at the feller wid me lef'. He gits nex'

HOW MR. MEERS AND MR. FOLEY BECAME FRIENDS

me breast an' the other feller lams 'im. Then I grabs 'im an' he breaks to the feller's neck. Wid that I grabs th' other feller. Just as I was knuckling 'im he comes at me from behin'.

"Then we all went to the floor togedder. Me head wuz in a spittoon, but I wuz knucklin' 'im an' callin' 'im all sorts of fools.

"Then we wuz pulled apart.

"'W'at yer mixin' fer?' says the bar-kip.

"'He's a liar,' sez I. 'An' nutty,' sez I.

"'W'at's he nutty fer?' sez the feller.

"'I'm rubed 'f I could remember—bot' of us wuz leary.

"So I done the han'some. I sez to him: 'I didn' call you no liar,' I sez.

"" 'At's right,' he sez; 'an' yuh didn't say nothin' 'bout nutty?' he sez.

" 'No,' sez I. 'What'll yuh have to drink?' sez I.

"An' sinst then me'n him's been good frien's."

Sophie's Sunday Afternoon

SOPHIE slipped out into the sunlight through the big oak side door of Mr. Hamilton Jefferson's residence and walked down the crooked path to the gateway, humming a little tune to herself.

Sophie was Mrs. Hamilton Jefferson's girl and Mrs. Hamilton Jefferson was proud of her. When there was a tea and Sophie in her puckered cap and dainty apron flitted about with the salvers Mrs. Hamilton Jefferson would lean forward and say to her guests behind her pudgy hand:

"She's a jewel of a girl and she sews beautifully. No, no, you can't have her at any price."

During all the week Sophie was just Sophie and she conversed with nodded "Yes m'm's" and "No m'm's," as any well-trained girl would do.

But on Sunday afternoon as soon as the dishes shone on the shelves of the china closet Sophie became Miss Sophie Johnson and she walked out of Mrs. Hamilton Jefferson's domain into a world of her own.

Sophie couldn't help humming. It was something to get out into the spring sunlight with a whole afternoon and the savings of a week to spend. And Sophie had a new hat—and wasn't that enough to make any girl hum? It was a mere bit of a thing—a knot of blue ribbons, a queer little twisted body and a red rose on a long stem nodding a perpetual "how-d'y-do" above it. The hat was perched on Sophie's yellow hair combed back straight and smooth and wound in a tight little knot at the back of her head.

Sophie wore a pink dress with ribbon bows playing hide and seek all over it, and a belt of leather with a shiny buckle, and her skirts kept up a bustling as she walked. Sophie's shoes

were new and squeaky and they hurt her a little, too, but she
wouldn't have admitted it for anything.

Sophie's face—a round, pink and white dumpling of a face—
beamed out from under her parasol with a soap and water
freshness and a consciousness of looking very well indeed.

When Sophie had walked several blocks she met a young
man on the sidewalk.

He stopped and smiled.

Now Sophie looked very much surprised. She had never
expected to see Mr. Carl Lindgren out there.

"Good-day," he said.

"Good-day," she answered.

Then they shook hands.

Sophie blushed a little. So did Mr. Carl Lindgren.

Presently he said something about Humboldt Park, and
Sophie laughed and nodded her head. Then she put her hand
with its silk mitt—a very neat silk mitt it was, too, only a
little old-fashioned—on his arm and they walked down the
street together under one parasol.

Mr. Carl Lindgren worked in a factory and he had bought
ten shares of stock in a building and loan association in Chicago Avenue with his savings, for Carl belonged to a frugal,
hard-working race, and he was thinking of getting married.

Carl's mustache—the color of raveled rope—bristled with
much brushing and his brown derby tilted back on his yellow
hair. He wore a shiny celluloid collar and a flat tie—one of the
kind crocheted from silk twist and presented by way of the
Christmas tree. His coat had been pressed until it shone and
the corner of a red silk handkerchief looked out with artful
carelessness from his breast pocket. A huge watch-chain with
a heavy fob dangled from his vest and a dandelion was stuck
in his buttonhole.

They walked to North Avenue and took the electric cars.
The car bumped along past the rows of small stores and houses
with the Sunday crowds strolling up and down the sidewalks
in front. There were children everywhere, romping, shouting
and playing, many of them bare-headed.

At last they reached the park. The trees were just leafing
out, the grass was green and inviting, with little patches of

THEY WALKED TO NORTH AVENUE

dandelions yellowing it here and there. Crowds of people, men, women and children, streamed into the park past the saloons, peanut stands and photograph galleries which cluster around its entrance.

Sophie and Carl strolled along arm in arm. They didn't have much to say—not yet, at least.

Now they were walking hand in hand. Carl had picked up Sophie's handkerchief and in returning it had forgotten to let go of her fingers. And Sophie didn't say a word.

The path led to the pavilion, the broad verandas of which swirled with children and young girls chewing gum and young men joking with them. In the lagoon boats, unevenly rowed, dragged about, splashing the water.

They sat down at a table in the basement.

"What will you have?" said Carl.

"Chocolate," said Sophie.

"One chocolate an' one wanilla," ordered Carl.

Then the waiter rushed to the counter where a man with the perspiration rolling down his face was dishing ice cream, twirling cakes across the counter and drawing sizzling soda water with almost frantic rapidity.

Carl and Sophie didn't say much. Sophie fingered her little handkerchief and Carl watched her out of the tail of his eye. Once she caught him at it and they both laughed. Carl took some money out of his pocket and paid the waiter with a little flourish. Sophie looked at him admiringly.

*   *   *

Just as they were going out Carl spied a fortune-telling machine—a gypsy with pointing finger and a knowing look. Carl produced some pennies and Sophie thrust one of them into the slot. The gypsy girl whirled around dizzily and finally stopped with her finger pointing to the words:

> YOU ARE NEARER GREAT DANGER
> THAN YOU ARE AWARE.

Sophie looked serious.

"I wonder what it is," she said.

"That's a bad fortune," answered Carl. "Try again."

The next penny brought better luck:

AN UNKNOWN LOVER ADORES YOU.

Carl laughed and Sophie blushed.
"It tells lies," said Sophie.
Then Carl tried. The gypsy bluntly pointed to the words:

YOU ARE IN LOVE.

"''At's the truth," said Carl, without looking at Sophie.

* * *

Then they went out and walked along the path until they
came to a popcorn booth. Here Carl bought a big sticky ball
for 5 cents, and he and Sophie went to a grassy spot on the
bank of a lagoon and sat down to eat it. A boy not far away
was dangling his bare legs in the water and some little girls
were rolling about on the grass. Ducks and swans nodded as
they swam in the lagoon. In the middle of a shawl sat a baby,
with her father and mother paying court to her not far away.
Carl talked now pretty steadily, but in a low tone, so that
no one but Sophie could hear him. Here are some of the things
which Sophie answered him:
"So?"
"Et's too bad about you!"
"Now, behave."
"Don't you tease."
"Sure."
When the popcorn was all gone Carl wanted Sophie to go
boat-riding. Sophie said she was afraid. So they walked
through the greenhouse and Sophie told Carl something about
the flowers.

Then they walked, hand in hand, swinging their arms just a little, down to North Avenue and went into one of the photographers' tents with the pictures hung in tempting array outside. Here a busy, nervous man seated Sophie in a chair, tipped her chin a little back and folded her hands. Sophie pulled off one mitt so that a ring would show. Then Carl stood up behind, put one of his big hands on Sophie's shoulder and the other behind him. Then he advanced one foot and looked up.

"Now look pleasant," said the busy, nervous man.

He clicked the plates into the camera, thrust his head under the curtain, jerked it out and pulled the slide.

"All right," he shouted, and then shot into his little darkroom.

Sophie drew a long sigh and Carl smiled reassuringly at her.

*   *   *

An hour later Carl and Sophie were hurrying from the park. A great black cloud reached out of the west and a stiff wind was blowing.

Sophie and Carl had been so much occupied that they had not noticed the coming rain. Just before they reached North Avenue a few big drops began to fall and they made a wild race for the car. But Sophie was laughing and holding fast to Carl's hand. By the time the car stopped at their street the shower was at its height.

Sophie and Carl crowded under the parasol and hurried down the dripping street. When they reached the residence of Mr. Hamilton Jefferson Sophie's skirts were soaking wet and her hair flew about her face. She had covered her new bonnet with her handkerchief so that it was fairly dry. The coloring from her parasol had dripped down Carl's neck and his coat was bedraggled and shapeless.

For a moment they paused in the entry where no one could see them. Then Carl came out with his face beaming and walked away regardless of the rain.

Olof Lindstrom Goes Fishing

OLOF LINDSTROM was going fishing. All winter long he had worked at his bench in the cabinet-shop. He made carved bureau tops from day's end to day's end. It was a hard, monotonous life—earn and spend, eat and sleep, week in and week out.

Olof was a little pale faced man, with a straw-colored mustache. On weekdays he wore a faded brown derby, white with sawdust. On Sunday, when he and his family went to the Lutheran Church in the next street, he changed it for a neat black derby, his coat was as smooth as Mrs. Lindstrom's flat-iron could make it and the corner of a silk handkerchief thrust itself into notice from his breast pocket.

The idea of going fishing had come to him suddenly, as it had done every spring for years. Perhaps it was the compelling sunshine that opened the doors of the wooden cottages and brought the children and the pet puppies swarming to the sidewalk, or, perhaps, it was merely the inherited instinct of a man whose fathers and grandfathers in Norway calked their fishing smacks each spring and mended their carp nets as soon as the sun had opened the rugged coves on the coast.

*   *   *

It was Saturday night. Olof had secured a fishing pole and bait. He was just setting out.

"To-morrow is Sunday," said Mrs. Lindstrom, as if warning him to be back in time.

Olof did not answer. He was going fishing and the fish were hungriest an hour before sunrise.

Oak Street runs as far as the lake wall with all the paved and guttered respectability of a great city thoroughfare. But eastward from the Lake Shore Drive it pitches off into a waste of ash-piles and garbage heaps which have usurped a part of the domain of Lake Michigan. Here it meanders around in an aimless, lawless way with a self-made, independent air, as if in contempt of the general orderliness and conventionality of city life.

Just at dark Olof followed Oak Street out among the garbage

piles. It was with a feeling of rebellious freedom that he left behind the carved bureau tops and Mrs. Lindstrom's strident voice. At the extreme point in the bumpy expanse of desert he found a newly dumped pile of paper, rags and broken boxes, and he set it afire. Then he built up a seat from some old bricks and a board and sat down with his face to the blaze, which he occasionally encouraged with a broken barrel hoop. There was not a human being within shouting distance, not even a policeman. Although the spot was hardly half a mile from the Lake Shore Drive it was quite as lonely as an African jungle.

Darkness settled down and every audible reminder of city life, except the intermittent screeching of tugboats, was drowned out by the thumping and mumbling of the waves among the ragged rows of piling. The lighthouse reflector began to wink crimson and yellow over the black stretch of water. A few dim squares and specks of light with a smudge of black above them, crawling along apparently through space, indicated the course of vessels outbound on their first voyage of the season. The city was a wall of black from north to south, with a few towers, spires and the huge bulk of a great building or two extending into the murky blue sky, where the moon hung—Olof didn't often have an opportunity to see the moon. He didn't care much about it either—it was only one of the things that united to make up a stolid sense of freedom, which he could not have explained. A long row of electric lights along the lake shore appeared like holes in the dark wall—as if the city blazed beyond.

A stiff, chilly wind sprang up as night deepened, and Olof set up a plank at his back and then sat quietly, unthinkingly watching the burning bits of paper scurry over the garbage heaps whenever he stirred the fire. Occasionally he nibbled a cracker from a bundle which he had brought with him.

Toward morning he grew cold and had to run up and down a hardened ash pile to keep warm. The wind cut through his thin clothing and pinched his shop-faded face. He had not dreamed that it would blow so cold.

At last, when the moon had gone down behind the waterworks tower and a faint gray streak of light cut the lake horizon, Olof baited his hook with a minnow from the pail and

"THE CITY WAS A WALL OF BLACK FROM NORTH TO SOUTH"

crawled carefully to the outer row of piling. Here he mounted, shivering with cold, and cast his line. The waves still beat heavily and the spray dashed up and drenched him.

At the end of half an hour he had caught one little perch, and half of his bait was gone. But the keen delight of watching that fish squirm on the bank was worth a great deal of misery— it gave him more pleasure than a thousand carved bureau tops.

An hour later the sun came up over the rim of the lake and

laid a ladder of gold across the water. But Olof didn't notice it—he felt a nibble at his line. He had never learned to revere sunrises—the nibble of a fish was ecstasy enough.

*   *   *

Later the church bells began to ring for early mass. For a moment they made Olof feel guilty and uncomfortable, but his joy was restored by catching a second fish, a shade larger than the first. He was still wet and chilly, and he knew that the twinges in his knees meant rheumatism.

At ten o'clock the sun blazed high and hot. The reflection in the water blinded the eyes of the solitary fisher and burned his face. At noon, after an endless series of nibbles, he caught one more fish and then his bait was gone. He felt hungry and tired, too—it had been a long night without a wink of sleep. His head ached.

Olof strung the three little fishes on a splinter and dragged himself back over the garbage heaps and ash-piles with his fish-pole on his shoulder. He met throngs of well-dressed people on their way home from church. He thought they looked at him chidingly for breaking the sabbath, and so he walked with his eyes cast down.

*   *   *

When Olof reached his home he found his wife in a temper. He laid the three little fish on the table as a peace-offering, but she only scolded him roundly. She said it was a shame, and that every one of the neighbors would be talking about him before the day was over.

"Can't a man have a little time to himself?" he said to her meekly in Norwegian. She did not deign to answer him.

The next day he went back to his bench and the carved bureau tops. He had a cold in the head and painful twinges of rheumatism in his knees. His face was red and sore with sunburn and his eyes saw green.

Yet he knew that if he was alive another spring he would go fishing again—even on Sunday if necessary.

It was in his blood.

The Glory of Being a Coachman

TWICE a year Chicago puts on display the best that it has of shiny vehicles, good horses and correct men in livery.

The Derby day parade is full of color and bright finery and is witnessed by thousands of spectators.

At the annual charity ball the equipages file along the Congress Street side of the Auditorium and are seen for a minute or two as they pass through the glare of electric light. The spectators are a few idle men and boys held back at a respectful distance and a faithful band of embarrassed policemen with white gloves. Between the hours of 9 and 11 practically all the swell winter turnouts of the town may be seen in front of the broad doorway. It is too bad that so much splendor is wasted.

The men "up" were white-legged and tight-coated on Derby day. Now they are hidden under top-coats and furs, but it is evident that under it all they are sitting bolt upright and preserving an unbroken dignity, even with the wind in their faces.

*　*　*

When the landaus, broughams and opera buses have been unloaded they drive away to return no more that night.

It has been found impossible to "call carriages" and send people home in their own conveyances when the hundreds in attendance at the ball suddenly determine to go home. The people are sent home in carriages furnished by the livery concerns. These are loaded in the order that they come, and when a carriage has delivered one party it comes back for another.

The midnight display is of plain black vehicles, blanketed horses and impatient drivers with buck gloves, ulsters and fur caps.

Between these drivers and those who come earlier there is a natural enmity and a natural contempt.

The genuine coachman does not regard the driver with the fur cap and red mustache as entitled to consideration.

The drivers from the stables pity the private coachmen who are compelled to wear high hats and can't talk back.

When these two distinct classes are brought into contact, as on opera nights, they hold themselves haughtily apart.

THIS IS THE OPERA BUS

The opera bus is growing in favor. It is a miniature of the passenger bus in general design, but with a mirror finish and upholsterings of leather and plush. The seats, extending the length of the interior, face each other and afford comfortable space for six persons.

There were eight of the opera buses in the glittering line on charity-ball night. Gen. Torrence and a party came in one of unusually elaborate finish. The buses cost from $1,200 to $2,500 each. There are seats on top, and when the windows are removed it is a correct summer turnout.

Chicago has been rather slow in adopting this style of turnout, which has been quite the thing in New York for two seasons.

No one can blame the private coachman for being austere and a trifle proud. He is more finely appareled than his employer inside the brougham.

It cost more to attire the coachman and make him ready for the box than it did to prepare the owner for the charity ball.

On the modern proposition that money has conversational powers the coachman is deserving of consideration.

That box-cloth top coat which he wears cost $95. It has four capes on it. A plain coat with no capes would have cost $65. His body coat underneath cost, to be exact, just $38. The trousers cost $14. He wears a silk hat of approved shape and standard make, cost $7, and the fur collarette to protect his

head and ears cost a trifling $12. Allowing $15 for the boots
and fur gloves and another $5 for incidental haberdashery,
and it can be computed that the coachman is wearing $186
worth of costume.

The footman beside him is similarly decked out.

There must be a footman if the excess of good form is to be
preserved.

The coachman who wears a cap in any kind of weather is
properly shunned by his associates.

The silk hat must be the invariable headwear, and the col-
larette is supposed to protect the ears. Those who know say
that under no circumstances should the rosette or cockade be
worn on the hat.

Only a few years ago this ornament was very common in
Chicago, but it has since been learned to the satisfaction of
inquiring minds that only the liveried servants of royalty are
privileged to adopt it. It is said that but two men in Chicago
cling to the cockade in the coachman's hat.

Both have lately acquired wealth—one in a mercantile way
and the other by means of the fitful roulette wheel.

*　*　*

There are between
forty and fifty swell and
absolutely correct coach-
men in Chicago. With
hardly an exception they
are English or Irish by
birth, and most of them
were in New York for a
time before coming to
Chicago.

These are genuine
coachmen of the first
guild. They hold nothing
in common with the

SOMETHING QUITE CORRECT

coachman who helps with the horses, does errands and perhaps runs the lawn-mower occasionally.

The coachman who grows any beard except the small patch
of side-whisker in front of each ear, who wears any article of

A MOMENT UNDER
THE ELECTRIC GLARE

headgear save the freshly ironed hat, who sits round-shouldered on the box and looks to the right and left—these are called "farmers."

A coachman who is married is usually given apartments for his family. He boards himself, and his pay is from $75 to $100 a month. The single coachman receives from $35 to $65 a month in addition to his room and board. Aside from driving, his only work is washing the vehicles and seeing that they are kept in first-class order. An inexperienced or careless man is never allowed to wash one of the carriages.

In a stable such as that maintained by Gen. Torrence, Potter Palmer or P. D. Armour, Jr., there are four men constantly employed.

The coachman and the "second man" or footman are the only ones who can appear on a turn-out. The stablemen and grooms care for the horses.

One of the questions that have more or less agitated those who have a reverence for good form is whether the colored coachman will do.

Both London and New York have decided that the coachman must be white and newly shaved, but there are families of influence that stand out against this edict.

George M. Pullman and the Lynches of Chicago still retain colored coachmen, who, however, are attired in the English pattern of livery. Mr. Pullman employs only colored servants at his big estab-

lishment in Prairie Avenue. The Pullmans and the Lynches are said to be the only families in the swell set of millionaires that have not engaged British servants.

The several hundred well-to-do families, each of which has its carriage and its man-of-all-work, do not discriminate so closely as to the birth and accent of the coachman.

The carriages passing before the Auditorium had men of varying nationalities and costumes on the boxes, but there was no mistaking when one of the "real" kind came up.

* * *

It might be expected that after a crowd of 3,000 persons had deserted the Auditorium there would be many lost articles gathered up.

After each of the two balls earlier in the season inquiries were made for lost diamonds, fans, lace handkerchiefs and the like.

The total amount of losses was several hundreds of dollars and only a few of the articles were found and returned to the owners.

At the last annual ball the only articles found after the crowd had gone away were a pair of rubbers and a white glove. These remained unclaimed. The only additional loss reported was that of a lace handkerchief.

Apparently the city detectives in evening dress effectively protected the diamond-laden women. One of the entertaining sights of the charity ball is that of the jeweled woman closely shadowed by the "fly cop" in evening dress. The "fly cop" cannot disguise himself, and therefore the jewels are safe.

Chicago High Art Up to Date

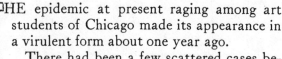

THE epidemic at present raging among art students of Chicago made its appearance in a virulent form about one year ago.

There had been a few scattered cases before that time, but the malady had not taken a firm hold and the bacilli were not yet generally distributed.

The disease should be known as "Beardsleyism," although its victims generally regard it as high art, up to date. Aubrey Beardsley, a young Englishman, deliberately started the trouble and succeeded in having himself talked about and imitated, which is practically the same as being successful.

Something like his pictures had been carved on the walls of the temple of Luxor many centuries ago. Japanese artists who decorated fans and vases had anticipated his style to a degree and generations of amateurs in all ages and countries made pictures of men with necks too long and bodies too short and whiskers done in scroll-work—little suspecting how near they had come to greatness.

*   *   *

The old-fashioned way of learning to draw pictures was to study perspective, light and shade, exact form, anatomy and a few other things. Students went to the Art Institute and sketched for hours at a time to get Hercules absolutely correct, with every tracery of muscle shown.

They studied the ancient models of statuary and the paintings which revealed the speaking likenesses of men and women.

That was before the malady appeared. Mr. Beardsley's pictures came along and the traditions of thirty centuries were shattered.

The new kind of art demonstrated that a woman's neck is shaped like a letter S, that the waist may be thin to nothingness, that the hair may radiate from the head in rigid ringlets, that the feet may be of the outline of pruning hooks.

Mr. Beardsley's strongest "things" consisted of great dashes of circling black lines with a pair of frightened eyes peering through the bubbling mass of spaghetti.

There were hands which had three tines each, like a fork, and there were figures which careened sidewise in violation of all known laws of gravity and had apparently been dried over a barrel.

This is not an art criticism. It is a simple account of the kind of pictures that allured the amateurs. They found that to be great they must forget all about anatomy, proportion or laws of light and shade, and let their imagination run amuck in circles and streaks of black.

The amateur who had despaired of becoming an illustrator suddenly learned that he or she could be a genius. In the new school it was possible for any student to draw things which were perfectly unintelligible.

One young man in Chicago adopted the boldness of the style, eliminated the utter insanity, utilized the decorative effect of striking contrast, and, by reason of the fad, made a reputation as a designer, bringing some good out of the mess of evil.

SKETCHING FROM A MODEL

But the ordinary victim of the epidemic was content to follow the weird suggestions of Mr. Beardsley. If it were an ear to be drawn he made it come to a point on top. Why? Because an ear isn't shaped like a Bartlett pear, and to draw it so suggests original conception. Besides, do the critics know that when the artist looks at the human ear it doesn't appear to him to be shaped like a pear?

Those stricken by the epidemic love to make pictures of cats—cats with bodies too long, with black pegs for legs and fish-spears for tails. Of course no cat ever had a fish-spear where the tail should be and probably is. The fish-spear notion is a flash of genius.

Be different. That's the motto of all who are taken down. At all times be so different that people laugh at your pictures. Then you have not only genius, but genius persecuted for art's sake.

"They'll come around in time," said an instructor. "Just now they're drawing shell-eyed women with worms in their hair, but they'll get over that all right. Most of them will. Others will have to be cared for. We had something of the same trouble when Oscar Wilde came over here."

THE CONDUCTOR OF THE CAR

How "Pick" Caught the "Battle-Row"

ONE day the regular patron of the shop was in the high chair having his shoes cleaned by Pickett, or "Pick" for short, when there entered a colored boy with a nose of exceeding breadth and two thick lips, betokening a strictly African ancestry.

"Pick" dropped his piece of flannel and asked, "Did you get 'em, Cla'ence?"

"I got 'em, sho' enough, but I don't tink yo' caught."

"G'on boy, g'on; I jus' got to ketch. I had 'em right."

"Pick" reached out a bony hand, the wrinkled crevices of which seemed dusty white, and took from "Cla'ence" a scrap of yellow paper on which were three rows of figures in pencil.

He carried the paper over to where the light fell from the street above and slowly whispered the numbers, one after another: "Fo'teen comes in Henry an' ole seven's theah—been theah eve' day fo' week—and six'-six—yes, seh, and theah's fo'ty-two in Frankfo't—Hm-m-m, dawg gone it. I didn' ketch aftah all. All my numbahs was theah, but not in the same book. Two paten' leathah shines gone."

Then with a sudden realization that he was neglecting his work he hurried back to the regular patron, who had been listening as if puzzled.

"What's the matter, Pick?"

"Nothin, seh, nothin; only I didn't ketch."

"What did yo' have—a ticket in a lottery?"

"Pick" turned toward the regular patron a grinning face, expressive of both surprise and amused pity. He chuckled deeply a few times and then said:

"Policy, seh."

"Oh, that's so—policy shops; I've heard of them."

"Pick" ran the brush around the heel and brought it back again, as he remarked, apparently to the shoe, that he had "he'rd of 'em, too."

"But I thought they were all closed," said the patron.

"I nevah knew the time I couldn't git action fo' my bit. One place around the cornah, three or fo' down on the levee and some mo' way out on State."

The patron became interested and asked many questions.

He was as ignorant as the average citizen concerning the game which is played daily by hundreds of people, mostly of dark complexion.

"Pick" confided to him that there were three books known as the "Frankfort," "Henry" and "Kentucky," and that the drawings took place twice a day at Louisville and the numbers were telegraphed to the main office in Chicago and then sent by messengers to the different "shops."

In each book there are seventy-eight numbers.

At the morning drawing twelve of the seventy-eight numbers are drawn from a revolving cylinder and at night thirteen are drawn.

The player must have faith. All that he really knows is that twice a day the lists of numbers are sent to the shop where he plays. If he plays three numbers in the Frankfort book and those three numbers come out in the lucky twelve he gets $9.50 for 5 cents. Playing three numbers is called a "gig."

He can play four numbers, and if three come out he gets $4.87 for 5 cents.

The "saddle" play is on two numbers, and if the two numbers are drawn he gets 45 cents.

If he can guess the first number drawn he wins the "capital" $20 prize. The "capital-saddle" play is to guess at the first two numbers, and the prize is $40, the highest for a 5-cent play.

On the ordinary "gigs" and "saddles" it is not necessary to catch the numbers in the order in which they come from the

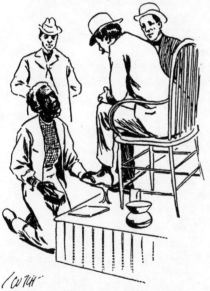

HE THOUGHT THEY WERE CLOSED

wheel. If the speculator puts 5 cents on the "lice row," 1, 2, 3, and all three numbers come out in the afternoon draw of thirteen he gets $9.50.

The regular patron slowly began to grasp the intricacies of the game, although Pickett's explanations were always clouded by technical phrases and references to "splits," "gigs" and "saddles."

"I don't see how the people who run the thing can make any money," observed the patron one day.

IT CAME IN THE WRONG BOOK

"Huh! Ev'y hotel an' resta'nt 'roun' here chips in a few dollahs. Cullud boys will take a chance. Ole people, too, an' plenty o' white folks. It counts up, suah. A cullud man has a dream an' he's got to play it—he's got to."

"What's the dream got to do with it?"

"Pick" stopped short in his work and said: "Well, sah, yo' ceht'nly don't know the game. Las' night I dreamt about a new paih o' pants, and to-day I plays fifty-fo'ty-thuhty-two. Tha's the pants row."

"How can you tell?"

"Pick" reached back into the drawer where he kept a reserve supply of blacking and brushes and brought out a small thumb-worn volume marked "Dream Book." He turned the pages until he came to the right place and then showed: "PANTS—If you are going to lend money be careful. 50–40–32."

The dream book, which is guide and friend to every policy-player, had an alphabetical list of objects which may appear in dreams, and every one of them had its corresponding number.

The graveyard rabbit, the full moon, the tombstone showing sickly white in the dusk, the gush of blood (5–10–40), the fierce dog (4–50, a "saddle"), the bouquet of flowers (1–29–63), the burning of a building (31–36–77)—all had their meanings.

When next the regular patron climbed to the chair he asked "Pick" about the "pants" combination and received the startling information that 50 and 32 had come in Kentucky and 40 in Frankfort, so that if 40 had been in Kentucky instead of in Frankfort, Pickett would have received $9.50 for his 15 cents.

He had been strong in the faith and had played 5 cents in each book.

*   *   *

"Pick" was not discouraged, however.

He had dreamed of money the night before, and was about to play a "greenback row" (12–18–44–61) which was not set down in the book but had been given to him in confidence by a friend who resided in Armour Avenue, who had received it from a lucky barber, with a record of two "gigs" and a "capital."

"What's a policy-shop like?" asked the patron.

"Jus' a small room an' a man theah to copy down yo' numbahs, an' some mo' settin' roun' seein' what's come up."

"What do you mean by that?"

"Well, seh, they keeps the drawin's in books, an' yo' can tell jus' what numbahs been comin' out. If some numbahs is comin' strong day after day mebbe theah good to play. Theah's always some one theah lookin' up the run."

"Where is this shop that you go to every day?"

"'Scuse me, seh, but I'd rathah not reveal the whe'bouts. It's been pulled several times, an' mos' the playin' now's done by a few that takes in money fo' the othahs."

The patron said he might want to play some time. "Pick" informed him that when he made his first play he should play his birthday numbers.

"Now, when was yo' born?" he asked.

"I was born May 14, 1863."

"What's the numbah of May?—le'me see—Janua'y, Febua'y——"

"May's the fifth month."

"Then yo' play five, fo'teen, sixty-three."

And the patron thanked him for the advice.

There was a new man at the bootblack chair.

He was young and smooth-headed instead of old and kinked with gray.

"Where's Pick?" asked the patron.

"Boss give it to 'im."

"Too much policy?"

The new man looked up in astonishment.

"Who tole you about it? Why, Thu'sday he ketches the battle row fo' nine plunks an' didn't show up heah o' at home fo' two days. Eatin' young pig and sweet potatoes 'long Cla'k Street and drinkin' nothin' but. Say, he were good—couldn't stop him. I s'pose he'll get work somewheres. Nothin' the mattah with that battle row. I'm aftah that myself."

Life on a River Tug

LONG ago there was an eddy in the Chicago River. It was caused by an ill-advised effort on the part of the north branch to beat the south branch to the lake. In the course of a few centuries, at a time when centuries didn't count, the eddy wore a bay in the earthy bank about the place where people would cross the Franklin Street bridge if there was one. Then Chicago sprouted in a patch of rag weed and prairie grass, and after awhile the river became a vast sewer, and was compelled to submit to the indignity of being sucked upstream as if it were a mere gutter rivulet.

But the eddy bay still remains as an evidence that the river once had powers of its own. It was a nick in the dock between a huge elevator on one side and a jutting piece of land known to rivermen as "the point," which is heaped with coal and rough building stone. The nick has really no good reason for existing, and some day when Chicago has another season of overflowing its edges like a honeymoon pie some outreaching corporation will fill it with piling, build a great factory or elevator over it, and posterity will never know that the river once had energy enough to make an eddy of its own.

Waiting that day the nick serves as a stall for the herd of

river tugboats when they come snorting homeward at the end of a long day's work to thrust their noses against the friendly dock. A single gaunt tie-post, its sides corrugated with the sawing strain of innumerable tie lines, stands sentinel at the apex of the nick. The first arrival of the day hitches to it and the next comer slides alongside and ties, and this is continued until the tugs lie in a solid mass like a pile of link sausages. Here they are within call of the tug-owners' offices across the river.

*   *   *

But it is only occasionally that a tug may rest in the nick, for tugs and their crews, like firemen, are supposed to be always on duty. They work as many hours out of every twenty-four as there are tows, and their Sundays and holidays all come in a bunch during the winter months. Yet, despite their hardships, the necessity of sleeping in such close proximity to the filth of the Chicago River and eating when there isn't anything else to do, there is hardly a healthier class of men in the city than the tugboat crews.

In spring, as soon as the ice has dropped the filth accumulations of the winter into the water below, the big men crawl out of their winter quarters, a little pale and gaunt, like a bear that has hibernated in a hollow log, and sit along the docks whistling and waiting. They are brawny men, men of quick decision, and most of them know every shoal and every tie-post from the lighthouse slip to the eddies at Bridgeport. So they wait, confident that some tug will come along and pick them up. Of course, there are more men than the boats can use—there are always two men for every position in the world —and some of them are not picked up. So they continue to sit on the docks and whistle and whittle, and a long row of them may be found there to-day explaining to one another why they don't go to work.

*   *   *

A tugboat crew consists of four men and a cook. Of course the cook is a man, but for some reason known only to the traditions of the river men he is never enumerated in the crew. But he is an important member of the company, as any hearty linesman will admit.

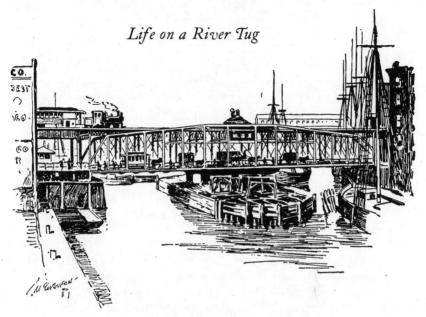

CROSSING THE RIVER AT LAKE STREET

The four men are the captain, the engineer, the fireman and
the linesman. The captain worked himself up from a linesman
because he was quick of decision and resolute, with an order
for every emergency. He is a young man, too, for after the
captain reaches the age of 50 he generally loses the "sand" to
bunt his tug through endless obstacles and hurl fantastic pro-
fanity at every one who attempts to oppose him. He is a valuable man, one who would make a general in war or a millionaire
in business if he was educated. For his services he receives $150
a month during the working season. The linesman spends his
time in casting tow ropes, cleaning the tug and longing to be
a captain. These three duties bring him $50 a month. Next to
the captain the most important man is the engineer, who receives $90 a month for sweltering in front of the boiler and
dodging hot mud when the safety valve foams. Under him
both figuratively and literally is the fireman at $50 a month.
He has a remarkable capacity for perspiration, as any man who
shovels three tons of coal a day into a red-hot boiler mouth
would have. He lives in the hope of being an engineer. The
cook—and a politic man he must be—receives $140 a month,
on which he feeds the crew and saves his own salary. He must

be a close buyer and a saving cook or else he will not have
enough money left to buy his clothes.

*   *   *

The firemen sleep in a little cubby-hole, "down aft," where
a landsman wouldn't have room to turn around. Sometimes
they have their clothes off once in two weeks, and sometimes
it is as many months, for there's no telling when one bell and
two jingles may summon them down the harbor. Not only do
they sleep in the boat, but they also eat there. The parlor,
dining-room and kitchen are in the for'd galley, a mere coop
of a place into which a man may drop from above. Here the
cook lives and oozes perspiration. At one side of him stands
his hot cook-stove and close against the bulkhead on the other
presses the boiler. Above, into the opening, beats the sun,
through the breathless, smoky air. On hot days it is one of
the hottest places in Chicago. When dinner-time comes the

THE CHICAGO RIVER AT FRANKLIN STREET

captain and his men dive down into the kitchen and get their
tin plates full of potatoes, pork and oily butter, bread almost
toasted in the torrid atmosphere, and climb out again to sit
on the rail and eat. Here the soot vomited from the stack and
the dust from the bridges settles down and peppers the potatoes and frosts the butter. But the tugman has a vigorous appetite and a light heart and the provisions slide quickly away.
Sometimes in shooting under a bridge the linesman holds up a
big potato on his fork to the crowd on the bridge and offers a
bite.

In getting a tow the tugs run down the river, one from each
of the four large concerns, and if there is a stiff wind from the
north a fleet may be expected, and the tugs shoot out into the
lake. Then there is a race, each prow cutting the waves of a
head sea. Sometimes the water runs so high that the doors of
the galleys have to be battened down and the waves sweep
the deck unrestricted. Frequently a man is brushed off like a
fly from the edge of a cream bowl. A tug sticks its toes deep
in the water, and that is why it cannot be capsized, why it can
steam so swiftly and with such tremendous power.

If a tow is not in sight the tugs keep racing northward, one after another, past Lake Forest, Waukegan, Kenosha and sometimes even to Milwaukee. Night and day they go, changing
watches from time to time, but never abating a pound of steam.

At last a tow is sighted—perhaps a lumber schooner from
Manistee. Instantly the tugs bite into the wind and begin the
difficult race for the schooner's tow-line. Each captain holds
firm to the wheel. He must run just near enough and not too
near—else he may be run down, and above all he must beat
his competitors. Wild excitement follows. The water foams
and splashes and the great ship flaps her sails and apparently
pays no attention to the race below. Each tug linesman sits on
his stern-post, eagerly waiting to catch the schooner's line.
Sometimes there are reckless collisions and wild shouting, but
at last one captain, more skillful than the next, runs in the
vessel's wake and catches her line.

*   *   *

On reaching the harbor mouth the sails are furled and the
tug snorts up the river with its burden. It is a difficult task.

Each tug must "blow through the bridges," and there are thirty-six of them from the mouth of the river to the end of the south branch and twenty-seven to the head of the north branch. Sometimes several big tows going up meet several big tows coming down. Then there is a jam very much like a street jam of vehicles when a drayman's horse falls down. There is much shouting, much blowing of whistles and clanging of bells, and at last the harbor master, who is the river policeman, is called, and he orders the boats about until the jam is broken.

Most of the big lines of steamers have contracts with towing companies for all their work, so that there is no racing for their boats. But a tramp steamer, of which there are hundreds on the lakes, is a prize to be raced for. The sailboats on the lakes are decreasing in number yearly, and it won't be long before there will not be a sail for tug smoke to blacken.

It costs all the way from $40 to $60 to tow a vessel up the river and take her out when she is unloaded. The price is regulated by the size of the boat and the distance to be towed.

Once in two weeks the tugs "lie by" to have their boilers cleaned. This is necessary because they use the muddy river water, and it doesn't take long for a tug to be in a condition to foam and blow showers of mud over everything. While the cleaning is going on the crew get a short vacation to go home to their families—if they have any.

* * *

When the insurance runs out in the fall, or the river freezes over, the work of the tugman is done for the year. Then, if he is industrious, he finds work on land. One captain teaches school in the winter, some work at the stock yards and in other places. But the great majority live in the sailor's boarding houses and hotels, and play cards and tell stories all winter long. The firemen lounge around the coal docks, as if seeking their element, the engineers frequent oil houses and saloons in their vicinity, and the captains while away their time about the ship-chandlers' places and in the tug-owners' offices.

Although the river is a good deal like a city street, with the ships for vehicles it is still largely a law unto itself. One rarely hears of the arrest of a tugman. Yet there are a great many family quarrels. The captain sometimes knocks down the cook and the fireman paddles the linesman with his shovel, and oftentimes men are "laid out" with calking mallets. Yet it rarely gets to the police. And it is most common for one tugman to "set out another's rings," which, interpreted, means to "blow him up."

*   *   *

The river men believe in the usual sea superstitions. If a rat leaves a tug on the run then trouble will follow, and if possible the crew leave the boat to save themselves.

"Why," said an old captain, "I remember I was on the tug Asa Ransom a number of years ago. One day we brushed the dock and a rat scurried out to the rail and jumped ashore. A week later the tug burned down in Sturgeon Bay. The rats know every time when there's going to be trouble."

A tug costs about $25,000 and there are fifty of them in the river.

Clark Street Chinamen

IN CLARK STREET, where all the nations of the earth dwell together in harmony, one has but to go downstairs to find a Chinaman. And when found he is washing.

This generalization applies only on week days, for on Sunday the Chinaman bubbles up out of his basement and discusses the silver question with other Chinamen who have bubbled up out of their basements. Or if it isn't the silver question— there's no way of proving that it isn't—it may be some other equally interesting matter. While he argues he smokes a good cigar, and occasionally he goes into a friend's house and sips rice brandy hot enough to scorch the throat of a wooden Indian. Or perhaps he goes visiting with a calling card of red paper about two feet long. Or if it is a bright day he and six or seven of his friends may squeeze themselves into a hack and be driven in state down the boulevard. To the ordinary Chinaman this is the height of spendthrift dissipation.

If by good fortune some Chinese neighbor has chosen Friday for dying then the funeral comes Sunday and it provides much opportunity for thorough enjoyment.

Sunday night the Chinaman goes back downstairs between his two white and red signs which advertise:

> FAMILY LAUNDRY

Any one but a Chinaman with his bobbed-off felt shoes must have a care how he descends these steps. Habitually sober men have been known to bump all the way down in a decidedly undignified manner.

*   *   *

The Chinaman is as frugal in sleep as he is in everything else except opium, and before most of Clark Street has rubbed Sunday out of its eyes he is up and ready for his Monday work.

Early in the day the bundles begin to come into the little office, which is partitioned off from the rest of the room by gently billowing red curtains. Why these curtains are always red no one has ever explained. Perhaps it is exciting to the Chinaman's imagination. It at least adds mystery to his surroundings.

"Washee?" asks the Chinaman in attendance, always in the same tone.

He takes the bundle and gives out a little slip of paper with some cabalistic signs on it.

Then the bundle goes with a great many others under the bench, and the Chinaman makes an entry in a big yellow account book with a camel's hair brush held straight up between his thumb and forefinger.

But the visitor with the bundle never goes behind the red curtain. It is a territory that few white men ever get an opportunity to explore, owing doubtless to the natural suspiciousness of the Chinaman.

The mysterious back room is commonly very dirty and disorderly and squalid. In it the three Chinamen—there are nearly always three in every laundry firm—live and do their work. Ordinarily there are three rooms—one in which the washing, ironing, and cooking are done, one in which the clothes are dried, and a small and stuffy closet where the proprietors sleep. Sometimes two rooms serve every purpose, and not infrequently the Chinaman, who has a great capacity for adapting himself to circumstances, can get along with only one.

* * *

In the middle of the main room there is a pudgy round stove with a broad ridge at the center, on which the flatirons rest upright. On the flat top a teapot is always simmering, so that the Chinaman may have his drink of tea at any time. He doesn't like water. At one side stands a big bin full of coke for the stove—coal is rarely used—and at the other is the box-like washtub, with a big wringer at one end.

And all about the room pails and boxes and brooms lie scat-

"THE VISITOR WITH THE BUNDLE NEVER GOES BEHIND
THE RED CURTAIN"

tered in confusion. There are rarely any chairs — an empty soap-box serves every purpose. The plaster has fallen from the walls in big pieces, and it is swept up with other accumulations into the corners, where it sometimes remains until the Chinamen are compelled to get rid of it on account of the lack of room. A barrel of rice is usually kept on hand, and the dishes in which it is cooked lie, when not in use, in a big sink half full of water. They are rust-eaten and dirty.

The room is always kept exceedingly hot, and the Chinamen potter around either bare-footed or in flapping, heelless slippers. The odors are far from pleasant.

Personally the Chinaman is cleanly in his habits, for when the clothes are all washed he strips off his own scant garments and slips into the washtub and polishes off his gaunt form with a scrubbing brush.

*   *   *

The clothes are hung in a big dark room, and kerosene-oil lamps are sometimes placed around on the floor to assist in drying. It is for this reason that garments washed at a Chinese laundry so often smell of kerosene fumes.

The Chinaman works nearly all the time. Mondays and Thursdays two of the firm wash while the other irons, often in the outer shop, where it is cool. On Tuesdays and Fridays all three iron, and on Wednesdays and Saturdays the laundry is delivered. In the middle of the day each Chinaman takes an hour's nap, and about 3 o'clock they have a hasty dinner of rice, tea, bread and a peculiar kind of cake, the members of the firm taking turns with the cooking.

At midnight the Chinaman bolts and bars his doors and windows, for he is always fearful of marauders. Then he prepares for bed.

The bedroom is usually small and cramped, and sometimes there are only two rough bunks for three Chinamen. In this case they cast lots and the one who loses sleeps on the floor. By the foot of each bed there is a little metal joss to which the Chinaman prays in his own peculiar way—a high, nasal monotone accompanied by much swaying of the arms and body. Here he flees first of all when he hears that the highbinders are after him, or when some one forgets to pay a laundry bill.

In spite of the foul air, the poor food and the long hours of work the Chinaman is unusually healthy. If he is sick he may go to a doctor of his own race who will give him a great many sweet and bitter herbs and say incantations, but in Chicago he has learned, as a rule, to patronize American doctors. Three or four physicians control most of the Chinese patronage.

From the Office Window

WHEN Ruggles was first given his seat in the office he felt thoroughly disheartened.

It was not on account of the desk, for that was of the latest pattern, with a rolling top, and the blotting pads were fresh every morning, and there were more pigeon holes and shelves and drawers than Ruggles had papers to fill. The chair stood close to the window, too, and Ruggles had always wanted a seat where he could look out and see the world move up and down.

He had the window, it is true, but it was a back window, and that is what made Ruggles feel disheartened. A score of feet across a narrow court rose the dingy brick walls of another building, an old building on which time and weather had wrought a thousand grotesque designs. From where Ruggles sat he could see four windows in the wall, and by leaning a little forward the edges of the scaling cornices at the top of the building became visible. Above this gleamed a narrow strip of sky as wide as Ruggles' window, which was very narrow indeed compared with the amount of sky that Ruggles had seen when he was a boy and lay deep in the tangles of a clover field.

* * *

From the top of the building a great many telephone wires, telegraph wires and electric light wires were woven in and out like a great cobweb. Ruggles imagined that it might have been spun to keep such buzzing, toiling flies as himself and Rogers and Hume, who sat at adjoining desks, from escaping.

In the morning of bright days a small, angular block of sunlight crept into the slit between the buildings, and traveled along the opposite wall from east to west, bringing out the stains and disfigurements of the weather with double distinctness. The sun did its best to reach its long arm to the bottom of the court, for it wished to pry around in the dampness and clamminess there, but it could never succeed, although Ruggles admitted that it was doing its best. As time passed Ruggles grew to understand what the sun said. When it reached the streakings on the wall, close between the windows—the spot resembled the hump of a camel—it said that Ruggles was hungry and that he had better go out to lunch, and when it reached the rusty iron hook, where an iron shutter once hung, it was time to rattle down the top of his desk and go home.

All of these things Ruggles learned little by little as he glanced up from his work. Gradually the wall assumed a comeliness all its own, and it smiled a welcome when he came down in the morning, and bade him a sad goodby when he went home at night. It was so companionable and sympathetic and silent. It wasn't as disturbing as the busy world in the streets would have been, and Ruggles often felt thankful for its protection.

*   *   *

And the windows—what a perpetual source of joy they were. When Ruggles first took his seat the two upper ones were dusty and uncurtained—they made him think of the staring eyes of a blind man. They were there to see through, but no one saw through them.

The two lower windows opened into some sort of a shop and Ruggles could see a long work bench and a table, where a foot-power saw often buzzed. Here an emaciated little man with a long leather apron spent all of his time bending over and tinkering at something with a hammer, pincers and small chisel-like instruments. Sometimes he had a visitor, who came and sat in the window and laughed a little and talked, but Ruggles could only make out an occasional word.

On bright and sunny mornings he started his whistle going merrily. It was evident that the emaciated man hadn't learned any new tunes for a great many years. So he'd begin on "Silver Threads Among the Gold" first thing in the morning and by noon he'd have reached "White Wings." Once or

ON CLEAR DAYS THE STRIP OF SKY WAS BLUE WITH RIFTS OF
SMOKE CLOUDS SCUDDING OVER IT (*Drawing by Schmedtgen*)

twice he tried to whistle "After the Ball," but it wasn't a success—perhaps it wasn't classic enough.

*   *   *

A few weeks after Ruggles began to be interested in his surroundings some one moved into the room behind the two upper windows in the wall. This was evident from the fact that
windows were cleaned and some pickle-colored shades put up.

A sprightly old woman, with a red-and-white bandanna handkerchief tied around her head, who came to the window every morning with a feather duster, was one of the inmates. The other—for Ruggles soon made up his mind that there were only two—was a fair-faced girl, with brown hair, and when she came to the window to get the fruit or the steak or the milk, which had been set on the sill to keep cool, she was always laughing and talking. On bright days when the window was open Ruggles could see the ornaments inside—a few cheap pictures, some artificial flowers and a home-made tidy on the back of the chair that rocked by the window. The old woman and the girl sewed a great deal, with their spools standing in a row on the window sill.

*   *   *

One afternoon about a week after the old woman and the girl moved in Ruggles looked up and saw a red-haired policeman standing at the side of the girl. She was looking up at him and laughing. Presently he sat down near her, and when the old woman went away he hitched his chair much closer and seemed interested in the girl's sewing.

Two days later a black-haired policeman—a big, handsome fellow—called. First he sat down by the old woman and talked with her as if he were much interested and she laughed and chatted gayly. After awhile she went out and the black-haired policeman crossed with his chair and sat by the girl. She seemed just a little shy, Ruggles thought, and when the policeman hitched his chair up she hitched hers back a little.

For the next three weeks the red-haired policeman and the black-haired policeman called at regular intervals. The girl always smiled on the red-haired policeman and the old woman smiled on the black-haired policeman. Once they came together, and Ruggles saw them scowling at each other, and the old woman was the only one that seemed at all at her ease.

Then for a time Ruggles looked in vain for the girl. The old woman appeared regularly at the window, sewing energetically, but the girl had evidently gone away. Then Ruggles himself was sent half across the continent, and was gone for nearly a year.

When he came back he slipped into his old seat with a feeling of comfort and satisfaction. The wall and the bit of sky seemed to welcome him.

Almost immediately he looked up to the windows opposite. There sat the old woman sewing, as usual, and Ruggles thought with a sigh of relief that nothing had happened. Toward noon he looked again. In the other window sat the girl. She looked a little older and not quite so merry-faced.

In her arms she was rocking a red-haired baby.

Where the River Opens to the Lake

IT'S CHEAPER to ride on the boat than it is to stay at home. Put plenty of lunch into the basket and weight it down with a paper-covered novel. Take an extra wrap, an umbrella, a camera and a pair of field glasses and get to the boat early.

It doesn't make much difference which boat you take. One will land you at Milwaukee and another at St. Joe, or you can take your choice of Michigan City, Racine, Waukegan, Kenosha, Sheboygan, Manitowoc, Algoma, Sturgeon Bay, Green Bay City, Escanaba, Gladstone, Grand Haven, Manistique, Macatawa, Ottawa Beach, Mackinac or Manhattan Beach.

The principal object is to get the boat ride. To be sure, the start is accompanied by certain penalties and difficulties. Your big boat lies crowded into the narrow channel of the Chicago River like a huge draught-horse in a pony's stall, and the black, oily river steams gently beneath the warm morning sun and does not charm any of the senses.

To the east there is a gap of clear blue water showing between the tall dingy buildings which line the docks, and beyond the smoke there is promise of real air.

There are a half-dozen white steamers lined in the muddy chute of the river and barriered between the bridges. They are very clean with paint and very patriotic with flags.

On one upper deck a band is playing "I Want Dem Pres-

"THE BLUE WATER AND THE CLEAR SUNLIGHT TO THE EAST"

ents Back." This is a lively tune, and the passengers who come flocking in from Wabash Avenue and River Street or emerge suddenly from under bridges or tumble precipitately from trolley cars all keep time to the music.

> "I want dat bran new cook-stove,
> I want dat chair,
> I want dat lookin'-glass,
> An' a comb faw to comb my hair."

The arriving passengers are in a state of apprehension.

Finally they are aboard and ready. Then they wonder why the boat doesn't start.

And now you hear the following:

"Ma!"

"Yes, dear. And you know I said to John, 'I just know I'll forget something, because——'"

"Ma!"

"Yes, dear."

"Why, ma, is—ah——"

"Now, I knew you didn't have anything to say. You mustn't interrupt mamma when she's talking. Well, after we got on the car I looked in my purse, and——"

"Ma!"

"Angel! I'll churn you in a minute."

"Well, ma."

"What is it?"

"Why—ah——is that another boat over there?"

"Of course it's another boat."

"Who is that man away up on top there?"

"That's the captain, I suppose."

"Who's the other man?"

"I don't know."

"Is he a captain, too?"

"Yes, I suppose so."

"Do they have two captains on a boat?"

"Darling! Listen, the band's going to play."

"Where is that boat going?"

"Across the lake, I suppose."

"Is it going to the same place that we're going to?"

"Yes, yes, I suppose so."

"Will it get there before we do?"

No answer.

"Ma!"

"Hush!"

"Ma!"

"Hush!"

"I'm hungry."

As there is sure to be an extended argument on the subject of food supply, it would be well perhaps to select a shady spot farther forward, but no matter where you sit, you will not escape the inquisitive child.

"Ma, is that Chicago over there?"

"After we get to Milwaukee are we going to come back home again?"

"Are there any fish in the lake?"

"Do all these people on the boat live in Chicago?"

"If a big fish came up and bit a hole in the bottom of the boat would the boat sink? Why?"

"How deep is the lake right here?"

If you are going for a ride on the lake, take a small boy along. He will be a sure preventive of idleness.

"Slim's" Dog

IN HIS earlier life he may have had a full-grown name, but around the docks he was always known as "Slim." The name fitted him quite well. He was muscular, but his was the strength of the tall and bony kind. His mustache was exceedingly red, harmonizing with his complexion, which was a combination of bronze and alcoholic flush. "Slim" drank heavily at times, but his habits never affected the goodness of heart that was born in him. If his habits were not commendable they were at least methodical. He had worked for eighteen years as a vessel-unloader. In his drinking bouts he patronized only one or two places. He had only a chance acquaintance with beds. Usually he slept on the dock or in a warehouse with a spread newspaper as a blanket and his dog for a companion.

The dog was an undersized mongrel which he had rescued from starvation. Between the two there sprang up a friendship which only death could sever. Death did sever it about three weeks ago. "Slim," after a weary illness at the hospital, during which time he was too weak to protest against the bed into which they had thrown him, stopped breathing one night. The dog had been with him, crouching near the bed, up to the very last. The news of "Slim's" death being carried to the docks, the men unloaded that day without singing over their task. Now that "Slim" was gone they began to realize that he had been the best man among them. Few had been in the work much longer, and none other had received such marks of distinction. Every year for fifteen years he had been the one to carry down the gang-plank the first crate of strawber-

HIS HOME WAS AMONG THE DOCKS AND WAREHOUSES

ries from Michigan. This crate always comes wrapped in the
American flag, and there is a crowd waiting to see its triumphal entry into Chicago. Who was worthy to carry the crate
now that "Slim" had gone?

The more they went over his record the more certain were
they that "Slim" had been a good fellow, a friend to man and
dog. Of course he had left no money, no effects. There had
never been another man more thoroughly without a fixed home.
No one had ever heard him mention relatives. Such a man usually goes into the paupers' field, but "Slim's" friends wouldn't
see him put there. They started a subscription list. Not only
the unloaders but the managers of steamship lines and the
masters of the docks put in money, until the amount was $60.
This was sufficient to give "Slim" a decent coffin and a place
in Calvary. A delegation in carriages attended the funeral.
The dog rode with the pallbearers. No one paid much attention to him until the mourners reached a road house on the
way back from the cemetery and lined up along the bar. Then
it was observed that the dog went along the line, sniffling at
the shoes. "He's lookin' for 'Slim,'" said one of the boys, and
the whole row turned from the bar and gave their melancholy
attention to the dog, who became embarrassed and went and
laid himself down under a table.

Next day the unloaders were at work again. The dog ran in and out among them, stopping for a moment now and then to wait for some one who didn't come. One of "Slim's" friends tried to adopt the dog, but the animal would not remain around the lodging house at night, but went roaming around the docks looking for a man asleep on a newspaper.

One night the hands on a tugboat heard a splashing in the water and the stoker rescued "Slim's" dog from the muddy river. The unloaders said the next day that the animal had tried to drown himself. Once or twice the dog has reappeared at the docks, only to take a hopeless survey of the working gang and then trot away. He is once more a pauper and a vagrant, just as he was before he found the friendship of his life.

"NEXT DAY THE UNLOADERS WERE AT WORK AGAIN"

Il Janitoro

MR. TYLER paid $7 for two opera tickets.

Although he slept through one duet he felt fully repaid for going, because Mrs. Tyler raved over the opera and wasted all her superlatives on it. The music was "heavenly" the prima donna "superb" and the tenor "magnificent."

There is nothing so irritates a real enthusiasm as the presence of calm scorn.

"Don't you like it?" asked Mrs. Tyler, as she settled back after the eighth recall of the motherly woman who had been singing the part of a 16-year-old maiden.

"Oh, yes; it's all right," replied Mr. Tyler, as if he were conceding something.

"All right! Oh, you iceberg! I don't believe you'd become enthusiastic over anything in the world."

"I like the music, my dear, but grand opera drags so. Then the situations are so preposterous they always appeal to my sense of humor. I can't help it. When I see Romeo and Juliet die, both singing away as if they enjoyed it, I have to laugh."

"The idea!"

"You take it in this last act. Those two fellows came out with the soldiers and announced that they were conspiring and didn't want to be heard by the people in the house, and then they shouted in chorus until they could have been heard two miles away."

"Oh, you are prejudiced."

"Not at all. I'll tell you, a grand opera's the funniest kind of a show if you only take the right view of it."

Thus they argued, and even after they arrived home she taunted him and told him he could not appreciate the dignity of the situations.

It was this nagging which induced Mr. Tyler to write an act of grand opera. He chose for his subject an alarm of fire in an apartment house. He wanted something modern and up-to-date, but in his method of treatment he resolved to reverently follow all the traditions of grand opera. The act, hith-

erto unpublished, and written solely for the benefit of Mrs.
Tyler, is here appended:

(*Mr. and Mrs. Taylor are seated in their apartment on the fifth
floor of the Bohemoth residential flat building. Mrs. Taylor arises, places her hand on her heart, and moves to the center of the
room. Mr. Taylor follows her, with his right arm extended.*)

Mrs. Taylor: I think I smell smoke.

Mr. Taylor: She thinks she smells smoke.

Mrs. Taylor: I think I smell smoke.

Mr. Taylor: Oh. What is it? She says she thinks she smells
smoke.

Mrs. Taylor: What does it mean, what does it mean?
            This smell of smoke may indicate,
            That we'll be burned—oh-h-h, awful fate!

Mr. Taylor: Behold the smell grows stronger yet,
            The house is burning, I'd regret
            To perish in the curling flames;
            Oh, horror! horror! horror!!!

Mr. and Mrs. Taylor:
            Oh, sad is our lot, sad is our lot,
            To perish in the flames so hot,
            To curl and writhe and fry and sizz,
            Oh, what a dreadful thing it is
            To think of such a thing!

Mrs. Taylor: We must escape!

Mr. Taylor: Yes, yes, we must escape!

Mrs. Taylor: We have no time to lose.

Mr. Taylor: Ah, bitter truth, Ah, bitter truth,
            We have no time to lose.

Mr. and Mrs. Taylor:
            Sad is our lot, sad is our lot,
            To perish in the flames so hot.

Mr. Taylor: Hark, what is it?

Mrs. Taylor: Hark, what is it?

Mr. Taylor: It is the dread alarm of fire.

Mrs. Taylor: Ah, yes, ah, yes, it is the dread alarm.

Mr. Taylor: The dread alarm strikes on the ear
            And chills me with an awful fear.
            The house will burn, oh, can it be

IT WAS HIGHLY IMPORTANT THAT THEY SHOULD "HASTEN AWAY"

That I must die in misery,
That I must die in misery,
The house will burn, oh, can it be
That I must die in misery?

Mrs. Taylor: Come, let us fly!

Mr. Taylor: 'Tis well. 'Tis well. We'll fly at once.
(*Enter all the other residents of the fifth floor.*)

Mr. Taylor: Kind friends, I have some news to tell.
This house is burning, it were well
That we should haste ourselves away
And save our lives without delay.

Chorus: What is this he tells us?
It must be so;
The building is on fire
And we must go.

> Oh, hasten, oh, hasten, oh, hasten away.
> Our terror we should not conceal,
> And language fails to express the alarm
> That in our hearts we feel.

Mr. and Mrs. Taylor:
> Oh, language fails to express the alarm
> That in their hearts they feel.

(Enter the Janitor)

Janitor: Hold, I am here.
Mr. Taylor: Ah, it is the Janitoro.
Mrs. Taylor: Can I believe my senses,
> Or am I going mad?
> It is the Janitoro,
> It is indeed the Janitoro.

Janitor: Such news I have to tell.
Mr. Taylor: Ah, I might have known
> He has such news to tell.
> Speak and break the awful suspense.

Mrs. Taylor: Yes, speak.
Janitor: I come to inform you
> That you must quickly fly
> The fearful blaze is spreading,
> To tarry is to die.
> The floors underneath you
> Are completely burned away
> They cannot save the building,
> So now escape I pray.

Mrs. Taylor: Oh, awful message
> How it chills my heart.

Janitor: The flames are roaring loudly,
> Oh, what a fearful sound!
> You can hear the people shrieking
> As they jump and strike the ground.
> Oh, horror overtakes me,
> And I merely pause to say
> That the building's doomed for certain
> Oh, haste, oh, haste away.

Mrs. Taylor: Oh, awful message.

How it chills my heart.
Yet we will sing a few more arias
Before we start.
Mr. Taylor: Yes, a few more arias and then away.
Chorus: Oh, hasten, oh, hasten, oh hasten away.
Mrs. Taylor: Now, e'er I retreat,
Lest death o'ertakes me
I'll speak of the fear
That convulses and shakes me,
I sicken to think what may befall,
Oh, horror! horror!! horror!!!
Mr. Taylor: The woman speaks the truth,
And there can be no doubt
That we will perish soon
Unless we all clear out.
Chorus: Oh, hasten, oh, hasten, oh, hasten away
(*But why go further? The supposition is that they continued the dilatory tactics of grand opera and perished in the flames.*)

Min Sargent

HER name was "Min." She came into the office of Morewood & Son one bright morning in August and broke the ice with young Campbell, who sat in the outer office.

"Where's the fellow that wants to hire a girl?" she asked.

"Are you an applicant?" asked young Campbell.

"Are you the man that wants the girl?"

"Well—no."

"He's the man I want to see."

"I guess you want to see Mr. Morewood."

"Well, where is he?"

"He's in his office."

"You tell him that I'm here, will you?"

"Certainly."

Campbell was rather dazed by the self-assurance of the visitor. He had been accustomed to patronize the people who called to see the head of the concern.

Having tapped softly at the door which had "Lemuel More-wood" painted on the flaky glass, he received a sharp "Come in." He cautiously opened the door and said: "A young lady to see you in regard to the position, sir." The gray and melancholy Lemuel Morewood was seated at a gigantic walnut desk, the tableland of which was strewn with papers and weights. All the pigeon-holes were choking full of blue-jacketed contracts, leases, agreements and abstracts.

The elder Morewood was a thin man with long and restless hands. He had a gaunt face set off with close side whiskers. Although of slender framework and seemingly aged and wrinkled before his time, his immense capacity for work had never failed him. He was a chilled-steel mechanism, operated by the energy of nerves.

"Friendship" meant business reciprocity to him. Only one man, his son, ever dared to take him familiarly.

*   *   *

The visitor slipped into the room and sat near the window. Lemuel Morewood, the great, his eyes rolling uneasily above his eye-glasses, muttered to himself as he scanned the pigeon-holes. His claw-like hands fumbled among the dry papers.

"Min" looked out of the window for awhile and then found it more to her enjoyment to watch the man at the desk.

Presently she said: "I believe I'll open the window. It's closer than an oven in here, mister."

"How's that? Oh, I remember."

He swung around in his revolving chair and looked at the visitor. He saw a girl of 18 or so, red-cheeked, bright-eyed, curly-haired, shirt-waisted, straw-hatted. Her nose had just the slightest tilt upward.

But did the great Morewood see all this? Or did he simply allow his mind to grasp the business fact that there was a Young Person seeking a situation?

"You desire employment?" he asked, gazing at her over his nose-glasses.

"Yes, I do, but I'd like to know just what you want. I can't short-hand, you know. What did you want, some one to copy and address envelopes?"

"Miss Lowell is our stenographer," said the great man. "We

want some one to relieve her of a considerable portion of the routine work. You operate the typewriting machine?"

"Yes, I can do that all right."

"Do you write a legible hand?"

"Well I can show you. Have you got a pen there? Why, but these pens are awful rusty. You ought to have a wiper."

She had arisen and come over to his desk, where she calmly sorted over the pens while the great man adjusted his eyeglasses and looked at her again, as if either annoyed or surprised.

"You have an awful nice office here," she said. "That's one reason I'd like to work here. Now where can I get a place to write? Let me sit down there just a minute."

Lemuel Morewood nervously smacked his lips and then arose from his chair. "Min" seated herself and began to write in a bold confident hand, with shaded capitals, every small "o" as round as a butter ball and every "t" crossed with precision.

The great man stood a few feet away and studied her as he would study a new Business Proposition.

"Read it," said she, handing him a sheet of her own heavily engraved paper.

"MIN"

"Well, I think it is hardly necessary to—"

"Go on and read it."

"Well, young woman, it seems to me— however, if you insist." He read aloud. "If I do not get a position somewhere I will have to wear my old cloak another winter. This is no joke.

"Very Truly, Minnie Sargent."

"You can read that, can't you?" she asked.

"Oh yes—yes, indeed. You live with your parents, do you?" and he resumed his place at the desk.

"Yes, sir, I live at 2618 Walworth Avenue. Do you want any letters from people who know me?"

"Well, really, young woman— my son Arthur should have attended to this matter. It's really out of my province."

"You're the head of the firm, ain't you?"

"Yes, of course," and he said it so suddenly as he turned to look at her again that his nose-glasses trembled.

"If you say I'm hired, that settles it. There won't be any trouble about that. Mr. Oh— Mr.—"

"Morewood! Morewood!" said the great man, sharply, once more scratching among his papers.

"——Mr. Morewood. I'll try to do the work and if I can do it, all right. If you don't like me after you try me you can say so. When a girl goes out to get a place she ought to be the same as a boy. If she can't do the work she ought to be fired— er, I mean she ought to be discharged. How much would you be willing to pay a week?"

"Really, young woman," said the great man, beginning to frown a little, "I had not fixed upon any compensation."

"If I'm worth anything, I'm worth six dollars a week, ain't I?"

Lemuel Morewood made a sound something like a gasp and he ceased to rummage among the papers. Here, at least, was a Business Proposition that could not be ignored. Once more he turned in his chair and stared over his glasses at the girl, who met the scrutiny with supreme calmness.

"You think that would be fair compensation?" he asked, pointedly.

"You can try me at that and find out," she replied, smiling.

* * *

Lemuel Morewood arose and moved toward the doorway, saying: "Come with me, young woman." She went with him into the outer office.

"Miss Lowell."

The typewriting machine which had been clicking behind a Japanese screen suddenly became silent. Miss Lowell, a thin woman of delicate beauty and a nurse-like smile, came forward.

"Miss Lowell. I have employed the young woman to help you. You take her in hand and show her what to do. She'll begin work—When can you start in?"

"I can start in now."

"You can come to-morrow morning," and Lemuel More-wood darted back into his office.

"What is your name?" asked Miss Lowell with a smile full of encouragement.

"Minnie Sargent."

"Miss Sargent, allow me to present Mr. Campbell."

"How do you do, Mr. Campbell?" and she held out her hand. The young man shook hands as awkwardly as possible.

"I'll be with you to-morrow morning, then," said Minnie. "Say, Mr. Morewood is an awful nice man, isn't he? I'll be here at 8."

"No need to come before 8:30," volunteered Campbell.

"He-ho! That's better still. Good-by."

As soon as the outer door was closed Campbell turned to Miss Lowell and said: "That girl's very fresh."

"It's a wonder Mr. Morewood didn't snap her head off. He's worried to-day over that Michigan failure."

"She said she thought he was a nice man. I didn't expect to see her stay in there two seconds. She must have hypnotized him."

Pink Marsh

WHEN the morning customer climbed into the chair he saw on the wall, within easy reach, a pasteboard box capped with a sprig of green. In the side of the box was a slit, large enough to receive a silver dollar. Below it were the words: "Merry Xmas. Remember the porter."

"What does that mean—'Merry Xmas'?" asked the customer.

Pink Marsh chuckled away down in his throat as he reefed the trousers leg. "You knows might' well wha' tha' means, mistah. If I on'y had yo' ej'cash'n I wouldn' be whippin' flannel ovah no man's shoes."

"I don't see what education has to do with it. What is it, anyway—that 'merry Xmas'?"

"Mistah Cliffo'd, on the secon' chaih, made it fo' me. He says that's 'me'y Ch'ismas'."

"MY GOODNESS, MISTAH, YOU AIN' GOIN' FO'CE ME TO COME
RIGHT OUT AN' ASK FO' IT, ARE YOU?"

"That's a funny way to spell Christmas. What does the
rest of it mean there, about remembering the porter?"

"My goodness, mistah, you ain' goin' fo'ce me to come
right out an' ask fo' it, are you?"

"Ask for what?"

In reply, Pink merely choked up with laughter and rolled
his head.

"Mr. Clifford did a very fine job there," observed the customer.

"Who, Mistah Cliffo'd? He can do an'thing. He's got a watch-chain made out o' real haih he made himself."

"He must be a versatile genius."

"I guess he—say, mistah, tha' was a wahm piece o' talk. Wha' was that you say—he——"

"I say he must be a versatile genius."

"A vussitle gemyus—genimus."

"Genius—versatile genius."

"Vussitle gen'us—tha's a lolly-coolah. If I on'y had a few like that I'd keep 'em ketchin' theah breaths, suah. Wha's the def'mmition?"

"That means a man of varied accomplishments."

Pink worked for a few minutes and allowed the definition to percolate. Then he observed, with a sigh: "I couldn't ketch them boys; not 'ith a laddah. Too high."

* * *

The barber at chair No. 1 shouted "Brush!" and Pink shuffled away to attend to a thin man with a powdered complexion and gummy hair.

First he brushed the thin man, front and back, becoming more earnest in his efforts just as the man received a handful of small change. Pink held the overcoat and, after the thin man had worked into it, he reached under for the inside coat and pulled it down so violently that the thin man was bowed backward. While Pink was brushing the overcoat the thin man walked over and took his hat from the hook.

But he was not to escape so easily. Pink gently pulled the hat away from him and went in search of the small brush. He stood in front of the thin customer and, holding the hat gingerly in the left hand, brushed it carefully, at the same time blowing off imaginary specks of dust.

While the thin man was waiting for his hat he casually put his right hand into the trousers pocket. Pink stopped brushing and scratched at an invisible spot or stain of some sort on the sleeve of the overcoat.

"Shine?" he inquired, softly.

"Nope."

So he continued to brush the hat.

The thin man withdrew his hand from the pocket. Pink turned the hat around right side forward and presented it to the customer with a low bow. The customer's right hand moved forward a few inches, but Pink's broad palm met it more than half way. The nickel passed.

"Thank you, seh," said Pink, in a reverential whisper. The thin man started toward the door. Pink seized the long whisk broom and pursued him, hitting him between the shoulder blades. As the man passed out Pink got in one final blow on the coat-tails.

*   *   *

"Well, did you land him?" asked the customer in the high chair, when Pink had resumed his work on the shoes.

In response, Pink dropped the nickel to the floor, as if by accident. Then he picked it up, turned it over and finally put it in his mouth.

"Money layin' all 'roun' heah to-day," he said, rattling the coin against his teeth.

"You can buy a loaf of bread with that," suggested the customer.

"You bettah make anothah guess on what I'm goin' to do with any nicks I get hol' of these days. Bread's fo' poo' people. I'm goin' eat chidlins, roas' pig, co'n bread, che'y pie, mash tu'nips, an'—ah—le' me see—"

"You'll be lucky to get snow-balls," said the wise barber, who had a disagreeable way of coming into the heart-to-heart talks between Pink and the morning customers.

"Don' lose no sleep 'bout me," retorted Pink, "I may be ba' foot an' need mo' undahclose, but I sut'ny will have chidlins on Ch'ismas, an' any man 'at thinks diff'ent wants to back up an' take a new guess. If that theah box treats me right I'll have mon fo' Ch'ismas."

The morning customer accepted this remark as a gentle and diplomatic hint.

*   *   *

While Pink was at work on the second shoe he began to sing very softly:

"Some folks get livin' with they han's
An' some get livin' f'm lan's,
But a little pa' of bones, all covahed with sevens,
Is s'ponsible fo' Dan's.
Some coons think they ah might' fly,
Try to read-ah my system in ah-eye,
But book say a suckah bo'n ev'y minute
An' nevah known to die."

"What's that, something new?" asked the man in the chair.

"Ain' that a wahm piece o' wo'k? Tha's new, fo' a fac'. My brothah gi' me that last night. He's a guitah-playah."

"Where does he play?"

"Anywheah that they's good to him. Yes, seh, tha's 'Crappy Dan, the Spo'tin Man.' If that theah box wins out fo' me I'm goin' to heah that Miss May Uhwin sing it some night. She's so wahm you can feel the heat up in 'e' gallery."

"You ought to save your money instead of spending it at the theater."

"Down theah whe' I live it ain' safe to keep yo' money. If they think yo' savin' yo' coin they stop yo' at night. If anybody's goin' to spend my money I wan' o' spend it myself, yes, seh."

"Why don't you put it in the bank?"

"Yes, seh, I'm goin' put some in 'e bank next yeah."

"Well, you want to bear well in mind that procrastination is the thief of time."

"Wow! Le' go, man! Tha's sut'ny the hottes' thing yo' handed me yet. Pocazzumalashum—prasticanashum—chenashalum—no, seh, theah's one too good fo' me. No, seh, don't try to gi' me that one. It keep me busy jes' foldin' kinks out o' that boy. I couldn' wo'k an' remember that at the same time."

"Why, that's very simple—procrastination. It means the habit of postponing action, putting off until to-morrow, as it were."

"'At's all right what't means, mistah. The wise boy 'at wo'ked all day gettin' up that wo'd nevah meant it fo' me. I am strong enough to swing them kind—pocrastumalation—timination——"

"Procrastination."

"No, seh, don' try it. I can't use that boy. They would'n' stan' fo' nothin' like that on Deahbo'n Street. Yo' keep that one an' use it yo'self—proclast-pocrasum-unn-unn—mistah, yo' sut'ny have wo'ds up yo' sleeve that ah strangahs to me."

"Procrastination is a good word," said the morning customer as he slipped a quarter into the Christmas box and descended from the high chair.

"Thank yo', seh," repeated Pink, three times.

"They ah sut'ny ve'y few man can use them wo'ds as you do," said he, as he was brushing the morning customer. "'Prastigumation is what steals away yo' time'—no, seh, don' tell me no mo'; it's too high. Good mo'nin', yes, seh. Same to you, mistah. Me'y Ch'ismas."

"Doc" as Lothario

TAKEN as a whole, the colony at the Alfalfa European Hotel would not have induced a modest woman to come across the street.

The members were not youthful, and, with one or two exceptions, the men who attempted to be dressy ran to fawn-colored gaiters, fly-front vests, ready-made cravats and other hyphenated articles properly belonging to the man who thinks he is while he really isn't.

The actor had a sort of reminiscent splendor, like that of a summer pavilion in the dead of winter, but here and there a pin had to do for a button and sometimes the cuffs wore an edge like that of a handsaw. The actor seemed to labor under the impression that he could atone for other shortcomings in his appearance by putting an extra shine on his shoes and allowing part of a slightly soiled handkerchief to protrude from his upper coat pocket.

The "lush," who, it was whispered, had wealthy relatives in the east and lived on an allowance granted by them, was the best-dressed man of the lot when he was sober enough to supervise himself. The race-track man favored the styles of his boyhood days. His shoes were rather box-toed and his cravat was a black string pulled into a bow. He had a large watch-chain looped across his vest, and the locket was necessarily a horseshoe.

As might have been expected, the lightning dentist sought color effects. When he came out to the street doorway in light checked trousers, saffron-colored vest and blue coat, his knotted four-in-hand cravat darting into the crack of his shirtbosom at a point some two inches below the collar, and his hands clammy from perfumed toilet soap, he seemed to feel that he was doing more than his share to make this world a pleasant place of abode.

THE COOING LOVER

* * *

"Doc" Horne, according to his own admission, was a most dangerous man with the women.

"Doc" was bald and ruddy, with a scattering of pimples, and his garments gave proof that on more than one occasion he had misplaced his napkin.

A stranger making a guess at "Doc" might have picked him for almost anything in the world except the cooing lover. Yet "Doc" had been a principal in love affairs, for he admitted it.

* * *

It is beyond all comprehension that women in passing the Alfalfa doorway of an evening should shy at the assemblage of men who were born to smile at women and lead them captive.

So far as actual observation went not one of the gallants had ever succeeded in winning a second glance from any female except the night waitress in the restaurant. She was on friendly terms with all of them and seemed to have an especial admiration for the lightning dentist.

As for invitations to social gatherings, it is doubtful if a square envelope has come to the Alfalfa in the last five years.

There has been nothing on the surface of events to prove that the Alfalfa European Hotel is a hotbed of society favorites.

It is necessary to engage in conversation with the members of the colony to learn of the hearts that have been broken.

THE "LUSH" IS SKEPTICAL

To be sure the "lush" had once met the lightning dentist clinging to a stout woman in State Street and had brought the news of it to the hotel.

When charged with the affair the dentist appeared to be greatly confused, and hinted that there was a mystery connected with the lady and he would not venture to tell the whole story.

In the presence of the lightning dentist the "lush" was compelled to admit that the stout woman possessed many charms. As soon as the dentist went away the "lush" confided to the other men that the stout woman was a "bear," whatever that may be.

*   *   *

From the stories told on several evenings it seemed that "Doc," the lightning dentist and the actor had been loved only by women of the first quality. Not one of the trio would admit of any entanglement with any female of blemished reputation.

"Doc" usually told of meeting his women at dinner parties. The dentist had made his conquests on the street and in railway trains, the woman usually seeking some pretext for addressing him, simply because she couldn't resist him.

The actor would say: "One night when I was playing in New York I observed an elegantly dressed lady in the stage box. She couldn't keep her eyes off of me. At the end of the third act, where I had my great scene—whole stage to myself —vengeance business, oath and quick curtain—got every hand in the house. I had to come out by this box and this lady threw me the lovely bouquet she had been carrying. Next day I received a note," etc., etc.

*   *   *

It must have been on account of the actor and his stories of smiling society women in the boxes that "Doc" was induced to tell of the season when he was singing in opera.

No one around the hotel had ever heard "Doc" sing. His voice was a "Tom gin baritone" and the "lush" declared it was "full of nails."

"What you givin' us, Doc?" demanded the "lush," glaring sleepily at the bland old falsifier. "You ain't got the nerve t' say you was 'n opera singer?"

"That's what I was, my boy. I sung one whole season through the south, down as far as New Orleans and back. My stage name was Sidney Dupont. I didn't want to call myself Calvin Horne on the stage because my family was very much opposed to my going into opera."

"They'd heard you sing, probably," observed the "lush."

"The story by our actor friend here," continued "Doc," untouched, "reminds me of an experience I had that season. I was singing in 'The Bohemian Girl,' at one of the larger southern cities, and I had observed for several evenings a strikingly beautiful lady who always leveled her opera glasses at me the moment I came on."

"She wanted t' see all the sights," said the "lush," who was in a quarrelsome mood.

"One night on returning to my dressing room I found there a beautiful cameo in a shell box, and with it was a note telling me to go riding again the next day. I don't know whether I ever told you or not, but I was a great equestrian in those days. I had been in the habit of going out riding every morning, and it was evident that the person writing the

THE RACE-TRACK MAN

note had observed me. Of course I was curious to know who had written, and just to follow the adventure out I went riding the next morning. As I was passing along a shady street in the suburbs I heard a clatter of hoofs behind me, and who should come riding up but the same lady I had seen at the opera house every night."

"Did you give her back the jewelry?" asked the "lush."

"She apologized for the manner of our meeting, but she said she knew of no other way of arranging it. She was one of the most beautiful women I ever met. I had no desire to encourage her, however, as I was engaged to an heiress in Cincinnati at that time. I started to ride beside her when there was a sound of hoofs behind us and up rode a young fellow with a black mustache. He came straight at me and tried to hit me with his riding whip, but I took the whip away from him and demanded an explanation. It seemed that he was her cousin and there was a family arrangement that he should marry her."

"What town's that?" asked the "lush."

"Doc" was a trifle annoyed as he replied: "There are prudential reasons why the town should not be named. This young man turned on his cousin and began to upbraid her,

THE CAPTIVATING ACTOR

but I said: 'Sir, I am willing to accept all the blame of this affair. Don't you dare to say another word to her.' He said he'd call on me later. I knew by that he intended to challenge me. Well, that didn't worry me much. At that time I was a dead shot."

"I c'n take you over to shootin' gallery and beat you fi' times out o' six," said the "lush."

"Did you have to fight?" asked the actor.

"Yes, I winged him in the right arm the first shot. I didn't want to kill him. The young lady never had anything more to

do with him after our adventure and I never saw her again,
although she wrote to me several times. She was a beautiful
woman and very wealthy and
could have selected her own
station in life but I understand
she went into a convent."

"Doc" paused and nodded
his head slowly, to think that
he had been the cause of it all.

The "lush" gazed at "Doc"
unsteadily and then said, with
an effort: "Doc, I'll betcha $2
you can't walk 'cross stage
'thout fallin' off into the bass
drum."

THE IRRESISTIBLE DENTIST

The Barclay Lawn Party

THE Barclays have had enough of lawn parties. Eunice
Barclay began the agitation, but in justice to her it
may be said that the other members of the family readily fell in with the plan. They were ready to welcome anything
that would break the dull monotony of a summer at home.

The Barclays are strict church people, and they shun the
places of summer-night resort where malt drink is served in
large quantities. Mr. and Mrs. Barclay are too old to ride the
bicycle. Eunice and Flora are of the opinion that bicycle riding is not consistent with modest demeanor.

The family is too frugal to waste money at extortionate
summer hotels.

Taking one consideration with another, the Barclays do not
have any variety of summer fun to offer themselves or any
one else. Mrs. Barclay and the girls keep up a course of sleepy
reading, and in the evening the family sits under the trees.

The Barclay home is one of the old-fashioned places on the west side. It has escaped the ravages of improvements, although the neighborhood is changed greatly from what it was in 1874, when the house was built. The ugly factories have sprung up on every side of what was a half-rural spot twenty years ago. Streets that were almost bare of houses have filled with small residences that stand closely side by side.

The Barclay place, with its pillared front porch, the big yard, the tall leafy trees and the clumped rose bushes, became an oasis, but Mr. Barclay held to the place because he couldn't imagine that he would be satisfied anywhere else. There are some good neighbors and old friends two or three blocks to the west, while the church which he helped to build and of which he has been a deacon for years is within easy walking distance.

*   *   *

Mr. Barclay offered no objection to the lawn party. He considered it highly proper that Mrs. Barclay and the girls should entertain their friends so long as there was to be no dancing or other trivial and worldly diversion.

The guests were to assemble at 6:30, and there was to be croquet playing in the area back of the grape-arbor. After that, when it came time for lighting the Chinese lanterns in the front yard, the company was to be seated at the small tables and provided with ice-cream, lemonade and cake. Two artists were to disperse mandolin music. After the serving of the refreshments and in the intervals between the mandolin selections Eunice Barclay was to play a violin solo and the minister was to give some of the dialect recitations for which he had become justly famous with the members of his congregation. The minister had a fetching dialect, which was neither Yankee, German nor Irish, but which he could fasten interchangeably on any kind of a character. Sometimes the minister would insert a dialect story into a sermon, and cause even Mr. Barclay to relax into an unwilling smile.

*   *   *

The lawn party started auspiciously, and the weather was perfect. As the invited guests came straying in Mrs. Barclay received them at the front porch and directed them to the

croquet game back of the grape-arbor. There were but four
players in the game, the other people sitting at the boundaries
and simulating a feverish interest. Flora and the minister were
partners against Mrs. Jennings and Mr. Talbot, who was the
basso of the church choir.

Flora convulsed the company when she exclaimed: "Oh,
Mr. Talbot, I kissed you."

Now, what Flora really meant was that her croquet ball
had kissed the croquet ball belonging to Mr. Talbot, but the
startling wickedness implied in what she said served to pleasantly horrify one and all. Afterward some of the women bit
their lower lips and seemed to feel that they had gone too far
in their laughter, but they were reassured to observe that the
minister was smiling and unruffled.

* * *

The Barclay girls did not realize the full triumph of their
plans until the guests moved in a loose swarm to where the
chairs and tables waited under the soft glow of lanterns. The
mandolin orchestra, literally a mandolin and a guitar, began
to tinkle in the shadow of the porch.

It was still early dusk as the company gayly took possession
of the small tables. The reserve which had marked the opening
of the croquet contest had gradually worn away, and bright
conversational flings went back and forth, from table to table,
many of them aimed at the minister, who was accused of in-
ordinate haste in getting at the ice cream. He laid the blame
on Sister Crandall, and said she had asked him to lead the way
to the refreshments. Mrs. Crandall protested in mock anger,
and Mr. Barclay indulged in hearty laughter at the minister's
cleverness.

* * *

A small boy had his head over the fence and was gaping at
the company. Eunice saw him and his presence annoyed her.
She went over to him and said: "Run away, now; that's a
good little boy." He backed away a few steps, staring at her
sullenly, and when she rejoined the company he again took
up his place against the fence.

The orchestra began to play a medley of variety-theater
airs, and if the music was wasted on the churchly people under

the trees it certainly aroused the neighborhood to the fact that something was happening. The boy at the fence was joined by three others. Two men in their shirt-sleeves walked across from the opposite side of the street, and a little girl, having peeked through the iron fence to take a frenzied observation, started away on a run to arouse her friends and bring them to the scene of festival.

By the time the orchestra had come to a rousing finish of its medley with "Henrietta, Have You Met Her?" there were nine male persons, varying in age from about 6 to 50, lined along the fence, and a moment later no less than six or seven little girls began to mobilize and excitedly point through the fence at the various objects of interest.

The Barclay guests pretended to ignore the outsiders until one of the men at the fence suggested in a loud voice to the mandolin orchestra that it "play something more."

The little girls also began to speculate earnestly as to the quality of the ice cream, and then Flora Barclay began to be annoyed.

"Isn't it dreadful to have these people standing along the fence?" said she. "Don't you suppose they would go away if you asked them to, Mr. Talbot?"

Mr. Talbot is a small man, and it must be that he was never born to wear the purple and command. Still, Mr. Talbot did his best.

He approached the fence, and, addressing the line of outsiders, said: "This is just a little private party, you know, and we'd be much obliged if you wouldn't stand here."

"We ain't hurtin' you," said one of the men. "Go on with your show."

"I know, but the ladies who live here would rather that you—that is, wouldn't congregate here."

The men looked at one another as if they were undecided how to regard Mr. Talbot's appeal, and then one of them said decisively: "I don't like to be drove away from a place while I'm behavin' like a gentleman."

"That's right," mumbled his neighbor.

Mr. Talbot rejoined Flora and said he believed the men would go away presently. But they did not.

IT WAS A PRIVATE LAWN PARTY

The orchestra played again, and the attendance increased. A crowd gathers itself like a rolling snowball. The larger it becomes the greater is its drawing power.

Those who arrived during the second music loudly asked what was happening, and some of them seemed to believe that the music and the display of lanterns had some political meaning.

*   *   *

It is hardly necessary to say that the Barclay guests were in a distressed state of mind. Mr. Talbot was especially worried. Flora Barclay had again asked him to "do something." What could he do but stand on a chair and make a speech to the assemblage?

Imagine his relief when he saw an officer of the law. The policeman had parted a way for himself and was leaning heavily on the fence, a thoughtful expression mantling his face as he listened to the music.

"Please, Mr. Officer," said Mr. Talbot, "can't you get these people to go away? This is a private lawn party."

"Do they bother you?" asked the policeman.

"I should say so."

"I don't know as I've got any right to move 'em."

"Haven't got any right? Of course you've got a right. I appeal to you, sir. What's your number?"

"Oh, well, I'll try to get 'em back," said the policeman.

So he started along the fence, saying: "Come, now, you'll have to move away from here." Every one retired before the majesty of his presence until he came to the man who had previously said that he didn't "want to be drove away." This man began to ask questions of the policeman. "Who owns this sidewalk?" he demanded. "These people here don't own the street, do they? You don't have to do what they say, do you?"

This policeman wasn't a bureau of information or a "questions and answers" department. He took the inquisitive man by the neck and attempted to throttle him. The next moment there was a whirlwind battle.

The timid women under the Barclay trees screamed and ran. Some of the frightened outsiders bounded over the fence to avoid the swing of the policeman's club.

That was practically the end of the lawn party.

As the flustered guests departed a few minutes later a patrol wagon was backed up under the street lamp at the Barclay corner and several hundreds of people watched the loading up of a battered prisoner.

But Eunice and Flora were in their rooms, squirming with hysteria.

Handsome Cyril; or, The Messenger Boy with the Warm Feet

I T IS the intention to present occasionally in this column stories which will appeal to the younger members of the family. These stories will deal, in a realistic style, with life in Chicago, and will be more or less permeated with adventure.

The first of the series bears the title:

HANDSOME CYRIL; OR, THE MESSENGER BOY WITH THE WARM FEET.

Chapter I. The Meeting

"Cyril!"

"Alexander!"

The two messenger boys clasped hands.

It was in Madison Street—that busy thoroughfare where many streams of humanity meet in whirling vortexes.

The afternoon sun lighted up the features of Cyril Smith, the courageous young messenger boy.

His steel-gray eyes glinted as he gazed at his friend and comrade, Alexander. He had regular features and a regular suit of messenger boy clothes.

"I hope you are well, Alexander," he said, a smile lighting up his handsome face.

"Oh, yes; quite well, indeed," responded Alexander.

There was a short silence broken only by the continuous uproar of the street. Then Alexander asked: "Where are you going?"

"I am delivering a death message," replied Cyril, thoughtfully.

"Well, I must ascertain how the baseball game is progressing," said Alexander, and shaking our hero by the hand he moved away.

"Alexander is a strange youth," said Cyril, musingly. "I sometimes think he must be pessimistic."

At that moment the shriek of a woman in agony smote upon his ears.

"What is this," he asked, "a woman in trouble? I must buy an extra and find out what has occasioned this disturbance."

For at that moment the newsboys were shouting the extras which told why the woman had screamed.

Such is life in a great city.

Our hero ran toward the corner.

He saw a beautiful woman struggling in the grasp of a fashionably attired man.

She was a magnificent creature. Great swirls of chestnut hair fell in profusion down her back. The alabaster whiteness of her face served to intensify her beauty. She wore a diamond necklace, diamond earrings, and her lily-white hands flashed with precious jewels.

She turned an appealing look at our hero and said: "Oh, sir, save me!"

Bing!

With a well-directed blow Cyril sent the fashionably dressed man sprawling on the pavement. With the other arm he supported the fainting woman. Then with the other hand he picked up the lace handkerchief which had fallen to the ground and presented it to her with a graceful bow.

"Curse you!" shouted the villain, struggling to his feet. "I shall cause you to rue this deed."

"Coward!" exclaimed Cyril, with a curling lip. "How dare you strike this woman?"

"We shall meet again," said Cyril's antagonist ominously, and with these words he stepped into a carriage and was driven rapidly away.

Our hero now turned his attention to the beautiful creature who reclined in his arms.

"Speak! speak!" he whispered.

Slowly the glorious eyes opened, and then she asked, in tremulous tones: "Where is he?"

"Gone."

"Where to?"

"That I cannot say, madam," responded Cyril, for though he was only a messenger boy he had been taught to be courteous.

"His name is Rudolf Belmont. He must be followed."

"Yes, madam."

"He has taken the papers which prove that I am the real owner of the Belmont estate."

A shudder passed through our hero's frame. Then, recovering himself, he said: "Madam, I will follow that villain and recover the papers."

"Oh, thank you," said she, and for a few minutes she wept softly.

Finally she lifted her tear-stained face and said: "Summon a conveyance and if you are ever in need of a friend come to this number," saying which she gave Cyril an engraved card and offered him a purse containing gold.

"No, madam," said Cyril, with dignity. "I will not take your money. My salary is sufficient to permit me to live in comparative luxury."

The cab which he had summoned arrived at this moment. He assisted his fair companion to enter the cab and then turned his attention to the carriage, which by this time was nearly a mile away.

"That wretch shall not escape me," he said determinedly, and without further ado he started in pursuit of the carriage, which was now a mile and a quarter away.

As he sped along the street he chanced to read the card that the beautiful woman had given him.

It read:

MRS. GERTRUDE FISHER

778 Michigan Boulevard
Second Flat

"Merciful heaven!" he gasped. "My mother!"

Chapter II. Treachery

It will be remembered that we left our hero pursuing the carriage containing Rudolf Belmont.

In a few moments he overtook the equipage and saw Rudolf Belmont enter a tall mansion in 12th Street.

Our hero secreted himself behind a large tree, determined to wait for an opportunity to enter the house.

An hour passed.

Cyril began to feel the pangs of hunger, but he was determined not to abandon his post.

"Ah, sir; you are a handsome youth," said some one behind him, and Cyril turned to behold a tall, handsome stranger.

Our hero acknowledged the compliment with a pleasant bow, and soon he was in conversation with the stranger.

Before departing the stranger gave our hero a box of crackerjack, which he devoured, with a relish, as it had been nearly two hours since he had tasted food.

Scarcely had he finished eating when he felt a strange faintness. Everything seemed to swim before his gaze, as though he were in a natatorium. He had to lean against the tree for support.

Suddenly the truth flashed upon him!

The crackerjack had been drugged.

The whole earth seemed enveloped in darkness. He sank to the ground.

He heard a voice, "Away with him to the basement."

It was the voice of Rudolf Belmont!

Then all was blank.

Chapter III. The River

When our hero recovered consciousness he found himself bound and gagged and being carried along a dark thoroughfare by two rough-looking men.

A drizzle of rain was falling and the sky overhead was inky black.

Cyril heard a voice. It was the voice of Rudolf Belmont. He was speaking to the two rough-looking men. He said: "Do your work well. Then meet me at the Rock Island depot and you shall have your money."

HANDSOME CYRIL

Cyril's heart seemed to stand still!

What were they going to do?

The two ruffians carried him along a dark wall. He heard beneath him the lapping of waves.

He knew the horrible truth.

The river!

The two men spoke in muttered oaths.

Our hero felt himself lifted.

Then he fell, down and down.

Splash!

The dark waters closed above him.

Chapter IV. Alexander to the Rescue

Just as the body disappeared and the two ruffians ran back into the dark thoroughfare a boat shot across the river.

"I thought I heard something drop into the murky river," said Alexander, for it was he. "I suspect foul play."

At that instant he saw the form of a man rise to the water's surface. He reached forth and pulled our hero into the boat. It was the work of a moment to remove the gag and ropes. "Cyril!"

"Alexander! What are you doing here?"

"I was taking a boat ride, when I heard a sound indicating that some one had been thrown into the river. What does it mean?"

"Quick! I have no time to tell now. We must get to the Rock Island depot. Have you your revolvers with you?"

"Yes," said Alexander, producing his trusty weapons and inspecting them carefully.

"Then come with me, for we have not a moment to spare."

With one strong pull the boat reached the shore. Our hero hastened up the bank, closely followed by Alexander, and ran toward the Rock Island depot.

Just as our hero and his companion dashed into the train shed a man with a slouch hat pulled down over his face ran for a train which was slowly moving out of the station.

That man was Rudolf Belmont!

CHAPTER V. THWARTED

Our hero, it will be recalled, saw Rudolf Belmont running to catch the train. He redoubled his speed.

As Rudolf Belmont swung on the last platform, Cyril followed closely.

He seized the object of his pursuit. They grappled and fell from the train.

Our hero fell underneath. "Curse you; though you had nine lives, like a cat, your time has come now," hissed Rudolf Belmont, drawing a revolver and pointing it at our hero's head.

At that instant a pistol-shot rang out and Rudolf Belmont emitted a cry of pain.

The revolver fell from his hand.

The faithful Alexander had put a bullet through the villain's hand.

The next instant Cyril was on his feet and Rudolf Belmont was in the custody of a stalwart policeman.

"You came at an opportune moment," said our hero, with a quiet smile, as he shook hands with Alexander. Then, turning to the policeman, he said: "Your prisoner has in his possession certain papers which I wish to secure, after which you may take him to prison."

The policeman touched his cap respectfully and Cyril removed the bundle of papers from Rudolf Belmont's inner pocket.

Rudolf Belmont was led away, cursing.

CHAPTER VI. UNITED

"Mother!"

"Cyril!"

It was indeed a happy evening at the magnificent home in Michigan Boulevard.

"I have brought you the papers, mother," said Cyril modestly.

"My brave boy!" she murmured, with pardonable pride. "We must not forget your friend, who so bravely came to your succor," and she handed Alexander a $1,000 note.

Little remains to be told. Rudolf Belmont served a life-sentence in Joliet. Cyril Smith lives happily with his mother, Mrs. Fisher, who is as young and beautiful as ever. Often, on pleasant evenings, they entertain at dinner a thoughtful man with a brown mustache and genteel suit of dark material. That man is a member of the Civic federation, but if we look again we will see that he is none other than our old friend, Alexander.

Clarence Allen, the Hypnotic Boy Journalist

THIS week's Nursery tale has the title: Clarence Allen, the Hypnotic Boy Journalist, or the Mysterious Disappearance of the United States Government Bonds.

CHAPTER I. TO WORK!

It was in the office of the Chicago Daily Beacon! J. Windsor Frost, the editor, sat in his palatial apartment, where the light fell softly through stained-glass windows and the walls were tastefully decorated with articles of bric-a-brac and vertu.

J. Windsor Frost was a handsome man and a neat diamond flashed in his shirt front.

Suddenly he aroused himself and an expectant smile came to his face.

A manly youth 12 years of age entered the room and stood facing the great editor. He had a strikingly handsome face and an eagle eye. On his breast glittered a star, indicating that he was a representative of the press. A notebook and a well-sharpened lead pencil protruded from his breast pocket.

This is our first view of Clarence Allen, the hypnotic boy journalist.

"Ah, you have come," said the great editor.

"Yes, Mr. Frost, I am always ready to answer the call of duty," said our hero, modestly.

Without further ado the great editor handed the following clipping to the boy journalist:

"GREAT EXCITEMENT

"Our city was thrown into a fever of excitement last evening by the announcement that Erastus Hare, one of our oldest and most respected citizens, had been robbed of $37,000 worth of United States government bonds by some unknown miscreant. The culprit entered Mr. Hare's bedroom through a window and attacked our old friend and subscriber with a knife. Afterward he took the bonds and escaped. As we go to press he has not been caught. Little knots of men may be seen standing on the corners discussing the topic in low tones. Great excitement prevails."

"The item you have just read was printed in this morning's Beacon," said J. Windsor Frost. "This is the greatest criminal case that ever came under my observation. Can you find the thief?"

"I can," replied Clarence, and, drawing his notebook, he hastily made a few notes.

At that moment he heard a suspicious noise outside the window. He ran to see what could have been the cause.

A masked man was rapidly descending to the ground by means of a rope.

They had been overheard.

CHAPTER II. THE FOOTPRINT

After providing himself with a dark-lantern and other needful articles, Clarence Allen, the hypnotic boy journalist, summoned a carriage and was driven rapidly to the Hare mansion.

Here all was confusion.

Our hero took immediate charge of the premises and made a minute examination of the room in which the assault had taken place. He measured the bedstead, counted the pictures and cut a small strip out of the carpet. Afterward he went outside and examined the ground. Suddenly he saw a deep footprint in the soft earth.

"Aha!" said he.

Taking the necessary articles from his pocket, he made a plaster cast of the footprints.

"I have a clew," said he, and, drawing his notebook, he made a few notes.

At that moment a bullet whistled by his head!

Chapter III. Desperate

With Clarence Allen to think was to act.

When the deadly bullet sped by his head he knew that the thieves had recognized him as a representative of the press, probably because of the star on his coat.

Without further ado he rushed to a telephone and called up the office of the Daily Beacon and expressed a wish to converse with J. Windsor Frost, the great editor.

"Hello!"

"Hello!"

"Who is this?"

"This is J. Windsor Frost, the editor. And you?"

"I am Clarence Allen, the hypnotic boy journalist. I desire—"

But J. Windsor Frost heard no more.

The wire had been cut.

Chapter IV. Quick Work

What was our hero to do?

For a moment only he hesitated. Then he rushed to the window.

It was thirty feet to the ground below.

A trolley car was approaching.

"I have no time to spare," he exclaimed, and jumped to the pavement.

Leaping to the trolley car he pushed the motorman aside, and, seizing the crank, sent the car flying along the street at a speed of twenty-five miles an hour.

The conductor of the car attempted to pull him away. With a well-directed blow our hero sent him flying.

Women passengers shrieked in terror and the street was in a panic.

Little cared Clarence Allen, the hypnotic boy journalist.

Suddenly applying the brake in front of the office of the Daily Beacon, he ran wildly into the office of J. Windsor

CLARENCE ALLEN

Frost and showed him what he had written in his note book.

"Great heavens!" exclaimed the great editor. "And now what do you propose doing?"

Clarence's eyes flashed as he replied: "I am going to put the bloodhounds on the trail!"

Chapter V. The Stone House

The Daily Beacon, like all other great newspapers, had a pack of genuine Siberian bloodhounds, to be used for tracking criminals.

Our hero, after making out an expense account, selected two of the largest and fiercest bloodhounds and showed them the plaster cast of the footprint which he had taken at the Hare residence.

The intelligent animals knew at a glance what was expected of them, and in a few moments they were on the scent, followed by our alert young hero, Clarence Allen, the hypnotic boy journalist, who carried a revolver tightly clenched in his right hand.

For nearly an hour no one spoke.

Then the dogs stopped in front of an old stone house, with tall elms surrounding it.

"This is the place," said Clarence Allen, concealing himself in a thicket to await developments.

After a few moments he chanced to look around, and his blood froze in his veins.

Some one had stolen the dogs!

Chapter VI. Hypnotized

It will be remembered that we left our hero concealed in the thicket.

He remained here for some time, and then, making sure that he had eluded his pursuers, he ventured forth and made a hasty examination of the old stone house.

It was a dark night and the wind rustled through the old elm trees.

Only one window was lighted, and it was on the second floor.

"They are there," said our hero, and, producing a coil of

rope with a hook in the end of it, he made a fastening to the ledge of the second-story window and climbed up until he could peer in at the window.

Three bearded men were sitting at a table talking in hoarse tones. Our hero felt a thrill when he heard his own name mentioned.

"It is understood, then," said the leader, "that we meet an hour from now at the blasted oak to divide the money."

" 'Tis well," said the other two.

"And then we will leave this country forever."

"Hold!" cried a stentorian voice, and, with a crashing of glass, Clarence Allen, the hypnotic boy journalist, leaped through the window and confronted them.

For a moment they were surprised, and then with fearful oaths they drew their weapons.

"Your time has come," snarled the leader of the gang.

Three revolvers were pointed straight at our intrepid young hero!

Could aught save him?

Clarence Allen did not flinch.

Gazing steadily at the leader of the band, he lifted his hands and moved them gently through the air.

The ruffian fell backward to the floor and the weapon dropped from his palsied hand.

Our hero turned quickly to the two other villains, who stood in mute surprise.

It was the work of a moment to put them under the hypnotic influence and take away their weapons.

"At last!" he said, and taking out his book he made full notes of the proceeding.

CHAPTER VII. JUSTICE

Having hypnotized the villains, it was an easy task for our hero to learn from the leader of the band the hiding place of the stolen bonds. They were found under a loose tiling in the fireplace and restored to their owner, who speedily recovered from his injuries.

Little remains to be told.

The Daily Beacon printed a half-column account, under

glaring head-lines, of the capture of the desperadoes by the hypnotic boy journalist.

As for the thieves, they were promptly sent to prison on the testimony of our hero, who achieved a great reputation by his courageous conduct and who was soon after admitted to membership in the League of American Wheelmen, a distinction which few merit and a glory which few achieve.

[THE END]

Rollo Johnson, the Boy Inventor

IT HAVING been urged that preceding tales for very small children were somewhat sensational in character and not calculated to impress any useful lesson on the juvenile mind, the story for this week will be made to contain some information in regard to mechanics. Perhaps it will excite children to attempt construction of useful and intricate mechanisms. The title of the story will be: Rollo Johnson, the Boy Inventor; or, The Demon Bicycle and Its Daring Rider.

CHAPTER I. THE SECRET

"At last!"

Rollo Johnson arose from his work as he gave vent to the above.

His friend, Paul Jefferson, who stood by his side, asked: "Are you sure you have succeeded?"

"Yes," replied Rollo, a proud flush coming to his cheek. "With this bicycle I am quite sure that I can make the fastest time that has ever been made."

Well might our hero flush, for now, at the age of 8 he had accomplished what Edison had failed to do. He had built a bicycle to be operated by electricity!

Standing in his workshop with Paul Jefferson by his side, he explained in a few words the secret of his invention.

He had filled the tubing with compacted batteries and had

joined them together by copper wires, thus utilizing the vac-
uum. At the point in the ball-bearing axle where the currents
conveyed, a flexo-lever had been placed, with the ohms oper-
ating directly on the hub. By this contrivance our hero was
enabled to use a gearing of 282, as easily as another rider
would use 68 or 72.

"It is indeed wonderful," said Paul Jefferson. "After four
years of incessant toil, you are to be rewarded."

"Yes," replied Rollo, musingly. "To-morrow I shall win
the mile championship on my wheel and then I will be
famous."

A grating laugh startled them.

They turned and beheld Hector Legrand, the millionaire
and capitalist.

A cold and cruel smile flitted across his face.

"Rollo Johnson, I heard the statement you just made,"
said he, insultingly. "If you dare to place this invention on
the market, you will ruin me and mine, and I will kill you."

Our hero laughed defiantly. With a muttered curse Hector
Legrand drew a dagger and sprang at our hero.

As he did so, Rollo stepped quickly backward and touched
an electric button connected with galvanic plates under the
floor.

With a maniacal shriek, Hector Legrand fell to the floor
and lay there quivering.

Chapter II. The Race

Rollo Johnson well knew that his enemies were desperate
and accordingly he had taken every precaution.

He had imparted the electric shock to Hector Legrand at
the critical moment, for the millionaire's dagger was about
to be imbedded in our hero's breast.

When Hector Legrand recovered from the shock he left the
place, much crestfallen.

Rollo bade Paul Jefferson an affectionate good-night and
soon after retired, for he wished to be well rested in anticipa-
tion of the great race for the championship of America.

Next morning he arose bright and early and proceeded to
the race-track, where thousands had already assembled.

It was known that our hero was the inventor of the demon bicycle and there was a buzz of wonder and admiration as Rollo came upon the track, attired in a neat costume of blue. To all appearances his wheel was the same as those used by the other riders.

Hooper, the favorite in the race, approached our hero and said, tauntingly: "You are a mere stripling, and it is presumptuous of you to enter the championship race."

"I will bide my time," said Rollo, for he was a gentleman at heart.

A moment later the riders in the championship race were called to the tape and the word "go" was given.

Eight wheels flashed away in the sunlight.

Hooper was leading, Gardiner was second and Smikels was third. Our hero was last of all, pursuing an even pace, a smile lighting up his pale and handsome face.

At the quarter-mile he was ten lengths behind.

At the half he seemed hopelessly beaten.

Suddenly there was a shout.

Rollo had touched the button and released the powerful current.

His wheel shot forward like a flash of lightning.

He passed the other riders in a twinkling.

The amphitheater rang with wild cheers. He had won by twenty lengths!

The last half-mile had been made in 14 seconds!

Chapter III. The Plans

With a light heart, Rollo returned home, having won the championship of America.

As he entered the house a sad sight presented itself.

His father and mother and his elder brother Claude were seated in the parlor weeping bitterly.

"Why so sad on this day when all should be joy?" asked our hero.

"Alas!" replied his mother, kissing him affectionately, "some one has stolen the plans."

"Stolen the plans!" he gasped.

"Yes, Rollo; the only copy in existence was left lying on

the table in your work-shop, and some miscreant has pur-
loined it."

"If I do not recover those plans my four years of investigation will have been in vain," said Rollo, thoughtfully.

"What do you purpose doing?" asked his father, wiping
his eyes.

"I will follow the thieves to the world's end!" exclaimed
Rollo, and, leaping on his demon bicycle, he rode away like
the wind!

Chapter IV. The River

It was dusk.

In a dingy basement near the murky Chicago River Hector
Legrand sat at a table with four swarthy men, heavily
armed.

Before them on the table were the plans for Rollo Johnson's demon bicycle. They were conversing in hoarse tones.

"I have the plans," said Hector Legrand, "but my revenge
is not yet complete. The boy must be put out of the way."

His four companions growled fiercely.

At that instant a bolt of lightning shot across the room.
There was a blinding flash, and the five men fell from their
chairs stunned by the shock.

Rollo Johnson had crept down the stairway and turned
upon them the full force of his portable automo-battery!

As the villains struggled to their feet they saw our hero
disappearing up the stairway. He had captured the plans.

With shrieks and curses they drew their weapons and pursued him.

Rollo mounted his wheel and dashed southward.

A dozen bullets whizzed by him.

He looked ahead.

The street along which he was flying led to the open river!

There was no escape to right or left!

Behind him were the murderous pursuers!

Ahead of him yawned the dark stream!

What was he to do?

ROLLO JOHNSON

Chapter V. The Escape

Hector Legrand and his villainous associates emitted yells of triumph when they saw our hero riding madly toward the open river.

Rollo heard their demoniacal cries and he knew that capture meant certain death.

Pressing the electric button on his wheel, he flew forward at a terrific speed.

At the river's brink he lifted his front wheel.

The bicycle shot into the air with the swiftness of an arrow.

Bang! Bang! Bang! went the revolvers.

Then there were howls of rage.

Rollo had landed safely on the other side.

Chapter VI. Retribution

After his escape from the would-be assassins Rollo's first act was to notify the police of Hector Legrand's attempt to steal the plans.

The police went to Hector Legrand's mansion to arrest him, but he had escaped, and was never again seen in Chicago.

His four associates were soon after arrested on another charge and sent to prison for life. Such is the fate of evil-doers.

As for Rollo Johnson, he took his plans home and had his mother put them in a safe place.

Little remains to be told.

Our hero received $1,000,000 for his invention and achieved just fame, but he did not relinquish his study, and every day he may be seen in his work-shop inventing some useful article for the betterment of mankind.

[The End]

The Fable of Sister Mae

ONCE there were two Sis-ters. They lived in Chi-ca-go. One was a Plain Girl, but she had a Good Heart. She was stu-di-ous and took first Hon-ors at the Gram-mar School.

She cared more for the Graces of Mind than she did for mere Out-ward Show. Her Sis-ter was a Friv-o-lous Girl. She cared lit-tle for Books, seem-ing to find more De-light in Bangs, Shirt Waists and Trin-kets of Gold and Sil-ver. This Sis-ter was fair to look up-on. In fact, it was a Pip-pin. But, as we have said be-fore, she was short on Men-tal-i-ty. Now when it came Time for these two Girls to seek Em-ploy-ment (for they were not richly en-dowed with the World's Goods), the Good Girl found work in a Hat Fac-to-ry. All she had to do was to sew Bands in Hats and she re-ceived for her services the Sum of Three Dol-lars per Week.

The Friv-o-lous Girl who had naught to com-mend her except a Beauty which fad-eth, be-came a Cashier in a Quick Lunch Es-tab-lish-ment and the Pa-tron-age in-creased largely. She chewed Gum and said "Ain't," but she be-came pop-u-lar just the same. The Men who sat at the Count-er eat-ing Sink-ers and Cocoa-nut Pie remarked one to an-other that she was all right. The Em-ployer of ad-ja-cent Es-tab-lish-ments came oft-en to have Bills changed.

Cus-tom-ers lin-gered aft-er hav-ing paid their checks, and
some spoke of The-a-ter Tickets and oth-ers spoke of Bicycle Rides.

And her Pic-ture was on many a But-ton. When she had
seen the Bunch she se-lect-ed a Young Man who owned a
Buck-et Shop. He was not as nice as the Young Men she
had read a-bout in the Ber-tha Clay Nov-els, but he was
Mak-ing the Money. So they were mar-ried and moved in-to
a Flat. She bought a Dog and a Thumb Ring and she had
her Hair bleached. Al-so, when she went out of Town she
had her name in the Pa-pers. She for-got the Price of Lem-on
Me-ringue and be-gan to be in-ter-ested in Vog-ner's Music.

Now when Wheat went to a Dol-lar her Hus-band didn't
do a Thing. She be-gan to feel that Life wasn't worth liv-ing
unless there was Cham-pagne on the Ice, and the Smell of
Cooking made her faint. Fur-ther-more, she wished to move
out of the Flat be-cause in a Flat One can-not be sure of
One's Neigh-bors. So She and her Hus-band moved into a
House and en-gaged a Coached-man named James, and She
had her Nose-glasses mounted on a Stick and couldn't see
where the Work-ing Classes came in.

Like-wise She be-gan to read Rich-ard Hard-ing Davis,
and she as-sem-bled the Pho-to-graphs of Her-bert Kel-cey,
E. V. Soth-ern, Mau-rice Barry-more, James K. Hack-ett,

Henry Mil-ler, Robert Hil-liard and John Drew, and after Eight Les-sons she could play "All Coons Look A-like to Me" on the Grand Piano. Hav-ing these ac-com-plish-ments she be-gan to won-der why the Doors of So-ciety did not open to her.

She went to the The-a-ter quite oft-en and a Box was none too good. The Hus-band oft-en wore a real Dress Suit, with a large sin-gle Dia-mond on his Shirt Front to show that he was a Prom-i-nent Cit-i-zen. She learned to talk gay-ly in the Box with-out be-ing a-ware of the Fact that Oth-er Peo-ple were pres-ent, and oft-en the Boys in the Gal-lery would look down and speak of her as the Real Thing.

Her Hus-band paid $12 for the Cut and had her Pic-ture put into the South-west Di-vi-sion So-ci-ety News with a line under-neath say-ing that she was a So-ci-ety Lead-er. She be-lieved it and sent Cop-ies to her Rela-tives in dis-tant States. Al-though she was get-ting on, she was not too Proud to re-mem-ber her Kin un-der the Cir-cum-stances.

Nei-ther did she for-get her Sis-ter at the Hat Fac-to-ry. Her Sis-ter was a Good Wom-an and was still get-ting her Three per Week. But the Good Sis-ter gave up her Job at the Hat Fac-to-ry and ac-cept-ed a po-si-tion as Cook for the Friv-o-lous Sis-ter. She re-ceived Six Dol-lars per Week, which shows that if One is Hon-est and In-dus-tri-ous One will sure-ly Suc-ceed in Time.

Moral—Never de-spise the Poor.

An Incident in the "Pansy"

THE "PANSY" saloon is directly across the street from the entrance to Sembrich's hall, where the Ludolfia Pleasure club gave its masquerade ball. "Matty" Swinton, Jimmy Flynn, "Butch" Hanton and "Fatty" El-dridge were sitting in the "Pansy" playing seven-up around a smeary table as the maskers arrived.

A masquerade ball at Sembrich's hall is worth going to see. It puts a few hours of actual splendor into the lives of hard-

working young men and young women. The laundry girl
reigns for one night as Marie Antoinette or else as the fated
Queen of Scots. The girls employed at the Southwest Division Louvre dry-goods store forget their gingham aprons,
their uniform dress and the wearisome clicking of the cash
trolley, for they are transformed
into flower girls, ladies of the
court, senoritas, Japanese beauties and what not that is be-
spangled and beautiful

There is a little shop just around
the corner from Sembrich's hall,
at which masquerade costumes
of the most astounding brilliancy
may be secured for a small consideration.

The young men seem to prefer
comic parts. They come to the
ball in the fantastic clothes of
harlequins, clowns, burlesque
German and Irish emigrants or
else as gaudy negro minstrels.
When they put on these fancy

"BUTCH"

costumes they seem to put on the carnival spirit, too, for the
gayety at a Sembrich hall masquerade is simply boisterous.
These young men, ordinarily shy and diffident in the presence
of young women, cavort and dance, beat one another with
slap-sticks, indulge in crazy pantomime and pay exaggerated
devotion to the masked beauties.

It must be confessed, also, that the girls enter into the
romp with no reserve of maidenly dignity. For John Swansen, the grocer's clerk, to put his arm around Hilda Jensen,
the little bonnet-trimmer, would be a subject of scandal, but
for the gallant bull-fighter to caress the senorita is mere ac-
curacy of romance and no one is shocked.

Be assured, too, that John Swansen and all the meek and
timorous young men have now become the most audacious
cavaliers. The young men of to-day in their somber store
clothes still have the fine manners and chivalry of the mid-

dle ages in their hearts, for when the opportunity comes, as at Sembrich's hall, they put on doublet and hose, velvet jackets, long tan boots, plumed hats, gauntlets, ruffled waists, chain armor, jeweled belts and hilts. Spanish cloaks, military helmets, Elizabethan ruffs and all the other finery to be rented at the little shop around the corner.

Certainly a masquerade ball at Sembrich's hall is worth going to see. One will be pleasantly amazed to find such a magnificent pageant so near the "Pansy" saloon, which fronts on a muddy street and stands in a row of hideously plain and commonplace wooden streets. Sembrich's building, the neighborhood pride, is a large box made of bricks.

* * *

"Matty" Swinton, Jimmy Flynn, "Butch" Hanton and "Fatty" Eldridge turned from their cards occasionally to

look at another noisy group of maskers passing up the lighted stairway across the street.

"They're goin' to have a great push over there to-night." said "Fatty."

"Ye-ah," said "Butch" Hanton, studying his cards. "I'm goin' over presently, and if it don't suit me I think I'll stop it."

"You'd better keep away," remarked "Matty" Swinton. "I seen you try to stop somethin' once before."

"Yes, you must like to ride in them wagons," put in the bartender, whose name was Joe.

Every one except "Butch" had to laugh. The bartender's reference to the "wagons" recalled the fact that "Butch" had been taken to the station one night for attempting to

JIMMY FLYNN

force his way into a wedding reception.

"I had my peaches that night," said "Butch." "They'll never land me that way again."

"Go on and play," growled Jimmy Flynn.

The four card-players in the "Pansy" were not the kind of young men to put on fancy costumes and go to masquerade parties. They were too hardened and experienced to care for such childish diversions, and they were glad of it.

They felt a superiority over the young fellows who acted as escorts to the laundry girls and those who worked at the Louvre. They would stand in front of the "Pansy" and watch the couples pass by and would feel a sort of malicious pity for them. They disliked the young men because of their guarded conduct and attempts at politeness.

CHRIS

The "Pansy" card-players knew that the young men over in Sembrich's hall considered themselves more decent and more worthy than any young men who loafed in saloons all the time and said insulting things to the working girls who passed. No wonder "Butch" and his fellows hated the masqueraders.

Think of your own hatred for some irritating wretch who complacently believes that he is your superior!

* * *

The door opened and "Butch" Hanton cursed fervently as he saw two clowns enter. They wore baggy suits of spotted design and little conical hats. Their faces were powdered and streaked. One was a large man, and he was especially ridiculous in such a costume.

"Hello, Choe," he shouted, and there was a rattling German guttural in his voice. "Let us haf two peers."

"Good crowd over there to-night?" asked the bartender.

"Fine—ef'rybody hafing a goot time."

The four card-players had dropped their cards and were gazing at the two strange visitors. Evidently their contempt was too deep for expression.

The two clowns drank their beer. The larger one benevolently laid his hand on the shoulder of the other and then began to sing. To the unaccustomed ear it sounded thus, and they did it with tremendous vigor:

> Hi-lee! Hi-lo!
> Hi-lee! Hi-lo!
> By untz gates immer,
> Gay-linger, Gay-schllimmer,
> Hi-lee! Hi-lo!
> Hi-lee! Hi-lo!
> By untz gates immer ve-zo!

As they concluded the last line "Butch" Hanton threw a piece of chalk (used for marking scores) and hit the larger clown on the ear. The big fellow turned to the four at the table and bowed. "Goot shot, poys," he said. "Come and haf a drink."

The four exchanged sullen glances and did not move.

"You fellows ain't stopped, have you?" asked Joe. "Come up and have something on Chris. Chris, these boys are all friends of mine. Shake hands with 'em."

Chris extended his hand toward Jimmy Flynn, who responded unwillingly.

"Say! Here!" Jimmy exclaimed, as he felt something close on his hand until the bones ground together.

Chris released him and seized "Butch" by the hand.

"For God's sake!" gasped "Butch," crouching half-way to the floor. With a backward leap he released his hand and rubbed it, while he chewed his lip with pain.

Chris started toward "Matty," who said "Nix! Nix!" as if in anger, and shifted toward the head of the bar.

"You big sucker, what are you tryin' to do?" demanded "Butch," glaring at the clown.

Chris smiled horribly through the chalk and said: "Ho! Sho! It is all in fun. You shouldt not get mat."

"Don't get sore about a little thing like that," said Joe, who was setting the drinks along the bar.

"I don't like them funny plays," said "Butch."

"Go on, Chris, and show him how well you can lift," said Joe, after the drinks had been disposed of.

"No you don't, objected "Butch," and he backed away.

"It iss all right," urged Chris, following him up. "It will not hurt."

He reached forward suddenly and caught "Butch" by the shoulder.

"Stant still," he said.

"Naw—naw."

"Go on!" put in the bartender, "Chris won't hurt you."

"Butch" looked sheepishly at the others, and

JOE

then, following directions, he stiffened himself and allowed Chris to take hold of him by the ankles and lift him into the air, very slowly, until his feet were on a level with the card table.

"Ah-h-h-h-h-h!" said Joe, admiringly.

Chris lowered his man a few inches, and then, with a sudden upward movement, he tossed "Butch" three feet or more toward the ceiling—as he would have tossed a ten-pound bell.

"Butch" fell on all fours and scrambled to his feet. Joe was doubled over behind the bar, screaming with laughter. The others were laughing, too—even Chris, who stood a few feet away, with his big shoulders heaving under the spotted suit.

"I won't stand for it!" exclaimed "Butch," rushing toward the big German. "Fatty" grabbed him by the arm and said: "Aw, come off! Don't start nothin'."

"I let no funny guy do that to me."

"On the dead, I never see a man get sore so quick," said Joe, his eyes full of tears from the attack of laughter. "Chris meant it in fun—huh, Chris?"

"Sure. All in fun. Goot-by, Choe."

The two clowns went out the front way, and Joe gave another howl of laughter.

"You put that guy on to me!" said "Butch," who was hot and nervous.

"What you talkin' about? He done that all in fun. Do you know him? Chris Schleger— the best weight-lifter on the west side. I seen him beat a professional one night. You can't tell about a guy just becuz you see him in one o' them funny suits."

"The Dutchman's all right," said Jimmy Flynn, and he laughed. Then all of them laughed—all except "Butch."

The Old Spelling School

I'M AFRAID there isn't going to be much sleighing," said the lightning dentist, as he joined the group at the Alfalfa European Hotel and kicked the steam radiator to get the loose slush off his shoes.

"What difference does that make to you?" asked the "lush," who was sober and melancholy. "If we had snow a foot deep you couldn't go sleigh-riding; you can't afford to pay $8 a minute for a cutter, can you? The only winter sport that you can get dead cheap in Chicago is a skate."

"Well, I don't know," said the dentist, seating himself and taking a cigar from a red leather case with a silver clasp. "I like to see good sleighing, whether I can go out myself or not." He snipped off the end of the cigar and remarked to the group, "I'm sorry this is the last one."

As it was well known that the dentist never bought more than one cigar at a time, his apology was received with polite silence. He would sometimes buy a cigar, put it in the case, walk twenty feet, take out the case and remove the cigar.

The dentist was a walking storehouse. He had a corkscrew and a patent nail-cleaner attached to his knife. He carried a folding toothpick, a card case, a small dictionary, a pocket-comb, a cigar-clipper, a pair of scissors and a letter-opener. His keys he kept in a hip-pocket anchored to a chain which looped around and fastened to a trousers button in front. It was his practice to pull out these useful articles and fondle them while engaged in conversation.

*   *   *

"Yes, sir, I like to see sleighing," continued the dentist. "It makes me think of the time when a crowd of us boys and girls used to pile into a bobsled and ride over to McKee's Tavern. That was about eight miles from home, straight out on the Langdon Pike. Why, we've gone out there some nights when it was colder than sin. But we never cared. Great Scott! We'd get down in the straw under the buffalo robes and snuggle up and have more fun than you could shake a stick at—sing and whoop and yell all the way out there."

"Somebody got hugged once or twice, too, I guess," said the "lush," with a mere flicker of a smile.

"Oh, well, I think I've reached once or twice and found another man's arm already there."

"You wouldn't let a little thing like that discourage you, would you?" asked "Doc" Horne, looking up and taking a sudden interest in the talk.

"Certainly not," replied the dentist, curling his mustache at the ends and chuckling modestly. "Those were great times. Yes, sir, that was when a man could have a good time without spending a dollar every time he turned around. We used to take oysters and crackers out with us and along about midnight, when we had all danced ourselves black in the face, we'd have an oyster supper. Why, we used to have more fun in one night than I can have now in a month. I'll bet

you went to many an oyster supper when you were a boy,
Doc."

"If you'll stop and think a minute you'll probably realize
that oysters didn't grow on trees out west here forty or fifty
years ago," said "Doc," with a quiet wink at the "lush." "I
went to as many parties as any young fellow in the state of
Ohio, but I had to get along without oysters. Still, roast
young pig and some wild game did pretty well as a substitute."

"Gee! I should say so," remarked the bicycle salesman,
with enthusiasm.

"You young men want to remember that we didn't have
as many railroads in those days," continued "Doc." "Every
neighborhood had to rely for subsistence very largely on
what it could produce. Still, I don't know that we suffered
any. Those were great days."

"Yes, indeed, doctor," said the book-agent, who had not
yet dared to use the familiar title. "What you say reminds
me of the lines:
" 'Backward, turn backward, O Time in your flight,
    And make me a boy again, just for to-night.' "

"That's great," said the bicycle youth. "Who is that by?"

"And then there's another thing that always struck me as
being very pretty," said the book-agent, dodging the question addressed to him. "It's that
" 'How dear to my heart are the scenes of my childhood,
    When fond recollection presents them to view.' "

"That is mighty purty," said the bicycle youth. "Let's
sing it. I guess we all know it."

"Nix! Nix!" said the "lush," authoritatively. "I've got
trouble enough now."

*　　*　　*

"Well, as I was saying, when I was 8 years old I could spell
down the school. My teacher, an eastern man named Fletcher,
began to brag about what I could do, and so the school in
the adjoining district sent over a challenge. I went over there
and spelled down the row in about ten minutes. They didn't
have as good spellers as some I had beaten right in our own
school. After that we had a good many spelling-bees in the
evening. Everybody could compete at these evening meet-

"BEGAN TO ATTRACT SOME ATTENTION WHEN I WAS 8 YEARS OLD"

ings—old folks and all. Well, it was just the same thing over, night after night. We'd run along for an hour or so, and then when we got over at the back of Webster's Complete Speller, and the fight had dwindled down to about six of us, Mr. Fletcher, the teacher, would begin to give out the hardest ones he could find, and I'd be left alone. I remember one night, after I'd spelled the others down, they put the teacher up against me, and we spelled back and forth there until the people couldn't think of any more words to give us. That Fletcher was a remarkable man—remarkable. He became very prominent afterward."

"I never was much of a speller," said the bicycle youth, sadly.

*   *   *

"The best speller in the adjoining county was a teacher who lived at Marion's Grove," resumed "Doc." "He had laid out everybody in his part of the country, and finally, when he heard of the boy wonder, as they called me, he drove all the way over to our schoolhouse one night to get my scalp. Well, I'll declare," and "Doc" had to stop and shake his head and laugh softly. "That was a great night. The schoolhouse was packed. Instead of starting in with the whole crowd, they just stood the two of us up and let us go at it. What do you think was the word he missed—a comparatively easy one, too?"

"I don't know. What was it?" asked the dentist.

"Peripateticism."

"That may be easy for you, 'Doc,' but I never heard it before. How do you spell it?"

"That isn't so hard."

"Well, how do you spell it?"

"Wait a minute," interrupted the "lush." "Where's a dictionary?"

"I've got a small one here," said the dentist.

"No, we want a big one. I'll get Steve's. He keeps one in there to decide bets." So saying, the "lush" hurried away to the bar, while "Doc" leaned back and contemplatively bit at his cigar.

After the "lush" had returned and hunted up the place in the book, he asked: "How did you say that was spelled, 'Doc'?"

"You've got it there, haven't you?"

"Yes, but I want to be sure the dictionary has it right."

This remark appeared to nettle "Doc," who said: "Oh, very well, sir. The word is spelled 'p-e-r-i-p-a-t-e-t-a-c-i-s-m.'"

"Not this year. It's 't-i-c-i-s-m.'"

"Well, I said 't-i,' didn't I?"

"You did not. You said 't-a.'"

"Well, I meant 't-i.'"

The "lush" said nothing. He slung the dictionary around under his arm and started for the bar, whistling "Razzle-Dazzle."

The "Lush" Tries and Fails

I UNDERSTAND that those southern floods are still rising," said the lightning dentist to his friends of the Alfalfa European Hotel. "If the rivers get much higher there'll be some terrible damage done."

"If they had built the Mississippi levees as I told them to, long before the war, they wouldn't be washed away every year," said "Doc" Horne.

"You've been through that flood country, have you 'Doc'?" asked the "lush."

"As often as you have fingers and toes," replied "Doc." "I think it was in 1857 that I went out from Cairo in charge of a relief expedition, and the river was so high that, as far as you could see in any direction, nothing but tree tops and the roofs of houses showed above the water."

"Those floods must be awful," said the bicycle salesman, with a serious shake of the head.

* * *

"My uncle didn't think so," said the "lush," with a palpable wink at the lightning dentist. "My uncle was living down south for his health. He had a small house a short distance from Vicksburg. He occupied an upper room, and his two negro servants slept downstairs. Well, when the flood season came his neighbors were uneasy, and some of them moved away, but he was never much of a man to worry about trouble until it actually came. He believed that the levee was strong enough to hold the current, and he said that even if there was an overflow it wouldn't do any more harm than dampen his front yard. He took his regular sleep every night, and didn't fret. Now what do you think? This will interest you, 'Doc.'"

"WE COULDN'T SAVE HIM"

"Yes?" said "Doc," inquiringly.

"Yes, sir, he awoke one morning and saw a tree just outside his window. He didn't know what to make of it. There
hadn't been any tree there the night before. He began to
think that some one had worked a miracle on him, so he got
up and looked out of the window, and there was a whole

clump of timber in front of him, and the whole country, as far as he could see, was inundated. You see, the levee had broken during the night and flooded the country for miles. The water simply lifted my uncle's house off of its wooden foundation and floated it a half-mile or so, and lodged it against this patch of timber. He slept through it all."

"Were the negro servants drowned?" asked the bicycle youth.

"No; they ran away. They were so frightened they didn't even stop to arouse my uncle, and he always said he was glad they hadn't aroused him, because he hated to get up in the night. If I remember it right, the two servants were found in a cottonwood tree the next day. It may have been some other kind of a tree, but I think it was a cottonwood."

"Your uncle must have had a hard time getting his house back to where it belonged," suggested the bicycle salesman.

"I suppose he waited until there was another flood, and then let it float back," said the dentist.

"Now, here; this is right—what I'm telling you," said the "lush," who pretended to resent these interruptions. "He didn't have to move the house at all. The new location over by the patch of timber suited him so well that he bought the land, had a new foundation put under the house, and it so happened that the flood set it down almost exactly on a north and south line, so that it didn't have to be moved more than three inches to make it face exactly east. The flood brought the stable along, too, and dropped it just a short distance from the house, so that uncle didn't have very many things to move over from the old location."

"Oh, you get out!" exclaimed the bicycle youth, who was beginning to be skeptical.

*   *   *

"Why, there's nothing so remarkable about that," said "Doc" Horne, as if in reproof of the bicycle salesman. "When I was out in charge of that relief expedition we picked up in midriver a cradle in which a baby was asleep. We learned afterward that the baby had floated some thirty miles before we found it. I presume that the water gave a gentle rocking movement to the cradle and kept the child asleep."

"I heard once of water coming into a house and lifting a bed in which a man was asleep, floating it out through a narrow doorway and carrying it away without even wetting the man," said the "lush."

At this the dentist arose hastily and walked to the front window, as if suddenly attracted by something in the street.

"Doc" Horne looked at the "lush" rather keenly and then said, with dry emphasis: "I hardly think so; I hardly think so."

*   *   *

There was a pause of a few moments, and then the dentist, sauntering back to resume his place, said: "Well, anyway, I don't like this wet season of the year."

"Yes, but we're better off here than they are out in the country, where the roads are muddy," said the "lush."

"That's a fact. Down in Illinois where I used to live we had the black prairie mud. At this time of the year it used to take four horses to pull a two-wheeled cart with a man and a sack of flour in it."

"Well, you know that other story they tell about the deep mud," said the "lush." "I don't suppose it's true, but I heard it. It's about the fellow who saw a hat in the street. He reached out and picked it up, and there was a man's head under it. This man under the hat looked up at him and said: 'Cheese it; I'm stealin' a ride on top of an omnibus.' Of course, I don't believe the story, but it was told to me."

"That story commands respect solely on account of its age," said "Doc" Horne, relighting his cigar, "but, as a matter of fact, gentlemen, anyone who saw this western country in the earlier days can tell you some remarkable stories. Why, right down here in Chicago, before they put down the corduroy roads, wagons used to mire down in Clark Street, and any one who lived as far out as Evanston or La Grange had to swim half of the way to get to Chicago at this time of the year.

"On the occasion of my first visit here a man named Simpson and I used to take a great many horseback rides out into the surrounding country. He was trying to sell me some tracts of so-called farm land, but it was really swamp and raw prairie, and I couldn't see my way clear to buy. Most of it is worth from $100 to $1,000 a front foot now, but that's neither here nor there.

"As I said, we used to take many horseback rides together. It was in May, and we were having some very warm weather, following a season of continued rains. The roads had been practically impassable for weeks, but they were drying rapidly, especially on top. You have doubtless seen, gentlemen, a muddy road with this dry crust. At intervals along the roads there were deep rucks, or 'mud-holes,' as they were called. When a mud-hole dries rapidly a cracked and flaky crust forms on top, and the large flakes curl up and warp in the sun. Often enough the crust will be as dry as a bone, while underneath are several feet of soft mud. I don't know that you ever heard the term, gentlemen, but in those days a mud-hole with this deceptive dry crust on top was called a 'lob-lolly.' Often it would require weeks of warm weather to dry out one of those places.

*   *   *

"Well, as I started to tell you, Simpson and I came to one of these low places in the road. It seemed dry, even dusty, on top, but I had had some experience in prairie country, so I told Simpson to go slow. He had been out from the east but a short time, and thought he knew it all. He started across. Of course, the dry shell broke through as if it were thin ice, and the first thing he knew he and the horse were stuck deep in the softest mire I ever saw. I jumped off my horse and threw him one end of my hitch-rein, and pulled him out. I supposed of course, that the horse could get out of the mud if relieved of the weight. He couldn't, though. The more he struggled, the deeper he went. I had heard of horses sinking in quicksand, but that was the first and only time I saw a horse sink right down into the mud."

"Did he go clear in under?" asked the bicycle salesman.

"Yes, he sank completely out of sight, and we had to stand there helpless. We couldn't save him. I understand that later in the summer some of the men dug down, out of curiosity, to see how far he had sunk, and they had to dig about five feet before they came to the saddle."

"'Doc,' that cigar doesn't seem to be burning very well," said the "lush." "Try a fresh one."

Only the dentist knew that this was a delicate act of surrender on the part of the "lush," who had prophesied early in the evening that he would tell a story that would keep "Doc" quiet all evening.

An Experiment in Philanthropy

BENTLEY was going to his home on the north side the other evening, whistling softly and comfortably, when a shadowy figure stepped out of a Dearborn Avenue doorway and slunk along beside him, mumbling some unintelligible request.

"What's that?" queried Bentley, stopping short.

"Mister, I'm hungry; I——"

"Well, what of it?" interrupted Bentley, tartly. "What are you telling it to me for? What makes you think that it's anything to me?"

In the light of a street lamp Bentley could see a flickering indication of humor in the young fellow's eyes.

"I might make you a lot o' trouble if I'd die yere on the sidewalk; you'd have to be a witness or somethin', wouldn't you?"

Bentley was in a good humor, and the tramp knew it, even before Bentley discovered the fact.

"I'll tell, you," said Bentley, compromisingly, "if you are hungry come along with me; I'll give you something to eat, but I won't give you any money."

Together they went into a Clark Street restaurant, where the young fellow demonstrated that he was hungry.

He also demonstrated that he could hold up his end of things at lying.

"Say," said Bentley, as the two turned into the street again, "How much money would have satisfied you in case I had shelled out when you asked me?"

"I'd been tickled to death with a dime."

"I MIGHT MAKE YOU A LOT O' TROUBLE"

"And yet I'm out 35 cents for what you've tucked in here?"

"That's it; yere I am wit' 35 cents worth of prog in me and it's a waste; w'y I'd 'a' lived t'ree days on 35 cents and had lodgin', too."

"See here," said Bentley, after a moment, "you look pretty seedy—if you'll come up to my room I'll give you something better than you've got on."

Bentley hauled out a lot of clothing from his closet, and, after a good deal of picking and sorting, he collected a full suit for his queer guest, which he wrapped up neatly in newspapers. It was about 11 o'clock; he opened the front door to let his alms-taker out.

"That's all right—that's all right," said Bentley, checking the tramp's thanks; "you're welcome to them, or you wouldn't have got 'em."

* * *

"By George, it's late," muttered Bentley, as he went back to his room and wound the little alarm clock. "I've got to be up early, too."

Five minutes later he was snoring, as only a man with a clear conscience can snore without awakening.

About 1 o'clock Bentley became conscious that somebody was pounding at his door.

"Who's there?" he called, sitting up with a snort.

"It's me," came the voice of his landlady; "there's a police officer wants to see you."

Bentley's eyes bulged, and he was out of bed in an instant.

"Me?" he faltered, gulping and trying to remember if he had done anything deserving of arrest.

"Yes; he's waiting in the parlor."

Tremblingly, Bentley dressed himself and went downstairs. A big patrolman was sitting there, with his cap on.

"Are you Mr. Bentley?" he asked.

"Yes."

"Well, we've pinched a friend of yours, who says that you'll go on his bail."

"What's his name?" queried Bentley, greatly relieved.

"He wouldn't give it; he says he's innocent and that you'll fix it all right."

"What was he arrested for?"

"I don't know; he's over there at the station, and it won't take you long to see him."

Bentley got his coat and hat.

"Pretty tough, getting a man out of bed at this hour, and asking him to put up some cold dollars to help another fellow out of jail."

The officer admitted that it was, and the two tramped on in silence, with Bentley wondering who on earth the friend could be and what he could have done.

At the station he was taken downstairs, and there, with his dirty face close to the bars, was the tramp.

"You!" exclaimed Bentley.

"Yes; pinched me for carryin' them clothes you give me. You give 'em to me, didn't you?"

"Certainly I did, but——"

"He was talkin' straight, was he?" queried the lieutenant on duty.

"Yes, about the clothes; I don't know what else he may have lied about, though," said Bentley.

"He wasn't answering very straight when he was picked up, so we run him in," explained the desk sergeant.

"Well, I guess we'll turn him loose," said the lieutenant, "but before we do you'd better give him a note to the effect that you gave him the clothes. He may call you out of bed again, if you don't."

"I'll tell you, Mr. Bentley," began the tramp, apologetically, "I thought as it was your clothes that got me in this box, you ought to help get me out and——"

"The devil you did!" returned Bentley, shortly, turning on his heel and walking upstairs.

*　　*　　*

"You can bet your life on this," said Bentley, winding up his hard-luck story the next morning; "if ever I give anything to a beggar again it will be either cash or nothing—probably nothing."

STATE STREET

In the Roof Garden

OLLIE and Fred were up at the roof garden one night
this week and it was just like getting into the younger
set to sit and listen to them.

Ollie wore one of his new summer suits, with the adhesive
trousers, and his soft white hat had been folded in from the
top until it was not much higher than the silvery hat-band.
Fred was in blue and held his gloves all evening. They tilted
forward as they walked along the aisle and both of them
stared seriously into space.

"Say, old man, where shall we sit?" asked Ollie, halting
suddenly.

"I don't mind, old chap."

"We might sit at this table."

"All right. Can we get a table to ourselves?"

"I don't know, old man. I think so."

"Well, let's sit here."

"All right."

"Well, you take this place."

"No, really, old chap, you know, I don't care so much for
the show."

"I'd rather you would."

"No, really, I'd just as soon sit here."

"Would you, really, old man?"

"Yes, I would, really."

So they seated themselves and Fred picked up a programme.

"What's on the bill, old man?" asked Ollie.

"I don't know who they are."

"I'll tell you who I'd like to see to-night."

"Who's that?"

"Vesta Tilly."

"That's right. I think she's great."

"She's dog-goned fine."

"I liked Yvette Guilbert, too."

"Yes, I think she's elegant."

"Did you think she was good-looking?"

"No, I didn't think she was, but Billy Pendleton says he thinks she's good-looking."

"The dickens he does! No, I don't think she is."

"Neither do I. She's good, though."

"Yes, I always thought she was elegant."

"You know when she sings those French songs, there's something—I don't know, but she has that—well, by George, she's fine."

"Yes, I always thought she was great. I wish Anna Held was here to-night. Don't you like her?"

"Yes, I liked her pretty well."

"I think she's elegant. There's something, you know, when she comes out and starts in—well, you know—er—. It's something in the—you can't hardly say what it is, but I think it's fine, don't you?"

"Yes, she's elegant. Did you buy a picture of her?"

"Yes, I've got mine in that frame where I used to have Della Fox."

"Say, old man, is Della Fox married?"

"I'll be dog-goned if I know. Somebody told me she was, and then I heard somewhere else that she wasn't."

"Lean over here, your tie's coming up."

"The dickens it is! If anything makes me mad it's to have my tie come up."

"I should say so. It's horrible."

"I used to have trouble all the time with my ties coming up, but, by George, you know, Crossley made me some new shirts that won't let your tie work up at all. They're great."

"I must get me some."

"That's what you want to do, old man. Tell Crossley I sent you."

"What did Crossley charge you for your last shirts?"

"I don't know. He sent the bill to the guv'nor. Say, tell that dog-goned waiter to come over here."

Ollie beckoned to a waiter, who came up briskly and asked: "Well, what will it be, gents?"

Ollie flinched as if cut by a whip, and then he gave the waiter a reproving look.

"What do you want, old man?" he asked.

"THEY TILTED FORWARD"

"Oh, I'll be dog-goned if I care."

"Don't you want some beer?"

Fred glanced apprehensively to right and left and then said in a careless manner, brushing his trousers leg with the gloves, "I don't care, old chap. Go ahead and order."

"Waiter, have you good beer here?" asked Ollie.

"Sure," replied the waiter. "How many—two?"

"Yes—I think so," said Ollie. "Say, waiter, now don't be in a hurry. Have you got mugs here?"

"Two mugs you want?"

"What do you think about it, old man?"

"Yes, I'd just as soon have mine in a mug."

"All right, waiter, two mugs."

The waiter dashed away, and Ollie looked after him, moodily. "Dog-gone!" he exclaimed. "It makes me mad to have a waiter try to hurry me."

"That's right."

"Do you see anybody you know?"

"No; I guess it's all right."

"Hat Elliott saw me drinking beer here one night last summer and she raised the dickens with me."

"Oh, thunder! A man's got a right to drink a mug of beer if he wants it."

"Well, that's what I said."

"Will Martin says that in the east everybody drinks beer out of mugs."

"Look out, Ollie, there's Mr. Kirby coming."

The two sat very quiet as an elderly gentleman passed along the aisle. Just as he was passing the waiter brought the two mugs.

"Do you think he saw us?" asked Fred.

"What the dickens do I care?" said Ollie. He took a gulp of the fluid and made a sour face. "Got a cigarette, old man?" he asked, throwing himself back in the chair.

"Yes, I've got a new Turkish kind here. I think they're great."

"I had some up at Burchard's the other night that were elegant. George Burchard got them in New York."

"Is that so?"

"Yes," and he lighted the cigarette which he had chosen from Fred's leather case. He timidly inhaled a draw of smoke and then said, hoarsely: "These seem to be nice."

"Yes," replied Fred, holding up one of the cigarettes and studying it with judicial calm, "they're fine."

"You're not drinking your beer, old man."

"Oh, I'll drink it all right. How is it—strong?"

"Not very. I don't like beer if it's too light."

"Neither do I."

They puckered their lips and took a sip apiece and then sat in silence for awhile, dreamily pulling at the cigarettes.

Then Ollie suddenly asked: "Say, old man, do you like my Tuxedo coat?"

"Yes; I think it's all right."

"Billy Pendleton said he thought it was too long."

"The dickens he did! He needn't talk, dog-gone it! You know those new shirts of his?"

"Yes."

"Uncle Bob got some exactly like them two years ago in New York. Billy thought they were something new."

Both of them smiled wearily at the expense of Billy Pendleton, and settled further down in their chairs.

Ollie resumed the conversation.

"Crossley's got some dandy hatbands," he said.

"Yes. I was looking at them. They're fine."

"I bought—"

But just then the orchestra broke in and the remainder was lost.

The Hickey Boy in the Feathers

"ME WITH a bunch o' the grip," said the Hickey boy. "Me the livin' drug store."

"But you're game enough to hit the cigaroot."

"Gee, I need my student's lamp now an' then, no matter how poor I'm feelin', but it looked for awhile as if I'd have to cut these little paper things for sure. They had me in the feathers with about seven kinds o' dope shot into me."

"I ain't seen you since Tuesday."

"Well, you ain't missed nothin', becuz I certainly have been a shellfish this week. The gong sounded Monday afternoon. I shook hands with one o' them microbe boys, and us mixin' it. Old Hickey's been on the ropes most o' the time since then. Say, ain't that enough to jar you? To think that this whole business is started by some little eight-legged dingus so small that you can't see a thousand of 'em. I thought it wuz a kid, on the level. When I went in to see Doc Tuesday morning I piped him about it and says: 'Is it right or is it Sunday-paper talk?' I been readin' them Sunday papers so long I don't believe nothin' no more. I says: 'Do you stand for it, Doc?' He says: 'Sure thing.' He says: 'For all I know there's seven million o' them grip things floatin' around in this room now.' 'Hully cheez,' I says, 'what chance has a guy got against the grip bazazas when they come at you a million in a bunch? There ain't a thing to it. No matter which way you dodge you find Mr. Grip Razmataz waitin' with a stiff left for you. They got that smokeless-powder game beat to a pulp. There's no gettin' away from it. They've got you in a pocket, an' it's a case of you busy with the quinine or else you're whipsawed to a horrible finish. Say, I wish I could give you the line o' talk that Doc passed to me about these grip umptaloriums—wha' d'you call 'em?"

"Germs."

"Sure! That's easy. All you got to do is to think of Germans. When I slipped him the dollar I says to him: 'Doc, you got past me with most o' them long boys, but any guy that can spring 'em an' make good, mind you, an' get away with 'em the way you do, is certainly entitled to his little old case note.' All about the mucous membranus and the broncho bazazas gettin' mixed up with the wallyollopis, down in the gazalium. Ooh! Madge! When he got through tellin' me about it an' spread me from the coin I says: 'Lead me back home an' do things to me. I'm a twenty-five hunderd to one in the winter book, an' not a thing doin'.' Then me to the house again. You ought to seen me. The lamps all red an' a tongue that felt like one o' them sofa pillows. I'm livin' at my sister's house, an' her, you know, wiser'n any doctor. Oh, easy! Out in the kitchen, cookin' up stuff for me. When she brought it in I looked it over an' says: 'No, not unless you hurry it into me while I'm asleep.' She says: 'You don't eat this. This is a poultice for your chest.' So me up against this stuff an' hollerin' plenty. I thought it wuz all off with me.

'Here,' I says, 'From now on we scratch the home doctorin'. I'll take the stuff that Doc give me an' let it go at that.' Could I stop her? Not for a minute. Think o' the handicap, too. Me laid out on the sofa an' her sneakin' on me every little while to get somethin' into me before I had a chance to holler. If I'd took the stuff she fixed up for me, say, me with the silver handles right now. That's right. When I couldn't stand it no longer, me up an' makin' my beller. I says: 'I don't want to start nothin' in the Hickey family, but if you try to shoot any more poison into me I can see myself swingin' on you.' She says: 'Now, I'm tellin' you, this'll do you good.' 'You give it to your husband,' I says. 'You don't know but what them microbes live on this stuff you've fixed up here.' I says. 'I'm after 'em with Doc in my corner, and if you don't keep out o' the ring I may forget that you're my sister.' Well, that held her for awhile."

"Did you have it bad?"

"I had it worse'n that. Monday afternoon I felt like I'd been run over by an ice-wagon three or four times. All the insides o' me wuz lumpy. I could 'a' swore I'd swallered a couple o' dumbbells and they'd settled in my back, an' the head was a lily. No eyes at all. Just a couple o' poached eggs, that's all. Me settin' around on my shoulder-blades lookin' like one o' these bamboo boys full o' the hop. I looked like the West Baden finish of an election bat. No, I couldn't see a thing to it. On the dead, I hoped it'd be a case o' die, becuz I couldn't see any other way o' ketchin' even with the blonde. Monday night it wuz all in-fightin' with the bedclothes an' dodgin' things that come up over the edge o' the bed. Me up tryin' to cool the nut with a wet towel an' seein' myself booked for the crazy house. Tuesday mornin' I says to the sister: 'Get on your nursin' clothes, for it's me to his whiskers,' and in an hour I'm back with all they could spare from the drug store. It's one kind every two hours and another every three an' another before I went to bed, to say nothin' of a nice warm plaster that was goin' to help some. It's a wonder I didn't get mixed on my dates an' land myself. At that, I think I'm dotty the minute I begin to feed myself the quinine an' all them other allypozacks in the blue boxerinos."

"Did it give you a ringing in the ears?"

INCIDENTAL TO THE HICKEY BOY'S SET-TO WITH THE GRIP

"It give me worse'n that. I think it had me scrambled between the ears. On the square, there must 'a' been knock-out
drops in it. Night before last I took a little of everything Doc
gave me, then into the sweater an' all wrapped up. It wuz a
new one on me, how you're goin' to sweat out anything like

them grip things with claws on 'em. I says: 'I think they can stand it as long as Hickey can.' But me under the blanket, becuz that's what the Doc orders. Well, I must 'a' reduced seventeen pounds, an' when I did get to sleep I had a dream that'd jolt anybody. When I woke up I had my head over one edge of the bed an' was tryin' to bite a hole in the pillow. Now, listen! Here's a poor one! Me a walkin' down the street, when I comes to one o' these gangs repairin' this block pavin', understand? You've seen 'em where they put down them blocks and push the gravel in between an' then pour this hot tar over the whole thing. There wuz a copper standin' on the corner watchin' the gang work, an' when they see me everybody hollers an' comes at me on the run. I didn't know what wuz doin', but I put up a swell race for about seven miles, then me in the gravel and about fourteen on top. Well, what do you think they done? This is just to show where the stuff put me. They drags me back an' chucks me into Mr. Big-iron-thing that they melt the tar in. Hot? Holy sufferin' mackerel! Me pushin' up the lid, you know, an' puttin' out the head to get a little fresh air, an' the copper givin' me an awful belt across the head every time an' sayin: 'G'wan, get back in there!' I'd duck back in an' do my two or three minutes settin' up to my neck in this stuff, boilin' hot—understand?—an' then up with the lid an' take another wallop. Oh, I wuz havin' a lovely time. I guess I must have hollered, becuz the first I remember wuz the sister wras'lin' with me an tellin' me to lay down an' keep quiet. I made a couple o' passes at her an' told her to give me a gallon o' water. She says: 'You seem to be a little feverish.' 'Oh, I don't know,' I says, all the time tryin' to crawl up on top o' the headboard. Oh, me up in the air! Say, if that's what them little grip things does to you, I'm glad they don't grow the size o' rabbits."

A Social Call

AFTER spending the evening at the home of Miss Flora Shadley the members of the commune came home on the last cable car and sat down to talk it over.

"A little request, Barney," said Jim. "The next time we go out for an evening of social intercourse, you kindly omit the bay rum."

Barney—"Could you notice it?"

Jim—"Could we notice it! It silenced the Welsh rabbit and the Camembert cheese. You know when Miss Shadley opened the window—well, you were the cause."

Barney—"I couldn't help it. The barber put it on."

Mac—"I suppose you told him that you were going to call on a lady friend."

Barney—"No; I didn't tell him where I was going."

Jim—"But you did tell him you were going somewhere?"

Barney—"Well, what if I did? I just asked him to do a good job, that's all."

Mac—"Well, Barney, if you are going to travel in our set you mustn't talk about your social engagements while you are having your hair cut. I may be a stickler for good form, but it is not what I would call the proper sort of thing. No offense, old chap, you understand? Merely a friendly suggestion."

Barney—"You go to blazes! I don't want to take any lessons in deportment from any man who spills things all over the table. Gee! but I was ashamed of you to-night."

Mac—"Somebody had to turn in and put a little life into the party. Why didn't you volunteer to dish out the Welsh rabbit?"

Barney—"Because you claimed to be an expert. Why, a person hearing you talk would have thought you prepared three meals a day on the chafing-dish. Say, Jim, did you hear what he told Miss Shadley? He said: 'We're going to get a chafing-dish for our apartments.' Not 'room,' mind you, but 'apartments.' By the way, Mac, when are you going down to pick out that chafing-dish?"

Mac—"Just as soon as you pay me for that hat of mine that you lost off the train."

Jim—"Now will you be good, Barney?"

Barney—" 'T was a cruel rebuff."

Mac—"But did you hear what Jim said when he was turning the music for her? She looked up at him and asked, 'Have you a piano in your apartments?' and Jim said: 'Not yet.' You know the way he said it. It meant that he had ordered the piano, but the men hadn't delivered it, although he was expecting them at any moment."

Jim—"Well, what did you want me to say? You began it by speaking of 'apartments.' It wouldn't have sounded very well for me to say, 'We can't afford a piano, and even if we had one there wouldn't be any room for it.' "

Barney—"Why not? Miss Shadley thinks we're sure-enough bohemians. I dare say she'd regard us with much more interest if she thought we lived in a garret with no light except a candle stuck in a bottle."

Jim—"We come near enough to the garret and the candle to suit me."

Mac—"I believe Jim is right. When you are in society a little judicious lying is a good thing."

Barney—"That's what I thought when I heard you talking about grand opera. As I understand it, Mac, you are intensely fond of grand opera, but you didn't get around to it as often as you desired, during the last season."

Mac—"That's right."

Barney—"You'll excuse my inquisitive persistence, I trust, but—how many performances did you attend, as a matter of fact?"

Mac—"Well, I happened to be very busy about that time."

Barney—"We understand that and I suppose it just happened that your dates conflicted, so that you didn't get around to grand opera at all."

Mac—"Perhaps not, but I love it just the same."

Jim—"I can understand that. 'Absence makes the heart grow fonder.' Now, the more seldom I hear Barney sing the greater is my admiration for his voice."

Mac—"I should say so! What in the world induced you to try and sing there to-night, Barney?"

Barney—"You did, both of you. You got her started and there wasn't any way out of it. Didn't both of you ask me to sing?"

Jim—"Yes; but haven't you learned to take a joke?"

Barney—"My candid opinion is that you fellows are jealous. I take notice that Flora told me I was all right."

Mac—"That isn't what she told me when we were out in the hallway. She said she thought you ought to take lessons."

Barney—"Now, be fair. She didn't say it in that way at all. She told me the same thing. What she said was that I had a good voice and ought to—to improve it."

Jim—"That's right."

Barney—"No—now don't interrupt. She said my voice was good enough to warrant me in devoting myself to vocal study."

Mac—"That isn't what she said to me at all. She simply said she thought you ought to study."

Barney—"About what time in the evening did you develop this conversational streak? I didn't see you do very much talking with her. For a man who is so free with his talk on the outside you are the clammiest man in a parlor that I ever did see. I, whom you derided, dashed right in and was up at the piano in less than no time, while you, supposed to be a high-toned composite of Beau Brummel, Lord Chesterfield and Ward McAllister—why, you didn't breathe for twenty minutes after we went into the place. You were sitting humped over in one of those Roman chairs that's shaped like a saw-buck and I thought for awhile you were asleep."

Jim—"Oh, no; he was awake. Didn't you hear what he said?"

Barney—"Did he speak?"

Jim—"Of course he did. He said one of the cleverest things. He looked over at Miss Shadley and said, 'Won't you play something?' "

Barney—"Yes, I remember now. That indicated great presence of mind."

Mac—"Well, I think there is such a thing as being alto-

Barney's Social Account

Receipts

	$
4 caviar sandwiches — — — —	.40
2 cheese ditto — — — —	.20
Salad, olives &c — — — —	.20
Welsh rabbit — — — —	.30
Beverages — — — — —	.60
Two cigars (estimated)	.10
	1 80

Expenditures

	$
Car fare — — — —	.20
Hair cut &c	.40
Soap — — — —	.10
	.70

Summary. $

Receipts —	1.80
Expenditure —	.70
Net profit	1.10

BARNEY'S IDEA OF A PROFITABLE EVENING IN SOCIETY

gether too much at home on short acquaintance. I prefer to dawn on people gradually."

Jim—"You want to break it to them gently, eh?"

Mac—"Well, I don't regard modesty as entirely unbecoming, and I don't like to overdo the eating the first time I am invited to a place."

Barney—"Say, that was a beautiful layout for a small lunch, wasn't it? There must have been five dollars' worth of stuff on that table."

Jim—"Great Scott! What do you think of that, Mac? There's one result of this restaurant education. As soon as Barney sat down at that table he began to count the sandwiches and estimate what they'd cost if he had to go out and buy them by the piece. Isn't that a nice way in which to speak of a light lunch served by our charming hostess— 'about five dollars' worth of stuff on the table'? Well, that beats anything I ever heard of."

Barney—"Oh, you needn't be sarcastic. I merely meant to indicate that it was a good lunch."

Mac—"After he finished I saw him feeling for his check."

Barney—"I'm glad I didn't find it."

Mac—"How much do you think you got out of it, Barney?"

Barney—"That's all right. I got what I wanted."

Mac—"I guess you did. A couple of dollars' worth, think you? Enough to pay you for your time and trouble?"

Barney—"I'm not complaining."

Jim—"I'm counting up here just how he came out. Of course he spent a little money, and that will have to be subtracted, but I should judge that he made a business success of the evening."

Jim had taken out his fountain pen and was figuring on a pad of paper.

Mac—"What did you say the total was, Barney—five dollars?"

Barney (with irony)—"Five dollars and ten cents. I forgot to count the pickles the other time."

Jim—"Now, wait a minute and I'll show you how the account stands."

He finished his writing and handed over an itemized statement showing that Barney had taken refreshments to the value of $1.80 and had spent 70 cents on account of his evening out.

Mac—"That 10 cents for soap hadn't ought to be counted, because that will last him for a long time. I think that he had three cigars instead of two. I saw him put one in his pocket to smoke after while. Barney must be at least $1.25 ahead. But I do hate to see a man take such a sordid and mercenary view of an evening call."   G. A.

At "Larry's Lunch"

THE place known as "Larry's Lunch" is a narrow hole in the wall between two frame houses. The buildings are so old and weak that they lean toward each other in their decrepitude. The street in front is muddy and cobbled. Street lamps are far apart. They burn low, as if there was not the oxygen in this neglected air to feed a cheerful flame. The sunken and rotting sidewalk of wood is slippery to the foot.

*　　*　　*

A kerosene lamp propped in the front window of "Larry's Lunch" showed as a mere smudge of light behind the dirty panes.

John Hazen lifted the loose iron latch, and there came into his nostrils, like the breathing from a foul creature, the smell of poverty, frying grease and bad tobacco.

But he had to eat. He had not eaten for twenty-four hours. A Jew dealing in pawns and junk had given him 10 cents for his pocket-knife, the last of his convertible property.

At "Larry's Lunch" he could get meat, bread, potatoes and coffee for 10 cents. He ordered and then leaned forward on the rough table, with his chin in his hands, while the meat sizzled in the pan and a rancid smoke filled the low room.

His uncle had been right.

"You take your share of the money and go to Chicago and you'll be broke within six months," the uncle had said. "You're a fool with money. Any man's a fool with money unless it's money he's earned."

"I know my business," he had said to his uncle.

After which they had parted, with the understanding that if John Hazen ever needed money he would not come to his uncle for it.

Yes, his uncle had been right. A fool with his money? Diamonds which he had worn clumsily—bravado betting at the racetracks—loans to new-made friends—experiments at the bucket shops. Six months of it and he had just sold his pocket-knife that he might eat a shred of carrion in this hole and be alive for another day.

Oh, what a triumph for those who had warned him—those who had told him he was a fool with money! What rejoicing there would be at home when they heard of it—and they would hear of it, because in small towns they hear of everything. They would be glad, he was sure—all except Aunt Ella.

"She was the only one who ever cared for me," he said, half aloud, grinding his fists on the table. "But I don't care."

Then, because he didn't care he let his head fall down into the angle of his right arm and there in the darkness which he had made for himself he cried. He was only 22 years old.

The front door clicked and slammed. Larry, who was both cook and waiter (in a red flannel shirt chopped off at the elbows), brought the meat and coffee. John Hazen pulled himself up from the table. Before him, talking to Larry, stood a very small young man, with square shoulders, a pointed nose, jet-black eyes and a mouth twitching into a smile whenever he spoke. This young man wore a plaid cap, with a short peak. His coat collar was turned up, and within it was a blue and white handkerchief knotted closely around his neck.

"If he comes around here, you tell him I want to see him," this young man was saying to Larry.

"All right, Eddie."

At that moment the young man named Eddie looked down and saw John Hazen's face, streaked with tears. Possibly he was surprised to know that a man may weep. Let it be assumed that he was prompted by impudent curiosity. He spoke to the young man at the table.

"What's the matter?" he asked. "Don't the steak suit you?"

"You'll have to excuse me," said Hazen, trying to laugh. "I'm hoeing a pretty hard row just at present. I s'pose I was kind o' weak from not eating or I wouldn't have ——" and he stopped.

"What do you think of that?" asked Eddie, speaking to the proprietor, who had gone back to his stove.

Larry nodded wisely and smiled. Eddie stood and watched Hazen tear at the fibrous strip of meat and take long gulps of the hot coffee.

"First to-day?" he asked.

"Yes," answered Hazen, who was divided between shame and hunger.

"How did you get the price?"

"I sold my knife."

"What if you hadn't any knife?"

"I don't know."

"How long you been in town?"

"About six months."

"Nice town, ain't it?"

Hazen shook his head dubiously and made an effort to smile.

Eddie threw back his head and laughed aloud.

"This is one o' the cases," he said, calling to Larry. "Is it any wonder they start out?" Then to Hazen: "Why didn't you stop some fellow and ask him to let you have a nickel or two?"

"Because I'm not a beggar."

"That's the way to talk!" exclaimed Eddie, and he laughed again. Hazen looked up at him, much puzzled.

"Where you goin' to-night?"

"I don't know. There are two or three places where I'm going to call again to-morrow to see about a job."

"The job you stand a chance of gettin' to-morrow or next week ain't very much help to you to-night, is it?" asked Eddie, with a quizzical grin.

"This is a new experience for me," said Hazen. "I've heard about fellows being up against it this way, but I never thought I'd come to it."

"You don't care much for it, as far as you've got, do you?"

Hazen looked up again, undecided whether Eddie was sympathizing with him or taunting him.

"I wish I had the money I had six months ago," he said bitterly. "They wouldn't take it away from me this time."

Eddie leaned across the table and gave Hazen a hard but playful blow in the ribs.

"You're all right," he said, laughing again. "I'll just stake you to a bed to-night."

When Hazen had eaten the last crumb of bread and drained

"NICE TOWN, AIN'T IT?"

the last drop of coffee he followed Eddie across the muddy street and up a dark stairway into a room that held a bed, a table, a chair and a zinc-bound trunk. The bed-clothes were in confusion.

"Roll in there next to the wall an' dream you've got all your money back," commanded Eddie, who had squatted on the trunk, giving the only chair to his guest. Hazen slept with Eddie that night and went to breakfast with him next morning, at a 15-cent place.

"If you don't strike anything to-day, come around to-night," said Eddie.

Hazen did come back that night to get food and a resting place. They were on their way to the room when two big men stood before them at a corner. One grabbed Eddie and the other held Hazen by the wrist before he had time to dodge or retreat.

"Hello, Mullen," said Eddie to the man who was holding him.

"Hello, Eddie," in a growling voice. "You can't stay away, can you?"

"Why should I, when this is my home? This is the dragnet again, I suppose?"

"I don't know. They told us to bring you in if we found you. Who's your friend here?"

"It'll do me a lot o' good to tell you, won't it? If I say he's a young fellow that's gone broke and that I just happened to meet him an' stake him for a day or two till he could pick up somethin', of course everybody over at the station'll believe me?"

"They may if you tell it good. Come on."

A few minutes later here were Hazen and the good samaritan bumping over the granite blocks on their way to the police station. Hazen was surprised to find himself indifferent to the shame of arrest.

He concluded that Eddie was known to the police and that any one walking along the street with Eddie was already a criminal in the eyes of the police.

"I'm sorry to get you pinched, young fellow," said Eddie, through the gloom of the covered wagon. "I ought to have told you you was takin' a chance when you went around with me."

"I don't blame you," said Hazen. "What right did they have to arrest either one of us?"

Eddie laughed and remarked: "You don't half know this town."

The wagon policeman, whose huge bulk was a barrier between them and the narrow door, gave a disgusted "aw-w-w," in token of the fact that he could not be deceived by their talk. He was possessed of a brutal unbelief, which, he thought, was a fine quality of discernment.

At the station they were separated. Hazen gave his right name to the man in the cage, much to Eddie's amusement. The man in the cage did not have to ask for Eddie's name.

Hazen slept on a bench and he slept, too, lulled off with a mild, impersonal wonder as to what his uncle and his aunt would say if they knew that their orphan charge was locked up in a police station and had not changed shirts for a week. Next morning he ate his heel of bread and drank his tin cup of coffee and looked out through the paralleled bars at the bedraggled men and women who were being mustered for the police court. He could not see Eddie anywhere. Some one was whistling at the other end of the corridor. He wondered if it was Eddie.

Then a turnkey in blue came and opened his cell door.

"Come on," said the turnkey, and Hazen followed upstairs into a hot room, where a big captain with a gray mustache sat at the desk.

The captain looked at Hazen intently and said: "I don't know him."

Other men with mustaches came in and looked at Hazen. They didn't know him, either, and they regretted to say it. It showed a lack of professional knowledge not to be able to identify any stranger as a professional crook.

"How long have you and Eddie been working together?" one of them asked.

"I've never worked with him," said Hazen. "I've been looking for work all week."

He told them his story—the truth of it. Five big men smiled broadly.

"An' you didn't know Eddie was a dip?" asked the captain.

"A what?" (Laughter.)

"A dip."

"I don't know what you mean."

"Did you ever hear of pickpockets?"

"Yes, sir."

"Well, a dip is a pickpocket. That's what Eddie is."

"I don't care what he is. He did me a good turn. I never saw him until night before last."

"This fellow can be vagged," said one of the big men. "He admits himself he's out o' money an' ain't got a job."

"That's why he ain't a vag," said the captain. "The vag has always got a job and plenty of money." Then to Hazen: "You keep away from Eddie an' his crowd." This meant that Hazen was free to go.

He started to leave the station and was attracted by the buzz of the courtroom. He went in, hoping to see Eddie again. The crowd around the magistrate was shifting and noisy. Cases were being tried, but Hazen could not follow them in the confusion of sounds.

At last he saw Eddie coming out of the throng, held by a turnkey.

He slipped forward along the wall and touched him on the arm.

"Hello, there," he said.

Eddie turned and grinned.

"Did you fix it?" he asked.

"They let me go."

"It's a wonder—bein' with me."

"Here, here!" growled the turnkey. "Come on!"

"I'm sent out," said Eddie.

"Where?"

"The Bridewell—I won't be there day after to-morrow. Good-by."

"Say, I want to thank you for——"

"That's all right."

"You never told me your name."

"You ask here at the station. They'll give you my history."

"Come on!" said the turnkey, pulling.

Eddie winked and the battered door closed behind him.

"Gondola" Wilson's Misfortune

G ONDOLA" WILSON was not a tramp, because he knew a trade and he had been known to work. He was a tramp in this, however, that he consistently refused to pay railway fares. Hence his name. "Gondola" is submerged tenth for "flat car."

He was a journeyman of the restless kind. When he had been three weeks in Milwaukee, then St. Paul seemed a more desirable place of residence. When in St. Paul he had a tired hankering to see the Narcissus lodging house in Chicago. After he had arrived at the Narcissus he began to watch the trains starting for Cincinnati and longed to curl himself on a truck and jolt away to where the muddy stream fronts the sloping warehouses.

Once he was away from the Narcissus for a whole year. During his absence he had been "put away." To be "put away" is to be held prisoner in a penal or reformatory institution.

The purpose of this story is to relate how "Gondola" Wilson, having no criminal intent, became a criminal under circumstances which are not usual.

On the day of his return to the Narcissus (the prison pallor on his face and his head cropped to show the white scars) six inmates were sitting near the windows reading a morning newspaper. They had torn the paper into sheets and divided it. The man who had drawn the small "ads" was discontented. He could find nothing on his sheet except "Help Wanted." He lowered his paper, and before him sat "Gondola" Wilson, seeming yellow in the filtered light.

"Where's the committee?" asked "Gondola." "Where's the triumphal arch, 'Welcome Home?'"

"You're alive, then?"

"Alive an' kickin'."

"If you're alive, it follows that you're kickin'. How long has it been?"

"A year—next month."

"We missed you when it come to the round-up last fall.

Nobody'd seen you. You've been under a roof, ain't you?
Hospital?"

"Put away—a year."

"You had to go crooked at last, did you?"

"Well, that's what they called it. I'm lucky they didn't
hang me. Some of 'em wanted to."

"Tell me what you done. I ain't the court."

"Say, listen, an' see if ever you heard the likes before. It
wuz in October—a year ago last October. I'd walked from
Loueyville over to Terry Hut with a nigger that played the
mouth harp. We hid in the
yards at Terry Hut an' got into an empty stock that we
thought wuz headed for Dan-
ville. Some time in the night a
brakeman seen us an' fired us
out. I'd been asleep, an' the
first thing I remember was
fallin' out o' the car an' lightin'
hard, with the coon comin'
after me. We didn't know
where we wuz, but could make
out a sidetrack an' a chute for
loadin' hogs. About a mile off
we could see some lights an'
we judged we wuz near a purty
goodsized town. Me an' the
coon started to walk toward
the town an' then I stopped
him an' says: 'Here, if we go to
drillin' around town at this
time o' night an' one o' them
country coppers gets a peek at
us, he'll shoot us first an' then
ask us our names afterward. Let's crawl in somewheres an'
sleep till mornin' an' then we'll go in town an' try to round up
a handout.' Well, just as I wuz sayin' this, we happened to be
walkin' along past a tall fence. I looked through the cracks
an' could see one or two lights quite a distance off an' right

HE COULD FIND NOTHING
BUT "HELP WANTED"

"GONDOLA" WILSON

near us wuz a long buildin' that looked somethin' like a barn. It wuz gettin' chilly an' I said to this pardner of mine, 'Coon, gi' me a boost over this fence an' I think we can find a warm place here.' So we skinned over the fence an' come to this buildin'. It wuz big an' I still thought it wuz a barn. We walked around, lookin' for a door or window, so't we could crawl in. At last this pardner of mine—his name 'uz Jeff an' I'll kill him if ever I lay eyes on him again—Jeff found a little door that wuzn't locked an' we went in, feelin' our way along, thinkin' you know, that we might find some hay or straw to sleep on. Purty soon Jeff fell over somethin' an' I landed on top of him. We felt around us an' discovered that we'd run into a lot o' watermelons layin' on the floor. I s'pose the coon was sorry to meet them melons, wuzn't he? The first thing I knew he'd split one of 'em open an' I could hear him chompin' in the dark. Well, I got up an' felt my way along an' purty soon I reached out an' what do you s'pose I took holt of there in the pitch dark? A plate with about a dozen biscuits on it. Now, I ain't no crook an' I never broke into a house to steal anything, but I'll leave this to you. If you hadn't had anything to eat for eighteen hours an' should happen to crawl into a barn at night an' reach out into the dark an' find a dozen light biscuits, would you eat 'em or throw 'em away?"

"I'd prob'ly eat 'em," was the reply.

"That's what I done, except what I give to Jeff. He found a match in his cloze an' struck it, an' we saw in front of us a wooden shelf covered with pies an' cakes an' all kinds o' cooked stuff. The match only burned for a minute, but we

made out that much. Jeff found a plate o' butter, an' we et
the biscuit with butter, an' I ain't tasted anything like it
since I ran away from home in Lowell thirty years ago. Then
Jeff broke a cake in two an' give me half of it. It wuz kind o'
dry eatin', but we put lots of butter on it. I s'pose I ought
to have stopped an' remembered that all this provender belonged to somebody, but I wuz so blamed hungry I didn't
wait to think of nothin'. An' I must say I never seen anybody
eat the way that coon did. I didn't exactly see him eat, neither, but I could hear him all right. After he et all the cakes an'
pies an' biscuits he could lay his hands on he went back to
watermelon, an' I could hear him sloshin' an' gulpin' there in
the dark. I started to feel around for a soft place to lay down,
an' what do you guess? I run into a lot of bed-cloze strung on
lines."

"Say, what kind of a pipe is this?" asked the listener, with
a sidewise turn in his chair, indicating skepticism.

"It's the truth, every word of it. There must a' been a
dozen quilts. I pulled 'em down an' me an' Jeff rolled ourselves up in 'em an' went to
sleep. We'd et a lot an' it wuz
a cold night, an' under them
warm covers we slept like a
couple o' logs. Well, the next
thing I remember somebody
was shakin' me good an' hard,
an' I looked up at a fellow that
had a tin star on his coat an' a
broomstick in his hand. I kin'
o' remembered what had happened an' looked around. It
wuz broad daylight. We laid
there in the infernalest mess of
eatables you ever seen. People
wuz pilin' through the doors
to get a look at us. I don't
s'pose you've figured out what
we'd done, so I'll tell you. This
place we'd got into wuz what

"I'D PROB'LY EAT 'EM"

they call Floral Hall at the county fair. All the stuff we'd been eatin' wuz the exhibitions of the best biscuits, the best watermelons, the best cake, the best butter, an' so on, of the whole county. You know the quilt I had around me. It wuz made out of about a million little pieces o' silk. The woman that made it put in fifteen years on it, an' it wuz supposed to be worth two hunderd dollars. That all come out at the trial."

"Well, there must a' been a sore crowd o' grangers around there," suggested the listener, after he had leaned back and laughed joyfully.

"Honest, it's a wonder they didn't kill us. We come mighty near bustin' up the whole show by eatin' them exhibitions. When they led us out o' the grounds an' took us in town to the jail there wuz a big crowd followed us an' hollered 'Lynch 'em!' 'String 'em up!' an' a few more remarks like that. That wuz the one time I wuz in a hurry to be in jail. Do you know what they made it when it came to a trial? Burglary! An' do you know what Jeff done? He got up an' swore that I'd hypnotized him. He testified that he didn't want to go into this buildin' at all, but I made him by threatenin' to cast a spell over him. You never heard such lyin' in your life. They sent him back to jail for three months an' put me over the road for a year. They bleached me just about right, ain't they? That's all right, though. Look here."

He put his hand into a raveled side pocket and brought out a copy of Henry George's "Progress and Poverty." He made a deeper reach and found a brass "knucks" with a blunt head and three staring finger-holds.

"I'm savin' that for the coon," he said.

Effie Whittlesy[17]

MRS. WALLACE was in a good humor.
She assisted her husband to remove his overcoat
and put her warm palms against his red and wind-
beaten cheeks.

"I have good news," said she.

"Another bargain sale?"

"Pshaw, no. A new girl, and I really believe she's a jewel.
She isn't young or good looking, and when I asked her if she
wanted any nights off she said she wouldn't go out after dark
for anything in the world. What do you think of that?"

"That's too good to be true."

"No, it isn't. Wait till you see her. She came here from the
intelligence office about 2 o'clock and I put her to work at
once. You wouldn't know that kitchen. She has it as clean as
a pin."

"What nationality?"

"None—or I mean she's from the country. She's as green
as she can be, but she's a good soul, and I know we can trust
her."

"Well, I hope so. If she is all that you say, why, for goodness' sake give her any pay she wants—put lace curtains in
her room and subscribe for all the story papers on the market."

"Bless you, I don't believe she'd read them. Every time
I've looked into the kitchen she's been working like a Trojan
and singing 'Beulah Land.'"

"Oh, she sings, does she? I knew there'd be something
wrong with her."

"You won't mind that. We can keep the doors closed."

* * *

The dinner table was set in tempting cleanliness. Bradley
Wallace, aged 8, sat at the left of his father, and Mrs. Wallace, at the right, surveyed the arrangements of glass and silver and gave a nod of approval. Then she touched the bell
and in a moment the new servant entered.

She was a tall woman who had said her last farewell to girl-
hood. She had a nose of honest largeness and an honest spread

269

of freckles, and yet her face was not unattractive. It suggested good nature and homely candor. The cap and apron were of snowy white. She was modest, but not flurried.

Then a very strange thing happened.

Mr. Wallace turned to look at the new girl and his eyes enlarged. He gazed at her as if fascinated either by cap or freckles. An expression of wonderment came to his face and he said: "Well, by George!"

The girl had come very near the table when she took the first overt glance at him. Why did the tureen sway in her hands? She smiled in a frightened way and hurriedly set the tureen on the table.

Mr. Wallace was not long undecided, but during that moment of hesitancy he remembered many things. He had been reared in the democracy of a small community and the democratic spirit came uppermost.

"This isn't Effie Whittlesy?" said he.

"For the land's sake!" she exclaimed, backing away, and this was a virtual confession.

"You don't know me."

"Well, if it ain't Ed Wallace!"

Would that words were ample to tell how Mrs. Wallace settled back in her chair, gaping first at her husband and then at the new girl, stunned with surprise and vainly trying to understand what it all meant.

She saw Mr. Wallace reach awkwardly across the table and shake hands with the new girl and then she found voice to gasp: "Of all things!"

Mr. Wallace was painfully embarrassed. He was wavering between his formal duty as an employer and his natural regard for an old friend. Anyway, it occurred to him that an explanation would be timely.

"This is Effie Whittlesy from Brainerd," said he. "I used to go to school with her. She's been at our house often. I haven't seen her for—I didn't know you were in Chicago."

"Well, Ed Wallace, you could knock me down with a feather," said Effie, who still stood in a flustered attitude a few paces back from the table. "I had no more idee when I heard the name Wallace that'd it be you, though knowin', of course, you was up here. Wallace is such a common name I never give it a second thought. But the minute I saw you, law! I knew who it was well enough."

"I thought you were still at Brainerd," said Mr. Wallace, after a pause.

"I left there a year ago November, and came to visit Mort's people. Mort has a real nice place with the street-car company and is doin' well. I didn't want to be no burden on him, so I started out on my own hook, seein' that there was no use of going back to Brainerd to slave for $2 a week. I had a good place with Mr. Sanders, the railroad man on the north side, but I left because they wanted me to serve liquor. I'd about as soon handle a toad as a bottle of beer. Liquor was the ruination of Jesse. He's gone to the dogs, and been off with a circus somewhere for two years."

"The family's all broken up, eh?" asked Mr. Wallace.

"Gone to the four winds since mother died. Of course, you know that Lora married Huntford Thomas and is livin' on the old Murphy place. They're doin' so well."

"Yes? That's good," said Mr. Wallace.

Was this an old settlers' reunion or a quiet family dinner? The soup had been waiting.

Mrs. Wallace came into the breach.

"That will be all for the present, Effie," said she. Effie gave a startled "Oh!" and vanished into the kitchen.

"What does this mean?" asked Mrs. Wallace, turning to her husband. "Bradley, behave!" This last was addressed to the 8-year-old, who had followed the example of his father and was snickering violently.

"It means," said Mr. Wallace, "that we were children together, made mud pies in the same puddle and sat next to each other in the old schoolhouse at Brainerd. The Whittlesy family was as poor as a church mouse, but they were all sociable—and freckled. Effie's a good girl."

"Effie? Effie? And she called you Ed!"

"My dear, you don't understand. We lived together in a small town where people don't stand on their dignity. She never called me anything but Ed, and everybody called her Effie. I can't put on any airs with her, because, to tell the

truth, she knows me too well. She's seen me licked in school
and has been at our house, almost like one of the family, when
mother was sick and we needed an extra girl. If my memory
serves me right I took her to more than one school exhibition.
I'm in no position to lord it over her and I wouldn't do it anyway. She's a good-hearted girl and I wouldn't want her to go
back to Brainerd and say that she met me up here and I was
too 'stuck up' to remember old times."

"You took her to school exhibitions?" asked Mrs. Wallace, with a gasp and an elevation of the eyebrows.

"Fifteen years ago, my dear—in Brainerd. I told you you
wouldn't understand. You're not jealous, are you?" and he
gave a side-wink at his son, who once more giggled.

"Jealous! I'm only thinking how pleasant it will be when
we give a dinner party to have her come in and address you
as 'Ed.'"

Mr. Wallace laughed as if he enjoyed the prospect, which
led his wife to remark: "I really don't believe you'd care."

"Well, are we going to have any dinner?" he asked.

The soup had become cold and Effie brought in the next
course.

"Do you get the Brainerd papers?" she asked, when encouraged by an amiable smile from Mr. Wallace.

"Every week. I'll give you some of the late ones," and he
had to bite his lips to keep from laughing, seeing that his
wife was really in a worried state of mind.

* * *

"Something must be done."

Such was the edict issued by Mrs. Wallace. She said she
had a sufficient regard for Effie, but she didn't propose to
have every meal converted into a social session, with the
servant girl playing the star part.

"Never worry, my dear," said Mr. Wallace, "I'll arrange
that. Leave it to me." * * *

Effie was "doing up" the dishes when Mr. Wallace lounged
up to the kitchen doorway and began his diplomatic campaign.

His wife, seated in the front room, heard the prolonged
purr of conversation. Ed and Effie were going over the family

"THEN A VERY STRANGE THING HAPPENED"

histories of Brainerd and recalling incidents that may have related to mud pies or school exhibitions. Somehow Mrs. Wallace did not feel entirely at ease, and yet she didn't want to go any nearer the conversation. It would have pleased her husband too well.

This is how Ed came to the point. Mrs. Wallace really should have heard this part of it.

"Effie, why don't you go down and visit Lora for a month? She'd be glad to see you."

"I know, Ed, but I can't hardly afford——"

"Pshaw! I can get you a ticket to Brainerd to-morrow, and it won't cost you anything down there."

"But what'll your wife do? I know she ain't got any other help to look to."

"To tell you the truth, Effie, you're an old friend of mine, and I don't like to see you here in my house except as a visitor. You know Chicago's different from Brainerd."

"Ed Wallace, don't be foolish. I'd as soon work for you as any one, and a good deal sooner."

"I know, but I wouldn't like to see my wife giving orders to an old friend, as you are. You understand, don't you?"

"I don't know. I'll quit if you say so."

"Tut! tut! I'll get you that ticket and you can start for Brainerd to-morrow. Promise me, now."

"I'll go, and tickled enough, if that's the way you look at it."

"And if you come back I can get you a dozen places to work."

*   *   *

Next evening Effie departed by carriage, although protesting against the luxury.

"Ed Wallace," said she, pausing in the hallway, "they never will believe me when I tell it in Brainerd."

"Give them my best regards, and tell them I am the same as ever."

"I'll do that. Good-by. Good-by."

Mrs. Wallace, watching from the window, saw Effie disappear into the carriage. "Thank goodness," said she.

"Yes," said Mr. Wallace, dryly, "I've invited her to call when she comes back."

"To call—here? What shall I do?"

"Don't you know what to do when she comes?"

"Oh, of course I do. I didn't mean what I said."

"That's right. I knew you'd take a sensible view of the thing—even if you never did live in Brainerd."

Notes

Notes

[1]Finley Peter Dunne ("Mr. Dooley") and Franklin P. Adams were born in Chicago. Ring Lardner was a native of Niles, Michigan. Eugene Field and Bert Leston Taylor came to Chicago as young men to seek distinction in the newspaper world. John T. McCutcheon and George Ade were native Hoosiers, Ade being born in Kentland, Indiana, February 9, 1866, and McCutcheon near South Raub, Tippecanoe County, May 6, 1870.

[2]Ade, George. "Looking Back from Fifty," in *Single Blessedness and Other Observations*, N. Y., 1922, pp. 49–50.

[3]The idea of "Port of Humorists" belongs to Thomas L. Masson, and was expressed in his book, *Our American Humorists*, N. Y., 1922, p. 110. The quotation is from the same source.

[4]Ade, George. "They Simply Wouldn't Let Me Be a High-Brow." *American Magazine*, December, 1920, Vol. 90, p. 50 et seq. Note that in the second reference (p. xxi) Mr. Ade confuses the order of the books with the order of appearance of the characters in the newspaper column, as discussed by the writer in the last paragraph of p. xxi.

[5]Ade, George. "I Knew Them When," in *Notes and Reminiscences*, Holiday Press: Chicago, 1940. Mr. Ade is not altogether correct when he says that the column was entirely anonymous. Ade's column was signed after September 3, 1898; and his initials "G. A." had appeared occasionally at earlier dates.

[6]The "Stories of the Streets and of the Town" were issued in eight series, as follows:

> First Series, April 1, 1894.
> Second Series, July 1, 1894.
> Third Series, April 1, 1895.
> Fourth Series, October 1, 1895.
> Fifth Series, July 1, 1897.
> Sixth Series, July 1, 1898.
> Seventh Series, April 1, 1899.
> Eighth Series, July 1, 1900.

[7]Ade, George. *One Afternoon With Mark Twain*. The Mark Twain Society of Chicago, 1939. Edited with notes by George Hiram Brownell. Pamphlet limited to 350 numbered copies.

[8]McCutcheon, John T. "George Ade" in *Notes and Reminiscences*, Holiday Press: Chicago, 1940. See also *Sigma Chi Magazine*, Sept.-Oct., 1934, Vol. 53, No. 4. Other quotations in this section are adapted from the same source.

[9]Carl Werntz, Charles Sarka, and Clyde Newman have kindly written letters of reminiscences to the writer, but lack of space unfortunately precludes printing them.

[10]McCutcheon, John T. "George Ade," *Appleton's Magazine*, November, 1907, p. 541. Also available in broadside form distributed by Mr. Ade.

[11]The illustrations in the Bandar Log Press pamphlets are entirely different from those in the original newspaper sketches which have been included in this volume.

[12]McCutcheon, John T. "George Ade," *Appleton's Magazine*, November, 1907, p. 541.

[13]Mr. Hosking writes that his little magazine (12mo in size) ran for only a few issues, and expired. The issue devoted to George Ade was October, 1898, Vol. 1, No. 5.

[14]Howells, William Dean. In *Literature*, July 2, 1898, p. 758.

[15]Howells, William Dean. "Certain of the Chicago School of Fiction," in *The North American Review*, May, 1903, Vol. 176, pp. 739–743.

[16]Mencken, Henry L. *Prejudices*. First Series, N. Y., 1919, Ch. IX, "George Ade."

[17]William Dean Howells has included this story in his anthology of America's greatest short stories, *Great Modern American Stories*, N. Y., 1920. In his Introduction, p. xiii, Mr. Howells says, "In this collection there is nothing humaner or more humane than Mr. George Ade's quite perfect study of real life, 'Effie Whittlesy.' It is a contribution to American fiction of a value far beyond most American novels; and the American small town which has often shrunken into the American City lives again here in its characteristic personality." The story "Effie Whittlesy" appeared originally in *The Chicago Record*, March 13, 1896.

The University of Illinois Press
is a founding member of the
Association of American University Presses.

University of Illinois Press
1325 South Oak Street
Champaign, IL 61820-6903
www.press.uillinois.edu